Roped In

Elle Jordan

Contents

Dedicated to the select 3% of us who got back with our exes and it didn't backfire. May we forever defy the odds.

Content Warning

Roped In is an open door novel, meaning there will be sexually explicit scenes and explicit language. If you don't like curse words, probably not the book for you. There is discussion of parents with addiction and parental abandonment. There is a side character who is pregnant.

Additionally this is fiction, some pieces of the story might be a bit far fetched for day to day life.

Prologue
WESTON

A deep ache settles in my chest as I drive. Probably because it'll be my last drive with her, and she doesn't even know it yet. Still, I'm the type of man who, once I've made up my mind, sticks to it.

I quickly glance in her direction and am struck by the sight of her hair tumbling around as she looks out the open window, my stomach turning sour. I love her hair, I always have. It was the first thing about her I noticed when we were little. Back then, it was innocent. I just thought it was pretty. Now, I can't help but notice how her hair is the perfect shade of brown, bringing out her green eyes. Since it's the end of summer, her tan olive skin makes them even more striking, accentuating the unique hues I could get lost in for hours.

"I'm going to miss this. I already can't wait for Thanksgiving. Maybe I'll be able to find a way to come home sooner, too," she says, breaking me from my thoughts.

Clearing the emotion that has me in a choke hold, I cough a little before replying, "That'd be nice."

Even to me, it sounds cold. I keep my eyes on the road, because if I look at her and the pinched expressions she's probably got on her face from my tone, I might crack. This is for the best. Maybe it'll even be the best thing for both of us.

I hear her seatbelt unclick and feel her scoot into the middle seat of my truck, her hand finding my thigh and giving it a gentle squeeze, and then she rebuckles herself. She knows me better than I know myself, I'd wager, so she knows something is up.

"You okay?" Her voice comes out soft. Everything about her is soft. Her heart, the way she looks at life, her skin.

"Yeah, just thinking about all the stuff I have to get done tomorrow is all." The lie tastes bitter on my tongue, but she doesn't push it. She just lays her head on my shoulder, and I squeeze my eyes shut for half a second. Memorizing the way she feels against me.

It's both too soon and not soon enough when we pull up to her house. The flowers I helped her plant brighten up the front lawn. The grass is cut short. I wonder if her grandpa will still want me to mow it after I go through with this.

She lives here with her Grandpa, but I know for a fact he won't be home right now because he's working on my parents' ranch. He's our farrier, that's how I came to know the girl beside me. She was eight when she moved to Windy Peaks. She came over to play, but ended up spending more time with my mom. One day, when I was thirteen, she came over, and I'm not sure what, but something about her had changed. She didn't look like the girl I chased around the ranch with worms or rode bikes with. She was beautiful, and once I realized that, there was no going back. She went from my best friend to my girlfriend when we were fourteen. I've spent the last four years loving her. There's a piece of me that will love her forever. How could I not? But it's time to grow up and do the right thing. Even if it sucks, and it feels like my heart is going to fall out of my ass.

I pull the key from my ignition and throw it on the dash, knowing I don't plan on sticking around long.

Swinging my door open, I hop out of the truck, Willow quick on my heels.

I take a deep breath to center myself. Fuck, I do not want to do this, but I have to. Even if it kills me.

"Hey, so you know I'm really happy for you, right?" I say as we walk to her front door, going up the few steps to the porch.

"Yes, I think you've told me a million times how proud of me you are. But it doesn't hurt to hear it again," she replies, amusement in her tone.

I finally brave looking at her face, and I swear I can feel my heart fracture. She looks so happy, carefree, and I'm going to ruin that.

"Well, I've given this a lot of thought, and I think it would be better if we maybe start college off as just friends. You know, with you being in New York and me staying here, I just don't see how it's going to work," I rush out, barely recognizing my own voice.

The smile that was on her face drops, and she steps back as if I slapped her. Her brows pull together as she starts shaking her head. "What are you talking about? It's not like I'll be in New York forever. I've already done a year of college classes; it's only a couple of years. You were fine with it when I agreed to go." Her voice cracks at the end, and I fight to keep my resolve and stay as formal as possible, because if she hates me, she will let this go. She may be soft, but this girl can hold a grudge like no one's business, and I was counting on that for my plan.

"Yeah, well, things change. I'm going to be busy working on the ranch, and my dad is forcing me to take a few college classes. We're both going to be too busy to make long-distance work," I lie, schooling my features into stone so she can't see that this is killing me, too.

She scoffs, shaking her head in disbelief. "What the hell is going on, West? This summer... This summer was everything," she says as a large tear falls, her lip trembling. "I don't even know you right now," she whispers.

"I know. I should have talked to you weeks ago, but I figured we could have one last summer together." That part is true; it was selfish of me, but I needed every second with her before I set her free.

She drops her arms as her hands ball into fists at her side. "You don't even want to try?" she asks in disbelief.

"This was inevitable. You and I both know this would have happened at some point. I just didn't want to drag it out." I shrug and kick my foot against the wooden plank to get some of this energy out.

Her eyes widen as her jaw drops. "You didn't want to drag it out." She shakes her head and looks down. When she looks back up, she takes a deep breath and studies me, and for a second, I worry that she will see through my facade, but she doesn't. She bites her lip as tears stream down her face.

"You know," she says, "I was dreading leaving. Dreading being so far away, but now I cannot wait to be on the other side of the country from you."

My hand subconsciously rubs the ache in my chest, but there is nothing that is going to make this stop. "I will always be there for you. If you need a friend or anything, you just have to call." There's nothing but truth there, because I would go to the ends of the earth to make sure she has what she needs.

"You can't pick and choose what parts of me you want, so no. I won't be calling. You might want to be my *friend*, but I don't want to be yours. This is the last time you will ever see me. I have no clue what the fuck is happening with you right now. Maybe there is someone else, maybe you want to experiment and screw someone else, I don't know. But when you pull your head out of your ass and realize that this was a mistake, don't call me." She points her finger at me before shaking her head one last time, turning on her heel, and walking in through the front door. I watch every step she takes, knowing this might be the last time I see her and needing to soak it in. When I hear the slam, I have to force down the sob that tries to claw its way out. I have to get out of eye sight before she sees me break.

Hopping in my truck, I put my hands on the steering wheel. My eyes catch on the bracelet she made me when we were thirteen. It was right when I realized I didn't want to be just her friend anymore, I wanted more. I didn't know how to flirt because at thirteen I barely knew my head from my ass, but I complimented her bracelet, and the next time she came over, she had made me one. It has all my favorite colors threaded together, and I can't look at it without thinking about how it's the first thing she gave me, the first step toward becoming something more.

I pull out of her drive and get on a dirt road as fast as I can. The road becomes blurry as my eyes fill with tears. I keep the windows down, trying to get some air because right now it feels like I can't fucking breathe. I just let the person I love most in the world go, and I don't think I'll ever be the same.

Chapter 1
WESTON

1 2 YEARS LATER

"Are you sure about this, son?" my dad asks, his grey bushy eyebrow quirking up at my newest idea for the ranch as he brings his cup of steaming hot coffee to his lips. We start most of our mornings this way, we have for years: breakfast at the house, and then we bust our asses for the rest of the day.

"Yeah, I think it could really work for us." Now, if I'm being totally honest, no, I'm not sure. There's about a million things I'm not sure of these days. How much hay I need to buy. What pasture I should switch to next month. Somehow, I forgot everything I knew about ranching the second my dad handed me the reins. It's been nothing but a year of second-guessing, but every Taylor man who has taken over our family ranch has done something to keep it going, and this is going to be my thing. "I'm tired of seeing ranch land get picked apart during tough times. This would help us generate some income without requiring much up-front investment. After that, it's just maintenance."

"I've spent the last year wracking my brain trying to think of something that would allow us to be more financially secure, even if it's just a little extra cash flow. If something were to ever go awry with the cattle, it would help keep us afloat," I add on. If I am nervous about this, it makes me worried he will be, too.

Running cattle isn't cheap, and all it takes is one bad year for everything to go to shit. I got the idea when one of my best friends' wives mentioned how she wished she could have visited a place like this when she was young. She wasn't exactly a city girl, but she had never seen the beauty that is the Wyoming mountains like you do when you're in Windy Peaks. We have a few run-down cabins around the property, and I can fix them up and use them as vacation homes. We get some extra cash flow, some city-bound family will get to enjoy the mountain air, and everyone wins.

"And your siblings are on board?" he asks, setting his cup down and leaning back in his chair, crossing his arms over his chest. I'm sure he thinks this is one of the dumbest ideas I've ever had, which is saying something because I tend to ask for forgiveness, not for permission. Thanks to my fully developed frontal lobe, I have actually thought this through.

"Yeah, I have Aspen working on finding a consulting company to help. I don't really have the time to juggle all of that, and I know it would be an extra expense, but I've talked it over with everyone, and they agree. Maverick has agreed to help with investments, Rhett can help with labor, and Aspen, well, she will stitch Rhett and Maverick up when they nail themselves to something."

My sister is a nurse at the local hospital, but when my dad handed down the ranch, it was split between me, my sister, and my two best friends, Maverick and Rhett. They've been like brothers to me for most of my life, having both lived with us at various points, so my dad thinks of them as sons. Aspen and I hold the majority, but to be honest, that pretty much means shit to all of us. We all take pride in this land, and this is where our hearts live. We give it our all and hope it works out.

"Well, son, I know you don't need it, but you've got my stamp of approval. You can tell me more about it on our ride out to the south pasture." He dips his head to me in a sign of respect and it still feels foreign. Getting up from the chair, he moves to the front door. Even retirement can't slow this man down. "The boys meeting us out there today?" "Yeah, I figured Rhett would have been here this morning, but he said he'd be ready to work by six, so I'm sure he will be around somewhere. Maverick and Ava had an appointment this morning, so he will be out to help us when they get back."

Mav married his one-night stand by accident in Vegas. Turns out luck was with him, because they stayed married and made the rest of us nauseous with how annoyingly in love they are. Now they've got one of their own on the way.

I'm happy for him, and a bit jealous. I wish I could have that.

"You coming, son? Or do you need the morning off too?" Dad's deep, grainy voice pulls me out of my thought spiral and back to the present.

"I thought you were supposed to be retired," I joke as I walk to the front of the house, opting for my ball cap instead of my hat. "Let's take the ranger, the horses rode pretty hard for us yesterday."

"Ain't got to tell me twice, my back is still yelling at me for sitting on that horse for so damn long."

I close the door behind me and get started on another day of my dream job of ranch life. I've always loved the ranch, but the older I get, the more gratitude I feel toward it, and the more respect I have for my old man for trusting me enough to hand it down. It being mine has changed me in ways I didn't think were possible. I'm in charge of keeping this legacy going now, and that's not something I take lightly.

Later that evening, the family all gathers around the large oak table for dinner. The smell of Mom's cooking has my mouth watering, and the fact that the only thing I ate after breakfast was some half-crumbled peanut butter crackers I found in the ranger. But it's almost the end of calving season, which means it's about to be a busy couple of weeks.

"We need to make sure we have everything ready for round up. I've got Dr. Wilhelm and Dr. Smith coming out to examine the animals and vaccinate. We still have quite a few calves we will need to tag as well," I say as I grab a glob of butter with my knife and smear it across my dinner roll. "Mom, you still good to cook us the dinner meal? Ava and Aspen each agreed to bring a couple of sides, so you don't have to worry about it as much."

"Honey, I've been cooking for that day longer than you've been alive. I've got it handled. We're planning on pulled pork and burgers. I'll make my potato salad. Your dad is going to run into town and buy the liquor store out of beer." She shoots my dad a wink, and he shakes his head. His eyes still have a little twinkle in them when he looks at her, and I can't help but feel a pang in my chest at the reminder that I once had that.

"Hey now, the three boys we've got just at this table will probably be drinking half." He gives Rhett, Mav, and me a pointed look.

"I'm a father now, I've learned how to slow down and be an adult," Maverick says, and Ava nearly chokes on the water she just drank as she laughs.

"Yeah, okay." She shakes her head and rests her other hand on her growing belly.

"I have to agree with Ava, sorry, dude," Aspen chimes in, before looking over at me. "Hey, by the way, I got that company booked. They're sending someone out on Monday at eight in the morning to come help. They'll be around for three months as a project manager, so you don't have to be as hands-on-"

I start to interrupt her by raising my hand and asking if they are going to help with the software and updating the books issue I've been having. My dad refuses to update anything to this century, and it's been a pain in the ass going document by document trying to digitize everything.

"And before you ask, yes, they will also help with the back office work." She smiles at me before shoveling a large bite of roasted chicken and gravy into her mouth.

A rush of relief pummels through me. "Thank you."

I wasn't sure how much Aspen was going to want to help out on the ranch, but she's insanely good at all the background stuff I never seem to find time for. Like calling people. I like people, mostly, but my sister, Aspen, can talk to a brick wall, so it's nice to have her handle it.

The five of us have done a pretty good job over the last year taking over the ranch. Getting to do your dream job with your family is something special. I have to remember that, especially on the bad days.

Chapter 2
WILLOW

My heels click against the tile floor in the lobby as I walk toward the elevator. It's a beautiful day in New York, which means I am already sweating. You know what no one warned me about twelve years ago when I moved here? Humidity. Wyoming was so dry when I was growing up, I never experienced humidity. Sure, I knew about it, but it was never something I put thought into.

But it's fine. The humidity makes my skin glow, and not a single thing can bring me down today. I've been working at Jones and Sons agency for four years. I've had to scratch and claw my way to where I am now. I started as an assistant, but today I get my very first assignment. Working for a consulting company comes with its challenges, like never really knowing what type of project you'll be roped into, but that also makes it exciting. I like the challenge. Struggle and pressure are where I shine. I step into the elevator and press the button for the twentieth floor.

When the elevator doors open, the air-conditioning hits my skin, and I instantly cool off. While I've done well for myself climbing the ladder, I am still not quite at the level to have my own office, so I drop my purse off at my cubicle and head to my boss's office. He's part owner in this firm. Someday I hope to sit beside him as an equal, but for now, I am content with where I'm at. If you had told eighteen-year-old me that thirty-one-year-old me would be happy with this, she'd laugh in your face. But life doesn't always pan out the way you think it will, and it's taken years for me to be okay with that.

I thought I would be married now, but I'm not. I have the ring, just not the last name yet. It's coming, but I don't think Josh or I are in a big rush right now for that. We've both been busy building up our careers, and I'm finally leveling up in mine.

It's taken me years, but this project is going to be it for me, I just know it. I knock on the door and pull on the cold metal handle to his office, peeking my head in.

"Hey, Tony. I'm a couple minutes early. Is that okay?" His fingers type away at his keyboard, and I almost think he didn't hear me.

"Sure, come on in. Please take a seat so I can get you briefed." He's straight to the point, which I can appreciate. No time wasted when you're living with New York minutes. "You're from Wyoming, right?" He asks the question and it makes every hair on my body stand up.

"Yeah. I lived there until I was eighteen," I say, my hands holding the arms of the chair a little too tightly.

"Great, it's good that you're familiar with the area because we're going to be sending you there for the next three months, potentially longer if you run into any setbacks."

Trying to hide the chaos wreaking havoc on my nervous system right now, I keep it professional because I really need this big break to prove to these guys I can get shit done better than anyone. That's how you reach the top here, you can't just outperform, you have to blow socks off. "Okay. When does the project start and where exactly in Wyoming?"

The creeping feeling up the back of my spine has me guessing where he's going to say before I even hear it, because that's how life has gone for me. Every time I finally start to get ahead, I get knocked on my ass.

It's exhausting. It's stolen a lot of the joy I used to have for life, but one thing about me is I'm always going to find my way back to my feet.

"It's on a ranch in Windy Peaks, Wyoming, actually, it's called Windy Peaks Ranch, so that should be easy to remember," he says nonchalantly, not knowing he just dropped a bomb on my life.

The blood drains from my face, and I can see his lips moving, but I can't hear a word he's saying over the ringing in my ears. That ranch holds so much of my childhood. And the boy on that ranch still holds more of me than I'm willing to admit. I shouldn't still have this feeling. It's been twelve years and we were just kids, but we were so much more than just kids together. And he ruined it. He broke me in a way I don't think I've ever come back from. I've been walked out on by my parents, and yet, him leaving me the way he did still cuts the deepest.

I've managed to stay as far away from that town as possible. I've only visited my grandpa five times since I left, because that man is all I have. He raised me on his own, but I haven't been able to enjoy a minute in that town since the day before I left for college and now I have to go back and stay for three whole months.

"You'll find all the information in this packet." His voice finally comes back to me, and I have to nod like I heard the last two minutes of his briefing. "Your plane will leave Sunday night, and you're expected at the ranch Monday at eight am."

"This Monday?" I choke out. It's Thursday, which means I only have a few days to prepare not only for the job but for my life getting flipped upside down.

"Correct, if anyone can do it on this late notice, it's you!" He looks annoyingly cheerful for how much of a crisis I am currently having, but no one cares about your feelings in this office. It's about money in and money out, so I plaster a fake smile on my face.

"Thank you for the opportunity. I won't let you down."

Grabbing the packet, I walk out of the office in a daze. When I get back to my cubicle, I stare blankly at the wall as my thoughts tumble through. If I want to prove myself, I have to do this. And even more than that, I need to prove to myself that I can go back there and see Weston. I'm engaged to another man, for god's sake. Josh and I's relationship doesn't make me feel the same as Weston and I's, and I like it that way. The way I loved Weston was all-consuming. He made my heart race and made me feel alive until he didn't. I learned the hard way what happens when you give every ounce of yourself to someone, and it's not good. Josh is comfortable and dependable, and that's what I need most.

Maybe seeing him again will be a full-circle moment. Although it felt like it did, the world didn't actually stop spinning when Weston decided I was old news. Showing up there and leading a project will be good for me. I've worked hard, and I deserve to be happy and proud of myself.

Taking a deep breath, I open the manila envelope and pull out the file. My eyes scan over the details. They need to update their filing and accounting systems. Maybe Jack is finally getting with the times, which is surprising, that old man is as stubborn as an ox. Kind of excessive to hire someone from New York for that. As my eyes read on, I get to the meat of it.

"Ohhhh," I say out loud to myself as I see their plans to renovate the run-down cabins into vacation rentals, which, honestly, is a great idea. That place is gorgeous and is a perfect destination for a fresh breath of mountain air.

As I finish reading through the file, it's clear this will be a big undertaking. They need a lot of help with project and business planning to bring the ranch into the twenty-first century.

"This is just a regular job. You're going to get in, make this an epic success, and get back to New York," I mumble to myself.

"What?" My cubicle neighbor pokes his shiny, bald head over, and I feel my cheeks heat. Guess I should keep the conversations with myself internal. My coworkers are going to think I'm losing my mind.

"Oh, just walking myself through this upcoming project," I explain as I pick up the stack of papers for emphasis. He gives me a look that confirms my suspicions about them thinking I'm crazy and he goes back in his hole.

Stretching my neck out, I log on to my computer and get to work. At least I get to surprise my grandpa. That is the silver lining, I tell myself, this time internally. I can't wait to see my grandpa's face when I tell him I'm staying with him for three months. He's always begging for me to visit, and now I can work, climb the ladder, and spend some much-needed time with my favorite person.

But first, I have to tell my fiancé that I am going to be out of town for months on end.

Chapter 3
WESTON

Monday rolls around faster than I can come to terms with. I helped deliver three calves in the middle of the night. Eight hours of sleep in the last three days has my eyelids feeling like sandpaper every time I blink. I need a stiff drink and a good night's sleep. Maybe I can convince Rhett to take the night shift with Maverick tonight. Sometimes I wonder how my old man did this when we were kids: up with babies or calves and still showing up as the best dad in the world.

My drive down the road is short. Usually, I get breakfast at the house, but I'm already running late, so I let my mom know I'll just be heading straight to the office. I can grab a bite to eat after I meet up with the consultant Aspen hired. It feels foreign to have to delegate like this. My dad has always figured it all out on his own, but I decided to branch into something new for all of us in my first year because, apparently, I love to make my life more complicated.

The gravel rolls under my tires as I pull to a stop in front of the barn. I grab my thermos full of coffee and head on in. Maybe I can talk Aspen into putting in an IV and getting this shit straight into my veins. I've only got thirty minutes to prepare for the guy coming today. Aspen hasn't given me a whole lot of information, which is right on par with her. I'm just grateful she got this set up. Hopefully, after working with this consultant, it won't feel so chaotic, and I'll be able to wrangle this ranch a little easier.

Looking around the desk, I try to make it look less like a clusterfuck of invoices, bills, and receipts. I don't want this guy to walk in and think I don't have my shit together. Which, in reality, I don't, but he doesn't need to know that immediately upon meeting me. They should find that out on their own, like everyone else.

I hear the unmistakable sound of tires coming down the road and I start to panic. Everyone who could potentially be coming up to the house is accounted for, which means the consultant is running early, and I'm going to have to shove this stack of papers into the desk and hide them instead of organizing them like I wanted.

Standing up from my chair, I stretch and shake out my hands, suddenly feeling a bit nervous. This is a huge step, and I don't want to let my family down. Maverick is investing a lot of money to make this happen, and I don't want my dumbass self to screw it up. I love this ranch, and I know I can run it successfully, but that doesn't stop the turmoil churning in me.

When I step out of the barn, I see Vern's old truck coming down the road, which is weird. It's been a long time since that old man has been here. Probably since I was in high school, when his granddaughter spent more time at the ranch with me than she did in her own home. We visit frequently, but I'm always the one to drive to him since his vision has gone to shit. Call it my public service: keeping other drivers safe on the road.

I wave, my hat doing a shit job of keeping the sun out of my eyes, so I lean against the old wooden ranch rail fence, waiting for the beaten-up Chevy to come to a stop. When I see a high-heeled foot swing out of the truck instead of a worn-down boot, my heart starts to race. I know without a doubt that it is Vern's truck. My head snaps up to catch sight of the girl stepping out of the truck. Or I should say woman. There is nothing girlish about her.

Willow.

My Willow. My girl. Until I broke her heart the day before she was leaving town, and I haven't seen or heard from her since.

But now she's here, and she's different. The softness of her features has faded, and her cheekbones now sit high on her face. Her brown hair is cut shorter, the natural curl gone, and instead it lays straight to her shoulders. You never would have caught her dead in a dress before. T-shirts and blue jeans are what she lived in, but now she's rocking a dress that clings to the curves of her body, curves that were not there twelve years ago, and heels. Not her boots, *heels.*

That light that has always drawn me to her is still there. I can feel it. It's like a beacon that calls me to her. It's been twelve damn years, and I can still feel it in my bones. The love I had for her. Who am I kidding, *have,* because the love I have for her is not in the past. The way my body reacts to being in her presence tells me I haven't done nearly as good a job of forgetting her as I had hoped. I've done everything in my power to squander the embers, but it seems the fire for her still burns.

While I am shocked to see her, I feel like my brain is short-circuiting, unable to form an entire thought. She doesn't look surprised to see me. She takes a big, deep breath before coming to me. Her heels wobble across the uneven ground, and when she gets to me, she holds her hand out to me to shake, like I haven't known her my whole life.

I take a moment to appreciate her up close. And damn it, she's even more beautiful now. My fingers twitch at my sides, itching to reach out and cup her face, draw her near me. God, does it feel good to be close to her again. What I wouldn't give for things to be different.

"Weston, nice to see you. I'm a little early for my eight o'clock meeting with you, but I wasn't sure if the truck would even make it out here." She looks over her shoulder at it, clearly avoiding my gaze.

I stand like an idiot, trying to form words, trying to comprehend how she's here, and how she's my eight o'clock. There are so many things I want to say to her. How I've regretted letting her go every single day since she left. How a piece of me has felt wrong and broken.

"What are you doing here?" is what I manage to spit out instead. I can barely hear anything over my pulse thumping in my ears.

She looks irritated, and I see that professional demeanor of hers slip for half a second as she takes in what I say. "As I said, I'm here for the meeting. I'm with the consulting company you hired to help you with updating the cabins and books."

I shake my head, trying to get a grasp of the situation. "You're a consultant?"

"I prefer the term project manager, but sure." Her voice lacks all the softness I'm accustomed to her having, and I hate it. Standing in front of someone you miss with your whole being, only to miss them more, is a special kind of torture. A torture I'd gladly put myself through if it means getting to see her again. Even worse, she seems so unbothered. She isn't really looking at me, but looking through me as if we didn't spend the majority of our lives at each other's sides.

The summer breeze blows a few strands of her perfectly styled hair into her face, and it's then that I see it. A fucking ring. She's wearing a ring. How did I not know about this? My world feels like it's collapsing in on me as I stare at it, the way it shines in the morning light. I hate it. My heart hasn't ached like this in twelve fucking years, since we were on Vern's front steps and I thought I was doing the right thing. God, if I only knew.

"Okay, well," I start, struggling to find the words, "let's head to my office and we can discuss what you need from me to get started." I use the short walk to try and form a cohesive thought. And to figure out how I'm going to survive this summer. We walk in silence. When we reach the barn, I pull the door open and usher her inside. Her eyes sweep over the barn; it's hard to call it that, because while it does have space to work and store the animals, it's also where our office is. It used to just have the corral and stalls, but as we grew, Dad added on to the barn. Now it houses a small office space, a place where we can load and store hay to keep it safe from the elements and wildlife, and park our bigger equipment. "Can I get you something to drink?" I ask as she continues looking over the place.

"Wow, it looks so different in here," she remarks. It's the first mention that she even remembers being a part of this place. She's so transfixed that she didn't seem to hear my earlier question.

"Willow," I try again, a little louder. "Can I get you something to drink?"

The tiniest furrow of her brow is the only indicator that hearing her name come out of my mouth stirred something in her. She starts shaking her head before saying, "No, I'm okay, thank you. Where is the office?" she asks, reminding me she's here strictly on business.

I usher her toward the door on the left side, and we make our way in. I look around and scratch the back of my head. "It's not much, but Mom was about ready to kill Dad with all of his papers stacked on the kitchen table, so he decided to add on to the barn and make it more of a shop-barn combo."

The office is about ten by ten feet, and on the walls hang pictures of cattle and some of our family during our summer barbecues when we brand cattle. The desk sits by a small window toward our back, where you can look out at the trees and a small pasture. It lets just enough light in that the place doesn't feel dreary. There are a couple of chairs for meetings or for the boys and me to hide from work and drink a couple of beers when a day has been particularly rough.

Willow takes in the space, revealing nothing in those green eyes of hers. "It'll work just fine, thanks. Let's take a seat. Today, I'd like to go over your expectations so I can better understand what you need from me. I'd like to be as detailed as possible so I can start work right away and ensure we hit the three-month deadline."

In short, she wants to talk to me as little as possible. I can't say I blame her. I always told myself if I ever saw her again, the first words out of my mouth would be I'm sorry. That I messed up and have regretted it every minute of every day since, but I get the feeling that wouldn't go over too well right now, especially since she's engaged. Maybe by the end of this, she won't hate me, and I guess that'll have to be enough.

"Okay, where do you want to start? I want to make this as easy on you as possible." I sit down in the chair opposite her and look over at her. She quirks a brow up at me, probably because I have never been known for making things easy for people. Not intentionally, I just have a bit too much fun giving people a hard time.

She takes out her phone and pulls up what looks to be a notes app. "Well, for starters, what's your goal for the books and back office?"

I let out a breath. "That one is easy. As you know, my father is as stubborn as an ox, and has been doing everything on paper, and I, well, have the attention span of a squirrel and cannot spend a whole day shuffling through papers just to see what our costs have been the last few years." This earns me a bit of a laugh, and the hair on my arms stands up. I haven't heard that sound in years, and god does it feel good to make her laugh again.

"Glad to hear some things haven't changed. So, you want to update things into a digital format and for it to be easily trackable?""Yeah, some kind of sheet where I can plug numbers in and go. I'm sure it'll be more complicated than that and need a few different forms for the costs of cattle, feed, and overhead. Basically, I want to unfile as many of these papers as possible. He's literally kept everything from the day he took over," I hitch my thumb over my back and point to a filing cabinet, "that only has, like, the last five years. I have boxes of years and years worth of invoices and bank statements."

Both of her eyebrows raise. "Oh, goody, and here I thought this would be the easy part. I'll work on a plan and give you a couple of different options. There's a way we can scan the last ten or so years' worth of papers into a file on the computer and then organize those by year, and I can do the last five into some sort of a file to make it easier for you."

"I'd appreciate that." I nod, shifting in my chair nervously. My heart is still beating like it's trying to pound its way out of my chest.

"And the cabins?" She types something on her phone before looking up at me.

"Well, from what Mav told me, one is currently livable, so I assume that one won't need as much work. But the other two will pretty much need ground-up renovations. I doubt they even have running water; only the one closest to us does. We can connect them to the wells, but it will need to be cleaned up first. For starters, it will need a construction team to get them up to code, and then someone to oversee decor, which is not my strong suit. My socks don't even match today." Socks? Smooth Weston.

A ghost of a smile turns up on her lips as she types, and my eyes get stuck on it. I am going to have to pull my shit together if I want this not to end up eating me alive by the end of the summer.

"Okay, and as we progress, we will need to touch base on insurance, an e-commerce site for bookings, and probably some staff for cleaning purposes."

I bob my head because words are hard today.

"What's your timeline looking like? My boss mentioned three months?"

"Yes, Maverick is the investor for the project, so I'd like to get the cabins up and running so we can start paying him back." Maverick spent his golden years tearing up the rodeo scene. He's retired now, but he'll reap the benefits of his success for years.

She nods as she writes some more. "Okay, and what's the budget?"

"I'd like to stay around the two hundred-and-fifty-thousand-dollar range, but if it needs to be more, just let me know. This is out of my ballpark. If you need to know what the price of cattle is this week, I could tell you that." I'm so out of my element with this conversation, it's not even funny. So much for my good first impression of adult Weston.

"I think I'm good, thanks," she says dryly. "I was told you would provide lodging? Is that correct?""You don't want to stay with your grandpa?" I ask, surprised that she wouldn't be staying with him, seeing as she doesn't have the opportunity to spend time with him, living out of state.

"My old room is a little filled up at the moment. If cost is an issue, I'm happy to work with the firm to expense it."

"There's no issue, I just figured you'd want to stay with Vern. He always-" I cut myself off before I give too much away. "Uhm, he always loved having you around," I say instead.

"He offered to clean out my room, but I know how physically taxing that is, and in truth, I'm going to be busy here. So does that offer still stand?"

"Yeah, of course." I didn't know Aspen offered lodging. Similar to how I didn't know the love of my life was going to show up on my doorstep out of the blue. Another thing my sweet, dear sister left out. She and I will be having some choice words later. Even if she didn't know she worked for this company, I need someone to blame, and little sisters are perfect for that. "Let me call the motel in town and see what I can get worked out. If you just give me one sec," I say as I reach for my phone and move to step outside the office.

Fifteen minutes later, and it appears there is no availability at our one local motel. I guess I can have her stay in that cabin; it's far from glamorous and not a place I would normally put her in, but maybe staying there would help give her some ideas. I don't know. Fuck. It feels like I can't think straight. I'd offer her a bed at my place or my parents but the cold shoulder I received today tells me she would shoot that idea down.

I come back into the office and brace myself to deliver the bad news. "Hey, so the hotel is booked, but I can put you in that cabin we have. I'll just need to run to my parents' house to get you fresh sheets, blankets, and a couple of towels. Feel free to hang out here in the office or explore the barn, I just need like fifteen minutes to gather everything," I say nervously before nodding and walking to my truck.

As I make my way inside my truck, I take a deep breath and try to center my spiraling thoughts. "Fuck!" This is *not* how I expected today to go. For twelve years, she's haunted me and shows up looking even more beautiful than I could have imagined, and with no warning. I need to figure out how to be around her again, how to form a coherent thought, and I need to do it quickly because it looks like this project just became my last hope.

Chapter 4
WILLOW

I hate him, I hate the way he looked at me like I was his salvation, and I hate this stupid dusty cabin. It smells stale and dirty all at the same time. It looks like no one has resided here in years. If this is what he considers livable, I am seriously dreading what the other cabins will look like. That reminds me, I'm going to need to coordinate time for someone to take me on a tour of the cabins. But I think I'll tackle some office tasks first and let myself get my bearings because being back here on this ranch brings back way too many memories. Memories that now feel jaded and wrong.

I made the rookie mistake of assuming I could use my old room and that Grandpa would be able to host me, so I was going to surprise him. Which I did, he was very surprised and when he gave me a tour of the house, I realized there was no way in hell that staying in that room was going to work. It's now home to every single thing he doesn't need, but refuses to get rid of. I'm sure you can find the Christmas ornament I made him in kindergarten there if you did enough digging in the totes and cardboard boxes. I didn't want him to feel bad, so I told him that work was providing lodging.'

My grandpa has done everything for me my whole life, and I don't want to make him do anything more, so I'm going to make this work. I grew up playing in dirt and loved living in the country, but that's not who I am anymore. That version of me died the night Weston broke my heart and I don't think I can see her making a comeback. Sometimes I miss that version of me. The version that trusted freely, even after everything I had been through as a kid. I blindly trusted that man with my heart. I'll never be that foolish again.

My heart is mine and I only give bits and pieces of it away now, preventing anyone from getting too close. Josh is the most I have let anyone in since, and I guess it was just luck that he was satisfied with the pieces I was willing to give to him.

My thoughts have me spiraling, which is usually when I work. While I would love to get started on work right now, it looks like I'm going to need to make a trip to town to get some cleaning supplies because there is no way in hell am I sleeping in this crumbling cabin without a whole bottle of bleach and a good hearty dusting and sweeping. I cannot believe he thinks so little of me that he would put me in a place like this and call it livable. I had a moment of hope when it seemed like my Weston was still there, hearing him talk about his dad brought a smile to my lips, but maybe the old Weston was just as good at lying as he is now. Being sweet, only to leave you face first in the dirt.

I look around and take stock of everything here. It's small, but when the work is done, I'm confident we can transform the cabin into a charming space that will bring flocks of customers here. The kitchen is directly to the left of the front door and is in an L-shape against the wall of the cabin. The dining room, which is just a small round table and two chairs with some cabinets behind it, sits connected to the kitchen. The living room is right of the front door. I walk past the dining room and see a small closet with a broom, a dustpan, and a trash can in it, all coated in a thick layer of dust. Lovely. The bathroom leaves a lot to be desired, it has a stand-up shower, the world's smallest vanity and a toilet that hopefully is in working condition.

I turn the outdated, gold knob and see brown water jet out of the faucet.

"You have got to be kidding me." I wonder how long it's been since water has been ran here. I leave the faucet going, trying to clear up the water, and peek into the bedroom, stopping dead in my tracks.

There is a bed, alright, but no mattress. I run my hands through my hair as frustration bleeds out of me. I look around at my new room. There's no bedside tables or dressers. Just a frame. My rage boils up inside me to the point where I feel like I might combust. What an ass. I was so nervous to see him again that I wasted so much time, constantly wondering about him and his life now. Before the breakup and after. I missed him so deeply it felt like my heart was physically breaking, but what doesn't kill you makes you stronger and I'll be damned if I make the mistake of trusting him again.

Well, I guess I will be adding a blow-up mattress to my shopping list, along with water, because there is no way in hell I will be drinking from that faucet until that water is tested by someone a hell of a lot more qualified than me.

Sweat drips down my brow, and I scrub the last bit of dust off the counter. It has been hours, hours that should have been spent working, but here we are. Sweaty, smelly, but at least this place is livable...ish. The water is running clear now. It only took an hour of running it nonstop, but at least now I should be able to shower, which is good because I smell like freshly boiled onions.

The only thing keeping me alive is the coffee I grabbed while in town. I had to dodge not one, but two of my old classmates. Dealing with people while I feel so...discombobulated takes more energy than I am willing to give. My high school English teacher, Mr. Warren, is now the cashier. Apparently, he got bored with retirement. I didn't even have to ask. He gave me a vivid, unprompted retelling of the last twelve years of his life.

No one randomly talks to you like that in New York, at least not anywhere I have been. They'll answer questions, sure, but not give you a PowerPoint on how their life has led them to that exact spot.

Now that all my housework is done, I should call Josh. We spoke briefly when I landed, and he said he would call me back as soon as he could, but it's now Ten PM in New York. I track down my phone by following the music blasting from it, and press pause before dialing his number.

It rings and rings until finally, he picks up. "Hello?" His voice sounds like I just woke him up.

"Were you sleeping?"

"Yeah, I went to bed an hour ago. I texted you goodnight." He sounds almost annoyed.

"Oh, sorry, I was, erm, working. I haven't checked my texts." I don't think I want to tell him the extent of the situation. He knows I'm working on the ranch and he knows Weston is my ex from high school. He's probably assuming Weston meant nothing because I never brought him up before. At least that's the only thing I could come up with for how nonchalant he's been about the whole thing.

"It's fine. Did you need something?"

I didn't need anything, I just wanted to hear his voice and fill him in on some of my day, but I guess I can just do that another time. I know he's strict about his sleep schedule. "Nope, just was calling to check in. You can call me back tomorrow."

"Okay, I'll talk to you then."

I go to reply, but the other end of the line goes dead. I pull the phone away from my ear to see our phone call information coming across the screen. Thirty-two whole seconds of talking. And not even an *I love you* but he's probably just tired from work. I know my brain is fried.

Guess it's time to see what this blow-up mattress can do.

Chapter 5
weston

Taking a long draw of my coffee, I skip breakfast at my parents' house again. I texted my mom last night to let her know I was going to work early, but in reality I'm not ready to tell people who's here. I'm not even sure if I've come to terms with it, seeing her here, on this ranch, again. They'll all know by the end of the day, someone will see her, and it'll spread like wildfire, but for now it's my secret.

Coffee isn't enough this morning, I need something stronger. I tried to convince myself that I'd be fine, but no matter how many scenarios I went through, there wasn't a single one where this wouldn't be the hardest three months of my life. I've missed her every second of every day she has been gone, and now that she's here, just out of my grasp, it's going to feel like constant torment.

When I open the door to the office, I stop dead in my tracks. Willow sits at my desk going through pages of paperwork. She looks lost in her own little world, so I stay back and just watch her. Her brow furrows as she looks between two pieces of paper, and I'm suddenly glad it's not just me that this paperwork frustrates the shit out of.

It's almost bizarre seeing her in business attire here on the ranch, the family and ranch hands always wear clothes made for getting dirty. In fact, I don't think I've even seen my mom in a dress. At this point I think that she was born in blue jeans. It's hard to have objections when the pink blouse gives me a perfect view of just a hint of cleavage. And now I feel like a complete creep gawking at my ex-girlfriend's turned business associate's tits. God, I have to get a grip.

Before I can humiliate myself, I tap my knuckles against the door frame, letting her know I'm here. She startles and the paper in her hand goes flying. I try and fail miserably to choke back the laugh. The glare she shoots me does no good to stop the laughter because she looks too damn cute when she's mad, always has.

I hold my hands up in front of me, indicating I mean no harm. "Good morning. Sorry, I didn't mean to scare you."

"Sure you didn't. I was just trying to get a head start on the back office work. My original plan was to knock this out before starting the work on the cabins but I'm realizing it'll be better to work in sync so we stay on schedule." She tidies up a stack of papers, holding them in her hand and tapping them against the desk to straighten them up. "Do you have a few minutes to touch base before I make some calls?" She tucks a piece of her perfectly curled hair behind her ear and I find myself getting lost in her beauty again.

She clears her throat, a reminder that she asked me a question and I realize I need to answer her. "Right, sorry, I've only had one coffee today, and it clearly didn't do its job," I offer lamely as an explanation for zoning out. "I have some free time this morning to help with whatever you need." My words come out rushed and even I can hear how idiodic I sound.

She raises her eyebrows and studies me carefully with those keen green eyes. I can practically hear her thinking about how fucking strange I'm behaving this morning. Trust me, if there were a manual for 'How to be around your ex who you secretly still love,' I'd be the first to buy it.

"Okay, first on the agenda, are there any contractors who you are against working with?" she asks as she reaches around to her bag and pulls out her laptop.

"No, I haven't really had to deal with any. I've heard John Beckman has been a little hard on the booze lately, so maybe not him."

"Glad to see the gossip mill is still turning out riveting information," she deadpans as she types a few things on her computer and I look around the room, not sure what I should do. "You can take a seat. This will take a bit."

The authority in her tone has me sitting down and my arousal perking up. "Yes, ma'am." Gone is the meek girl I said goodbye to, this version of Willow in front of me isn't afraid to take charge and I can't say I'm hating it. My fingers tap nervously against the arms of my chair as I wait for further instruction.

"Okay, so things I need you to have to me by the end of the week are an email containing the following: what your goals and inspiration are for these cabins, and if you have any pictures that would be helpful." She types on her computer again before she looks back up at me. "Oh, and are you planning on hiring a property manager or will you be handling that?"

It is in this exact moment that I am in over my head. I hadn't even thought about a property manager, but I guess you would need someone to keep on top of bookings and questions. My confidence wavers as I realize how naive I was. I don't want to admit that I'm in over my head and haven't considered all the details. I did a lot of research on the process of getting started, not so much on the day to day.

When my eyes rise to meet hers, I feel a rush of embarrassment. "I will talk to the team and get back to you." I say it like this whole thing has been a team effort, but really, I thought it was a good idea, ran it past them and started looking into it. I don't regret the idea, I do think this is a good plan and would be really beneficial for the ranch and our family, I just wish I had the ability to form a complete thought before jumping ship.

"Okay, I am going to get a list of potential contractors and start writing up a business plan. I can make some spreadsheets to keep all the information, costs, and plans in one place. No one should have to deal with those damn filing cabinets ever again."

Her phone starts ringing on the desk, and on it I can see a picture of her with a man. He looks like he's wearing a dress shirt, he doesn't have a single hair out of place. Their smiles look practiced and almost robotic. I've seen a real smile from Willow, and that ain't it.

"Oh, sorry. Do you mind if I take this?" She looks up, her cheeks stained a pretty shade of pink. Not sure why she feels embarrassed.

"Not at all. Do you want me to step out?" I go to stand, but she shakes her head.

"I'll go. It should only be a minute." She quickly walks away, shutting the door as I sit here and try to mind my own business. For a whopping three seconds. I almost gave in at two, but I know I'm stronger than that.

I slowly turn the knob on the door, cracking it a little to try and hear.

"Well now isn't a good time, I'm meeting with my client." She paces around the space outside the door. "Yeah, I know I said I wanted you to call but-"

I see every bit of light drain out of her and it's right then that I decide I hate the man who put a ring on her finger. Not because he took her off the market, but because she doesn't shine when she's with him. She deserves that.

Her brows knit in together, and she ends the call and starts walking back, shoulders slumped and gloomy.

I haul ass back to my chair before she can catch me and start thinking of ways I can turn this day around for her. If that fuckface won't put a smile on her face, I will.

Chapter 6
WILLOW

The ache in my back causes me to finally give up on my dream of a full night's sleep. I've been here a full week and it feels like I am drowning. Probably from the lack of sleep I've been getting. My air mattress is slowly leaking air, so I spent the night half-asleep in a blow-up taco of a bed. At least it's Sunday and I get to visit my grandpa and get the hell off this ranch. A little space between Weston and me wouldn't hurt either.

Every day that I wake up with a part of my body hurting due to my shitty sleeping situation, or the ice-cold shower I am forced to take every day, I am reminded of how good it was for me that he ended things, even if seeing him still feels like a dagger to the heart. It's been so many years, but I still don't feel like that piece of me has let go. Weston was my best friend which made losing him that much harder. Being here again makes everything feel fresher, and it feels like I'm reliving it all over again. So, a day at my grandpa's is exactly what I need.

The drive to town takes a while. The truck doesn't go over forty-five, so I don't push my luck and choose to make the most out of it. With the windows down, I take the path I've driven a million times. The flowers on the side of the road are in full bloom, lots of woods' roses and geraniums, adding a splash of color to the sagebrush and weeds growing in the ditch. The fresh air fills the cabin and I can feel my grumpiness slowly fading. Not all the way, but enough that I can breathe again and have a good time with my grandpa.

When I pull up to his house, his grass is neatly maintained and the flowers next to the mailbox on the sidewalk add pops of yellow and white. It still looks exactly the same as it did when I was a kid. This place will always be my home. Some might have been embarrassed about being raised by their grandparents, but I was so lucky. My grandpa has the kindest heart, and if I get anything from him I hope it's that. Sometimes I feel like I've lost that piece of myself a bit over the years, but maybe spending more time with him will bring it back.

I walk up the front porch steps, and the top stair creaks just like it always does, which was really inconvenient when you were seventeen and trying to sneak back inside. Eventually, I started using my bedroom window, even if it meant potentially falling into the rosebushes we had growing in the backyard.

Out of habit, I pull the door open and walk right in like I still live here. My grandpa sits in his recliner on the chair in his living room.

"Gramps, I am so sorry, I should have knocked!"

"There's a lot of people in this world required to knock before entering my home, my sweet grandbaby is not one of them. Thanks for coming by, I was hoping you would be making time for this, old fart."

"You're not that old." Unfortunately, his barely there grey hair that he has combed over disagrees with me. As do the wrinkles on his face. He was always smiling and you can tell by the smile lines surrounding his mouth and eyes. The one thing that hasn't changed about him is his love of glasses and suspenders that don't match anything in his closet.

"I ain't that young either, I've got more artificial joints and teeth than the bionic man."

I can't help but laugh at him, his old age hasn't changed him a bit.

"What do you have going on today, Gramps? Got some time for breakfast and maybe a walk around the block?"

"Can we get breakfast and skip the walk?" he asks, looking hopeful.

"No can do, but we can eat first if that takes the sting out of it.""Only for you, Lolo." My grandpa is the only person in the world who calls me that and hearing it in person settles something in me.

I get to work on making something for breakfast. I do my best to find something healthy, knowing this man probably has not been taking the best care of himself. If he had it his way, he would live off fried eggs, bacon, and cheeseburgers from the diner downtown.

When I set down the veggie omelet in front of him, he grimaces before looking up at me, "There's a whole lot of green shit underneath those eggs."

My whole body shakes as I try to hold in my laugh. "Yeah, those are called vegetables, and they were about one day from growing new friends; it's a good thing I came over."

He uses the tip of his fork to pull apart the top of the steaming omelet, inspecting it, "Cheese would have sufficed," he mutters.

"Cheese probably would have added to your cholesterol problem. Eat the damn omelet." I point my finger at him, scolding him the same way he used to do me about the same things.

"New York made you mean," he says before finally putting a piece of the omelet in his mouth.

"See, not poison. New York made me not be a doormat." Which is only half true, but he doesn't need to know that. I put my hand on my hip and look at him expectantly, waiting for him to tell me it's delicious, because I know it is.

I turn back to the stove and plop the veggie omelet onto my plate, my stomach grumbles as the smell wafts up. Turning around, I set my plate down and sit down at the table, ready to dig in.

"How is it going on the ranch? I bet it's got to be a bit hard being back there again." The humor is gone from his eyes, and concern replaces it.

It's my turn to play with my food, because I don't know how I feel about being back. My living situation is the worst, and seeing Weston is just...hard. But actually, spending my days on the ranch has felt good. I've missed being back home more than I was willing to let myself admit. Being surrounded by nature makes me feel grounded and steady. Plus, this right here, having a bad day and getting to come sit at my grandpas is more healing than any therapists chair I could sit in. Being back in Windy Peaks is strange, like I'm coming back to a version of me that I don't know exists anymore. Part of me misses that old me, before everything happened, but I like the walls I put up around myself.

That's a lot to say to my elderly grandpa, who probably needs to be reassured that his baby is doing okay, so I settle for, "It's good, actually. I've got a lot to do and you know I like being busy. Plus, I get space for myself." The cabin is less glamorous than a prison cell, but he doesn't need to know the details.

The day with him passes by way too fast. I take advantage of the hot water at his house and enjoy a shower. It may be summer but that doesn't mean that cold showers at the crack of dawn are pleasant. He, of course, thought it was weird that I shower here when I have my own place over there, but I told him Weston was working on the plumbing and then ran away before he could see through my life. Very mature of me, I must say.

"Okay, Gramps, I will be back to see you sometime this week. If you need anything just let me know."

"You do the same kiddo, can't wait." We hug and he kisses my cheek before squeezing me one last time. With each little one, an old piece of me snaps back into place.

When I get to the truck, its old familiar smell fills my nose. There is a distinct aroma that old trucks with fabric seats have, it's hard to explain, but it's one of my favorites. When I turn the key in the ignition, it makes a clicking sound but doesn't turn over. "Huh, that's weird."

It takes a few tries, but it finally roars to life, and I breathe out a sigh of relief. A moment too soon, because within seconds smoke is piling out of the hood and I know it's bad.

My grandpa must hear the commotion and comes outside, with more of a limp than I would like, and pops the hood. "I'm no mechanic but I am pretty sure it's not supposed to be smelling hot like this. It's been burning oil like crazy lately. I'll call my mechanic and see if they can get it towed and into the shop. Sorry, Lolo." I rear my head back in surprise. "What are you sorry for? I just blew up your car."

"She's been on her last leg for a while. This isn't your doing."

It's now that I realize I am completely stuck here. "Gramps, I'm going to call Weston to pick me up, okay? It's all good. Go inside and get back to your game shows! He'll be here before you know it."

I tell myself I'm doing it for my grandpa, but a smaller voice inside my head says I'm a liar. My draw to him is in the past, or at least it should be.

Dialing his number feels foreign and all too familiar at the same time. I never deleted his contact. In the beginning I was sure he would call and say he made a mistake. But as time went on and the call never came, I didn't have the heart to delete the one last connection we had.

Now here we are.

He picks up on the first ring. "Hey, Willow, is everything okay?"

I clear my throat and try to get my brain to catch up, suddenly feeling all too nervous. "Yeah. Well, actually I kind of need your help if you're available. If not don't wor-"

I'm cut off before I can even get my sentence out. "I'm always available for you. What do you need?"

A lot, a drink, or maybe a grip because hearing him say he's always available for me causes a flutter in my chest.

"Something happened with my grandpa's truck and now it isn't running. Is there a chance you could come get me and bring me back to the ranch?"

"Are you at Vern's?"

"Yeah, do you need the address? I know it's been a while since you've been here."

"Nope, I'm on my way to you. I should be there in about fifteen minutes."

Up until now, every interaction with him I've had has been about work with a safe distance between us, now I'm going to be stuck in the truck with him.

My brain wanders to the last time I was in a truck with him. He walked me to my door and broke my heart seconds later. Sometimes I wonder what life would have been like if he hadn't.

I was always convinced he was my person. Like we were born two halves a whole. I can still feel it when he's around, the familiarity. It's been years and somehow my soul can still find him in a room of a thousand.

I was dead set on staying mad and as distant as possible, but maybe we can try being friends. With as many years as we have between us, it would harder to fake indifference than it would be just to try and be friendly.

It's taken two whole weeks here and my resolve is already crumbling. What will happen when I'm here for three months?

Chapter 7
WESTON

"I've gotta go," I call over my shoulder as I pocket my phone and make my way to my truck.

Rhett's voice hollers out from behind me, "Where are you going?"

"Willow called, she needs help." I leave it at that because none of them need an explanation. If she calls, I come running. This time, literally.

We had just finished checking out the east pasture, and I've been debating on moving the cows to some newer land to give some of the old grass time to grow back. My heart about stopped when I saw her name with the contact picture come up. We were eighteen, with our hoodies on and her in my lap at a bonfire in high school. The best days of my life.

I hop into my truck and get the key in the ignition. I haven't had enough time alone with her, and maybe this can be my shot to show her I'm not an ass. We've talked about work a lot but I've been terrified to ask about her life now. Terrified to learn more about the man who put a ring on her finger. I need to know if she's happy. If she's going to be here, I want to get to know her again. Really, I want things how they were then, but if I can't have that then being her friend will be better than being her enemy.

I've made it to town in record speed many a time, but this might be my new record. I pull in front of her grandpa's house in exactly fifteen minutes from when she called. The ranch is just a little more than twenty minutes away.

She sees my truck and hops off the front porch step. Today she looks like the Willow I know and love. A T-shirt, pair of jeans and some sneakers. While I will admit, her ass looks phenomenal when she wears heels, to the point where I've had to recite the alphabet and think about anything else when she's walking by me to distract my wandering thoughts. Her in blue jeans will always be my favorite.

Getting out of the truck, I swing to her side and open the door as she walks up, ready to hop in.

"I can get my own door." She says it as if she's trying to educate me.

"Not if you're riding in my truck." I nod my head, indicating for her to climb in. "You look good today."

Her head whips toward me and a rush of color spreads across her cheeks. "Oh, uhm, thanks. It's laundry day."

"The work wardrobe is great, but you've always looked good in a simple pair of jeans."

She nervously bows her head, something she did when she was feeling shy or at a loss for words when we were kids and I wonder if I've gone too far. I close the door and walk around the truck, getting back in.

"Thank you for coming to get me," she says quietly from the passenger seat.

"Like I said, it's no problem," I respond before putting the keys in the ignition and starting the truck.

"How's your grandpa doing?"

"Judging by his fridge I'd guess he's got some high cholesterol and high blood sugar, but he's good." Her lips tilt up in an unintentional smile as she looks out the window. There's probably not a person in this world she loves more than her grandpa.

"I'm sure he's doing just fine. Every time I've seen him, he's still sharp as a tack." We pull out on the road. All the houses on this block are brick. The lawns are all manicured, and aspen trees fill the rest of the space. I can't believe there was a time in my life I didn't love this little town. Its charm is unbeatable.

"Have you seen him a lot?" she asks, surprise lacing her tone as she turns her head to study my face.

Not wanting to show all my cards and potentially make her mad I reply with the safest answer, "It's a small town, bound to run into each other a lot." Not a lie, but not the whole truth.

"That's true. I almost forgot what it was like, everyone always knowing everything about you. Secrets are basically illegal."

"Yeah, but that also means you have a lot of people ready to drop everything and come help you."

"It's not like that in New York. Well, some people are kind and helpful, but it's rare to run into people you know. Most of the time, you're just a nobody in a sea of strangers." There's a sadness to the way she says it, and I feel a slight pang in my chest knowing that she might not have a community of people supporting her in there as she did here. Her response sparks the question, "Are you happy in New York?"

"Are you asking as someone who used to be my friend or as my client?" She turns her head toward me with her left eyebrow arched high and her voice inquisitive.

"We both know I'm more than just a client. At least, I hope so. I may not know you anymore, but I'm not a stranger. I don't want to be." Conviction rings out of my tone.

She lets out a deep sigh and chews on her lip. That usually means she's overthinking.

I reach my hand over and put it on top of hers to get her attention.

Her gaze snaps down to where my hand is laying on hers before her eyes shoot to mine. It takes everything in me to pry it off her. I just want to be close to her, feel her touch again.

"Listen, I know I have done some things in the past that you hate me for. And it's well deserved, but I would really like to move forward and at least be friends. It's nice having you back here, and I'd like to make the most of it."

I'm almost expecting a full-on ass chewing, to be honest, I'd deserve it. But she shocks me instead by simply saying, "Okay."

I wasn't quite prepared for the conversation to go this way. I had mentally argued with her in my head for forgiveness and for all the reasons she should be willing to be friendly, so now I'm stumped into an awkward silence.

Smooth, Weston, smooth.

"Okay." I mirror her response because it's the only thing I can think of for a few seconds. Now that I have the door to her cracked open, I want to hear more.

"So, tell me about your life in New York. Is it everything you hoped it would be?"

She looks at me and stares for a few seconds. I can visibly see a few of her walls falling by the softening of her face. The relief I feel at getting to do this with her, talk about life, is staggering. I wasn't sure she'd ever consider letting me in. I just need a crack in the door, just a small piece of her to mine again.

She crinkles a brow before looking up to the ceiling of my truck, letting out a weighted sigh, "Honestly, not really."

"In a good way or a bad way?"

"I don't know anymore. I have friends, but we're all in a race to climb the corporate ladder. I just thought my life would look different by now."

Part of me wonders if she, too, envisioned me there. My life doesn't look the way I planned either. I'm not lonely per se, I've got the best friends in the world, but everyone is starting to move on and I feel... stuck.

"That's okay, you've still got plenty of time left to paint your life the way you want. You're Willow, you're capable of anything," I assure her.

"Okay, Oprah," she says sarcastically with her eyebrows high, but her shoulders noticeably relax, and I'll take it as a win.

"First of all, I take that as a compliment. Second of all, I'm serious. If you're not happy, find out why, and change it." I take another turn, now on the road to the ranch. I love this part about being in a small town. Town is close, but if you need a getaway to the woods, it's right here. Pine trees line the road as we make the faintest incline up to the ranch.

"I have always loved your positivity, but sometimes it doesn't feel that easy. It's not always black and white." She starts picking at her nails again as she looks out the window, as if she's lost in thought.

At least she's admitting she still likes things about me. "I never said it would be easy, but you're in control of your own life. And if you feel like you're not, take back the reins."

She looks over, her features visibly softer. The corner of her lips even turns up ever so slightly. "Yeah, I guess you're right."

"I'm always right," I say with a playful wink, "and could you repeat that again so I can get it on camera. No one ever thinks I'm right and this would be great evidence."

Her laugh is silent, but it's there. I see her chest shake in my peripheral vision, and her smile makes a full appearance. It's been years since I've been the one to make her smile, and damn does it feel good.

We pull up to the entrance of the ranch, I drive under the Windy Peaks Ranch sign, and down the bumpy road. The setting sun begins to cast rays through the treetops. It's almost metaphorical of how I'm feeling. There's a little peek of light coming through, and her name is Willow Rae.

I pull in front of her cabin and see she's even cleaned that up nicer. The small porch it has is all dusted and there's a small planter of flowers.

I put the car in park, and as she unclicks her seatbelt, I fly out of the door, rushing to get to her side, and open the door up. I'm going to make her remember all the reasons she used to love me.

When I open her door, she deadpans at me and rolls her eyes. "You don't have to do that every time, you know."

"I'll decide and I decided that I want to." With a shake of her head, she jumps out the truck.

"Okay, well thanks. I guess I will talk to you tomorrow."

I walk back to the driver side and get in. My eyes find her again as she stops at the door and turns to wave to me and I feel a rush of nostalgia. All those times I dropped her off at her doorstep.

I pull out and start my drive to my house, replaying every last minute I've had with her. We're getting somewhere, and we might be moving slower than molasses but at least it's something. My thoughts of the past get interrupted by a vibrating sound from the passenger seat.

Willow's phone is halfway wedged where the bottom of the seat meets the top. I pull it out and see the new bane of my existence ringing. Should send his ass to voicemail, but I'm working on being her friend, which means I have to answer.

"Hello, this is Weston. Willow accidentally left her phone. I was just turning back to take it to her." I pull over and flip a U at the spot where the road gets a little wider. We used to pull off here to walk to the river just through the trees.

"Sounds like her. I have no clue how she manages businesses just fine but can't seem to keep track of her own things." He sighs deeply, as if her accidentally leaving her phone in my truck is a major inconvenience to him.

So, it's official. I fucking hate this guy.

"Well, she's doing a great job at the ranch. We're all very appreciative to have her help." I try not to insinuate it's just me who's happy to have her here, because I don't want to cause problems for her.

"Let's just hope she's better at remembering the things she needs for you than she is herself." He laughs a little this time and it sounds like nails on a chalkboard.

He so freely brings her down. No fucking wonder she seems like a shell of herself, I bet this assbag has put her down so much she's lost her spark. My anger courses through me so hotly that I have to squeeze my steering wheel to keep myself from chucking this phone out the window.

I don't know who the fuck this guy thinks he is, but over my dead body will he speak about her like this. Is this what she has been going through while she's been gone? The thought makes me sick to my stomach.

"Yeah, to be honest with you, city slicker, I don't think I like the way you're talking about her. She's amazing at what she does. Even better, she's a good person all around. You might want to pull your head out of your ass before she wises up and realizes she's too good for you, not the other way around."

"Excuse me?"

"Did I stutter? Respect your damn fiancée and quit trying to shit talk her under the table. That's pathetic. If you can't treat her right, I know a guy who can."

"Is this some backwoods way of trying to insult me?" he asks incredulously. As if no one has dared to ever put him in his place before. Well, today's the day, mother fucker.

"No, if I was insulting you, you'd know it. This is a man's way of calling out another man for being a bitch. Step up and have your woman's back. Unlike you, I have things to do besides talk shit about your fiancée, so I'll be sure to let her know you called."

I hang up the phone before he has a chance to answer. It's a good thing I have a minute to clear my head because right now, I want to ask what the hell she sees in that guy. But that will only lead me to being the overbearing ex-boyfriend, and that won't get me anywhere.

I pull in front of her cabin, a faint glow comes from the window. Jumping out of the truck, I head to her front door and knock, holding the phone out in front of me.

She swings the door open and looks at me, and then down at my hand. "Oh, thank God. I was wondering where the hell I left that thing. I was hoping it wasn't on the curb at my grandpa's house."

"Nope, it must have fallen out of your pocket. Josh called. He seems..." I can't quite find a word to describe him. He oozes little dick energy and arrogance.

"Please tell me you were nice to him." She snatches the phone from my hands.

"I was very nice. I told him you would call him back and that you're doing an amazing job." This is the loosest version of the truth known to man, but I don't want her worrying.

"Oh, well, thanks," she says, a faint blush coating her beautiful face, and I make a mental note to compliment her more. It's clear she's not getting any praise from her fiancé and I'll be damned if she doesn't feel appreciated for everything she's doing to help me on the ranch.

"You really are doing great. I'm going to head back, but just holler if you need me."

"Okay, thanks, Weston." She holds the phone up.

"No problem." I put my hands in my jeans to stop myself from reaching out to her. It feels too natural, regardless of the time that's passed. It's taking all my willpower not to pull her into my arms, breathe in her scent, and hold her like she's mine.

The good news is now I know my competition, and he can't hold a candle to the way I know how to love her. She's going to learn that she deserves to be loved the way I treat her every day. It comes as easy as breathing for me. This dumbass doesn't know what he's started. I'm a man on a mission and I'm gunning to get my girl back.

Chapter 8
WILLOW

Monday morning, I wake up still replaying the conversation with Weston over and over in my head. While no part of me feels like the same girl I used to be, *that* felt exactly like it used to.

Weston was always my safe place to land. He always had my best interests at heart and would tell me what I needed to hear, not what I wanted to hear.

But I'm left feeling confused because if he wants to be friends, why did he put me in this dilapidated cabin? There's no way I would put anyone I had any respect for in place with no hot water or mattress. I suppose he can have one brownie point for at least providing me with blankets and sheets.

This is a good reminder for me to keep my guard up. We can be friendly, but that doesn't mean we are friends. Friends don't make friends live like this. Though I have to admit, this is still a step up from my first apartment in New York. It was moldy and musty, and the cockroaches and mice were best friends who refused to vacate the premises, but it was all I could afford.

Stepping out of the shower, I shiver as I reach for my towel. The good news about cold morning showers is that they freeze the tired right out of you. All the exhaustion I was feeling before is nowhere to be found, but a fresh bit of "fuck Weston" has been restored.

My phone rings on my bed, and I tiptoe across the creaking floor. I hate being barefoot in here; it feels like a sliver waiting to happen. I need to grab a pair of slippers on my next visit to town. When the time comes to fix this cabin up, I won't need any guidance from Weston. I'll be able to tell the contractors exactly what needs to be worked on.

My phone lights up on the bathroom counter, and Grandpa's name appears alongside one of the few photos we have together. A wave of anxiety comes over me when he calls out of the blue. He's not exactly young, and I'm terrified I'm going to lose him before I'm ready. Not that anyone is ever ready or mentally prepared for that.

Fumbling with my phone, I bring it to my ear. "Gramps, is everything okay?"

"Good morning, Lolo, everything is just fine. Well, besides my truck. That old hunk of junk might not be repairable."

"What do you mean?" I try to keep my voice level, but I can hear the shrillness behind it.

"When Eddie came by to pick it up this morning, he took a look under the hood and told me it might not be worth it to put any more money into fixing it. So, I'll have to let you know. But don't plan on having it back in driving condition anytime soon."

Son of a bitch, I was supposed to be meeting with some contractors tomorrow. I need a vehicle, but I can't tell my grandpa that because I don't want him to worry. He spent too many of his golden years worrying. He deserves to be carefree. And I can't tell my boss I need a rental now, because I told him I didn't need one since my grandpa had offered his up.

"That's okay, Gramps, I'm sure I'm going to be able to figure something out," I assure him, trying to make my voice sound as calm as possible. "Sorry, sweetheart, I know it's not the news you were hoping for, but my girl always makes it work. I'm going to head down to the diner and get my coffee and breakfast with the rest of the old geezers. I'll see you soon, love you."

"Love you, too." Pulling the phone away from my ear, I plop down on the bed, still wrapped in the towel.

The thought of what I am going to have to do rips away the fresh and rejuvenated feeling I was relishing a few minutes ago. The urge to stay in bed and pretend this isn't yet another roadblock coming on too soon is strong.

I wanted to put some distance between Weston and me, but it seems the universe has other plans because I'm going to have to ask for a favor...again.

Walking into Weston's office, I prepare myself for how I am going to ask for help. During the walk over, I ran through about a million different ways this conversation could go in my head. I didn't, however, prepare for the sight of Weston at his desk in a backward ball cap. Don't get me wrong, he looks great in a cowboy hat, but I always had a soft spot for him in a ball cap. At eighteen, he was still baby-faced, but now, he has stubble covering his strong jaw. He looks the same as he did back then, only older, and more handsome, because apparently the world likes to make my life hard.

He notices me staring and shoots me one of his crooked grins. My heart thumps erratically in my chest, and I feel like I'm a teenager again.

I try to form a word or two, but not a single thought strings together in my mind.

He clears his throat before breaking the ice. "Morning, I got you a coffee. Hopefully I made it right." He goes to hand it to me, but the motion is choppy, and if there wasn't a lid on it, half of it would have sloshed onto the floor. Apparently, I'm not the only one who is nervous this morning.

My jaw hangs open awkwardly, and I open and close it like a fish a few times before finally sputtering out, "You made me coffee?"

"Yeah?" he questions, still holding the coffee out to me.

"Why?" The fact that one of his first thoughts of the day was something to make mine easier is hard to wrap my head around. I'm usually the caretaker when I'm in New York. I think I might have forgotten what it's like to be cared for in this way. With the little things.

"Because it's a Monday and Mondays usually suck, and I wanted to?" He shrugs one shoulder up. At this point, the arm holding his coffee has to be getting tired.

"Oh. Uhm, thanks," I respond before accepting the cup from him and taking a sip. It warms me up from my frigid shower and slightly melts the icy feelings I have toward my new business partner and ex-love of my life.

"Did I do okay?" he asks tentatively, his thick eyebrow crinkling with concern, and I can't believe he cares this much about my coffee.

"It's perfect," I assure him. This gesture is so incredibly sweet that I lose the fight of hiding my smile.

"More creamer than coffee isn't perfect, but I'm glad that I still remember how you like it." His smile is genuine and warm and makes the wilted piece inside me perk up a little. It's been twelve years and he still remembers how I like my coffee. It makes me wonder if my own fiancé knows how I like my coffee.

Clearing my throat, not really wanting to dig up that bag of worms, I set the coffee down on the desk between us and sit in the chair. He follows my lead and picks up a stack of papers. "So, I hate to do this, but I need a favor...again."

He stops flipping through his papers and looks at me with no hesitation before saying, "Anything you need, consider it done."

"You don't even know what I'm going to ask?" If I thought the coffee thing had me discombobulated, this tops it. How does he say exactly what I need to hear without me having to clue him in?

"I don't need to. You need something? I'll find a way to make it happen. Always." He says it with such conviction it's almost staggering. It *is* staggering, and so damn confusing.

There was a time in my life when I would have believed him, but that was before he crushed the thought that maybe not everyone who comes into contact with me would leave. My dad left me before I even graced this side of the earth, my mom left when I was a toddler, she couldn't stay away from the bottle, and eventually that led to harder substances. I've only ever had Weston and my grandpa, until I didn't. He built my trust through years of friendship just to bulldoze it down with a half-hearted goodbye.

Averting my eyes, I grab my coffee cup and fiddle with it in my hands. "As you know, my grandpa's truck broke down, and the mechanic checked it out first thing this morning, but it doesn't look good. Do you guys by chance have an extra vehicle I could borrow, or could you drive me into town so I can pick up a rental car?"

"How long would you need it for?" he asks.

"Realistically, the rest of my time here. I know it's a lot to ask, but I can totally rent one." We may have history, but he still is a client, and I need to tread carefully here.

He shrugs like what I'm asking is no big deal. "You can drive mine and I'll drive the old ranch truck."

His truck must cost more than I make a year and the thought of driving it around is slightly intimidating, especially if something happened. "That's really not necessary. I can drive the farm truck or your old truck from high school. Does it have tags? I can pay to register it if it's a problem."

"I got rid of that truck a long time ago." He stops, as if lost in thought, and I wonder if he's thinking about all the memories he and I created in that truck. I know I am. It shocks me how sad I feel knowing it's gone. He snaps out of it. "The farm truck is all up to date, just old and dusty. Which is why I'll drive it." He looks at me like what I'm suggesting is laughable. Considering the hunk of junk cabin I'm staying in, a dusty truck might just be a step up.

"Driving your truck is way too big of an imposition, and I'm pretty sure my boss would lose his shit if he even knew I was asking this," I say, nervously playing with my engagement ring.

"Then don't tell him," he replies, looking down at the ring with what looks to be a scowl and then back at me like it's the obvious choice.

"Or, you could just let me drive the old truck," I counter.

"It's a manual." He leans back and quirks an eyebrow up at me.

Pursing my lips together, I groan internally. "That's not a problem."

"Yeah, I'm going to go ahead and call bullshit. When was the last time you drove a stick?" he asks with a smirk. Now he just looks downright amused, and I hate it.

"You should remember, you were there."

"You last drove a stick when you were in high school and you expect me to believe that you still can?" He crosses his arms, and I decide to lie through my teeth.

"It can't be that hard, you do it." I quirk a brow up and match his stance, crossing my arms.

He has the audacity to laugh at my insult. "Okay." He digs in his drawer and grabs the keys before tossing them to me. "Prove it."

Well shit.

Chapter 9
WILLOW

We get in the truck, and he was not wrong, it's dusty and smells of cows and smelly men. Worse than that, I truly remember next to nothing about driving a stick. I know there are three pedals instead of two: the clutch, the gas pedal, and the brake. Really, it can't be that hard. Weston does it.

"Alright, show me what you got." He slaps his hands down on his lap excitedly.

Turning the key in the ignition, the old cab begins vibrating underneath us as the engine roars to life.

"Okay," I stall, looking around the dash of the truck as I try to figure out what I am looking at, besides the layer of dust. Unlike modern cars, most of the dash is shiny red metal. The gauges look like they are straight out of an antique shop. The pindley orange needle bounces with the rumble of the truck. "Just let me get acquainted with the truck."

"Take all the time you need, I've got all day." His tone inches on cocky; he's enjoying this...thoroughly. He makes a show of stretching his legs out and folding his arms behind his head.

Well, I certainly don't. I already feel like I am running behind, and I have a video meeting with my boss tonight to go over the progress of the project, and I can only imagine how well that's going to go.

Hey, Willow, it looks like you're already behind. Care to explain?

Ugh, I can hear it already.

So far, I have yet to figure out the contractor; I do have it narrowed down between two. We do have a basic idea of what he wants, but we haven't dug deep into his vision for the cabins. I should probably schedule time with him to walk through them together so we're on the same page. I've made some progress on the bookkeeping end, though, and that was the part that I was least looking forward to. So, that's a small win. Everything else, still lost. Confused as hell when it comes to Weston, too. Trying to be friends with someone you thought you were going to spend your life with turns out to be just as difficult as I thought it would be. Realizing that I am stalling, I press my feet down on the clutch and the brake, and I shift the car into reverse. I slowly take my foot off the brake and move it to the gas and slowly let off the clutch. To my surprise, and Weston's, judging by the way he sits straight up, we begin to reverse. "Ha! Told you I could do it."

The car slowly backs up, and then it's time to go forward. I keep my game face on, and put my foot on the brake and promptly stall the truck mere few seconds after my brief back out victory. The engine hops and then splutters until it is completely dead.

My cheeks heat as I suck my lips between my teeth and I refuse to look over at Weston. The vehicle starts to slightly shake, and I just know that asshole is laughing at me. I know it, and honestly, if I wasn't so hell bent on proving him wrong, I would laugh, too. But he's still kind of on my shit list.

"Well, I'll give you a point for moving us a whole five feet. I was willing to bet that you were going to kill it by throwing it into reverse."

Well, that makes two of us, but he doesn't need to know that. "In my defense, it's been twelve years since I've even thought about a manual vehicle. So, I was bound to be a little rusty." I readjust in my seat, shaking off my minor failure.

If I can survive New York as a naive eighteen-year-old, I can remember how to drive a stick shift. Trying again, I try to run through all the steps. At this point, I'm just winging it. He could have at least given me time to sneak watch a YouTube video or something.

When I put it into drive again, we move forward, but my joy is once again short-lived as I kill the engine, again. Unable to hold back my frustration, I grunt in annoyance.

"What am I doing wrong?" I throw my hands in the air as frustration runs through me like a pack of wild horses.

"Well, first of all, the golden rule of driving a manual is to not let it know you're mad or afraid, the engine can smell that from a mile away and will shut down at any sign of incompetence."

"You think I'm incompetent?" I rear my head to look him dead in the eyes, and the flash of panic I see there shouldn't bring me as much joy as it does.

"Honey, I am going to need you to take a few deep breaths before we continue today's lesson. I'd like to live to see my next birthday, and you're madder than a cat in a bathtub."

"I'm not mad, I'm just..." My words trail off because I'm not sure what I am at this given moment. A little stressed, a little unsure of myself as it feels like I'm already failing at my first solo project, everything around me seems to be making it harder, and to make matters worse, Weston looks so damn good today it's making it hard to concentrate on anything, much less the fact that I have a fiancé waiting for me back home.

"Frustrated to the point of annoyance, I've seen that look in your eye before. How about I drive for a little bit, and I walk you through what

I'm doing, and you can get a refresher course. I promise not to even tease you about killing the truck twice in a thirty-second time frame."

The independent New Yorker in me wants to tell him that I don't need his help, but I do. I need a car that I can move more than two feet without it sputtering to a stop. And the sad sap in me loves that he still knows me like the back of his hand.

"Fine." My voice comes out in a bite, so he knows I'm not happy about it. My hands fumble with the square seatbelt lock, but the stupid thing is stuck, and no matter how hard I press down on the center of it, it doesn't come undone.

Weston comes around to my side and opens the door; the half smirk on his face quickly disappears when he sees me seething. "Here, let me help."

His large body comes across mine, and I think I forget to breathe for a second. Surrounded by his woodsy scent, it's hard to think straight. It smells like comfort, strength, and the home that I've been searching for since the day I left. I take a deep breath through my nostrils and feel my body's tension melt away. His scent and touch ignite a piece of me that I thought had withered away. I used to love when he would do things for me; it was never because he didn't think that I could. I was always more than able; it was because he wanted to do everything in his power to make my life easier. And here he is doing it again.

"I forgot to tell you, it jams." The sound of the seat belt releasing is almost inaudible over the thundering of my heart. He pulls back, and my eyes track his every movement. His hand stays propped up on my other side, and now we're face to face. Close enough for me to count the flecks in his eyes. They're like little pools of shimmering moss that I could get lost in. I think I am lost in them. He seems lost, too.

My eyes track down to his full lips. Lips that part as soon as he realizes where my attention is. I shouldn't be doing this. Just because he's making me feel safe and cared for like he did last time doesn't mean I should fall right back into the trap. He left me, and he hasn't given any indication that he still has any feelings left for me at all besides the type of love that comes from having someone around for a long time. The staring contest we're engaged in right now is certainly blurring some boundaries, and I have a fiancé waiting for me back at home. Clearing my throat, I look down. "Noted."

The mood in the truck changes in an instant, and he pulls back, giving me space. The brightness that was just there is now shaded with furrowed brows.

I get in the passenger side of the truck and click my seatbelt, unsure of how to shake the awkwardness in the cab. "So, I'm assuming I am doing something wrong with the clutch?"

"Yeah, you can't just take your foot off it all at once, or you kill the fluid that gives engine power, and as we get faster, you're going to have to shift to higher gears." He looks over to me, all evidence of his prior frustration is now gone, and he's ready to be my teacher.

He spends an hour walking me through and making sure I can walk him through. I have to ditch the passenger seat so I can get in the middle and see what the gauges are reading, so I can prove to him I know when to shift.

Fire burns through me where our legs touch. Thank goodness I chose today to wear dress pants. It could be all in my head, but I swear I almost feel a little bit of pressure coming from him where our legs meet. Like he's trying to be closer. Which is bad. What's even worse is I feel myself leaning into it, too. Looking over to the dash just to get another hit of his intoxicating smell.

It didn't even take me a whole month before the ice I froze around myself began to thaw out. I can feel it happening, the softer piece of myself coming back out. "Okay, I think I'm ready to try again." Mostly, I need to get out of this truck and away from him, even if it's just for a couple of seconds.

"You've got this. There's no shame in asking questions, either." He's having more grace right now than I would if the situation were reversed, so I have to give him some credit for that. On top of all the other nice things he's been doing. Would it kill him to be rude once or twice so I could keep the fire of my rage nice and hot?

The gravel crunches under the tires as he pulls us off to the side. Thank goodness we are on an old abandoned dirt road, and it's doubtful there will be any traffic coming our way anytime soon.

Weston stays by the door after he hops out and closes it behind me while I get seated in the driver's seat. Like a coward, I avoid his gaze, needing these few seconds to not feel like I'm being suffocated by the man he is, the man he has become since he left me.

To both of our surprise, I get the truck going just fine and manage to shift it into higher gears, no problem. He points me to a road with a steeper incline so I can get some practice. Living in the mountains, I will need it, especially in this old, rusty thing. "I knew you could do it."

Taking my eyes off the road, I level him with a stern look. "I'm fairly confident you're lying to me, but thanks anyway.

The shit eating grin on his face confirms my suspicions and sends a wave of warmth through me. I turn my head back to the road, thinking way too hard about how badly I want to be around him again. Because right now? I think I'm happier than I've been in a long time. But this time, I don't want to give him the power to take that away.

Chapter 10
WILLOW

Saturday morning rolls around, and I wake up feeling refreshed. Maybe this cabin isn't so bad after all. Being tucked away in the woods, with plenty of privacy, has been better than I expected. I've come to terms with not having the bells and whistles here, and the simplicity of it all is calming. The only issue is I am officially out of coffee, and that's a must. A hot cup of coffee and a folding chair on my porch are more relaxing than one would think. So, I need to head to town.

I take the world's coldest shower, which I have yet to grow fond of, and get myself ready for the day. Jeans and a T-shirt are the most effort I'm willing to put into today. My first stop is the coffee shop and then I'll go to the store. My fridge needs restocking for the week, and I think I need some time off the ranch to clear my head. Get some distance from... Well, who am I kidding, Weston.

I hop in the dusty old truck and head down the road. I like that the road to the cabin is the same one that leads to the ranch house. I love getting to see it and be near it all the time; it's like a piece of me gets to still live in my golden years. The house is new, but the feeling I have here is the same. Jack and Mabel must've built this one while I was gone. The old one was my home away from home growing up. I really want to stop by and see Weston's parents, but I'm worried it'll be awkward. My memories here are filled with happiness and laughter, and I don't want to ruin that by showing up at their home unannounced.

When I drive past Jack and Mabel's, I see a car that's a little too shiny for these neck of the woods. Not to mention, everything here is either Ford, Chevy, or Dodge, and there's a BMW parked in front.

As the caring tenant of one of their cabins, I decide to investigate. I let my foot off the pedal to slow the truck, driving slowly down the gravel road, the sound of my tires crunching over the rocks. I'm not being nosy, I'm making sure they are safe. The first thing I see is Mabel. The urge to stop is even stronger now. I've been avoiding them, partially because it hurt that they cut me off when Weston walked out, and partially because I'm afraid they'll treat me differently, and that would hurt even worse.

Oh, and she's waving.

I can't even roll down the damn window because this thing was made when dinosaurs roamed the earth. I take back what I said about simplicity; some things make life less simple. It's then that I see a familiar face

Oh my God, that's Josh, in the small town of Windy Peaks, and not New York City, where he just was two days ago when we last spoke. My heart starts racing, and I suddenly feel nervous. Why am I nervous? Probably because we haven't seen each other in a month. I have a million questions going through my head, but the one I can't ignore is *why* is he here?

Speeding up, I press my foot down on the gas pedal and whip into their paved driveway up to their house, turn the truck off, and hop out.

"Willow girl." Mabel steps around Josh when she sees me walking up and opens up her arms for a hug.

My face hurts from how wide my smile stretches at her gesture. She smells faintly of fresh cinnamon and bread. If I had to guess, she's spent her morning cooking. I guess some things haven't changed here at all. "I have missed you."

"You too, sweet girl. I've been wanting to talk to you. I hope you know we only distanced ourselves because we thought it would be easier for you after Weston, well, anyway, it's great to see you. It appears we have some catching up to do." She nods her head over to Josh, and I let her go and walk to him.

I'm not sure what I was expecting, but after a month apart, I expected him to wrap me tight in his arms and squeeze. Instead, I get the lovely gesture of a side hug.

"Great to see you, sweetheart." His voice sounds different, like he's on the phone with one of his clients, he's trying to schmooze. I hate this persona of his, it's like nails on a chalkboard with how unauthentic he comes across. Besides my boss and Josh, I haven't had to talk to anyone in corporate in a month, and it's right now that I'm realizing I liked it better that way. "Are you going to introduce me to your friend?" His smile is tight and doesn't reach his eyes, almost as if he's annoyed with me.

"Of course, this is Mabel. She's pretty much the community mom. Mabel, this is my fiancé, Josh."

He wraps his arm around me now and gives my upper arm a squeeze. I don't miss the way Mabel's eyes are tracking everything. Now, Josh's smile isn't the only one that is forced. Mine feels borderline painful. We all stand together, and my fear that things would be weird when we reunited has officially come to fruition.

"Well, we are having family dinner tonight. We would love to have you guys." Mabel clasps her hands together and looks at each of us with a warm smile.

It's on the tip of my tongue to turn down the offer. Sitting in a room with Weston and Josh together is my exact definition of hell.

My fiancé loves nothing more than a good dinner party. He really shines when it comes to the way he can talk to people; it's why he's so good at his job. "We'd love that, wouldn't we?" Josh prompts when I don't respond, lost in my thoughts.

I shake my head and reinforce my now very painful phony smile, "Of course. You're in for a real treat; no one can cook quite like Mabel." That part isn't a lie. Her food is to die for, and that's something to look forward to.

"Alright, well, I need to go water the chickens out back. I'll see you guys back here tonight around six or so." She waves and walks around the house to the back, where I'm guessing her coop is.

Now that we're alone, I turn to Josh. "This is such a surprise! What are you doing here?"

"Well, we've never been apart for this long, and I missed you," he says before leaning down and kissing me. "This place was kind of hard to find. I couldn't remember the name of it, so I had to pull it up on my phone when I got into my rental car." He then looks over to the truck I'm driving. "Speaking of rentals, why did your company not reserve you one?"

He looks at the truck with such disdain that I immediately feel defensive of it. This farm truck has worked harder than probably everyone on this ranch combined in its years. "My grandpa offered, but then his truck had some issues. I thought I told you this?" I vividly remember both conversations.

"No, I think you're just imagining that. You're so forgetful, sweetheart," he says with a chuckle. I have been forgetting to call him at night, exhausted from working all day to meet the deadlines. The nights I do remember are too late with the time change, but now that he's here, I can finally show him my hometown.

"Well, I was just heading into town. Do you want to tag along, and I can give you the Windy Peaks tour?" The excitement in my voice isn't forced at all. I love this place, and now that he's finally here, I can't wait to show him all my favorite places and people.

"I'd love to. The town looks charming." His smile is so tight that I wonder if it's a bit forced, but right now, I'm too excited to care. It's nice having him here and getting to merge my two worlds together.

I turn to walk us to the truck, but he grabs my arm and stops me. "What are you doing?"

I look around, genuinely confused, because we literally just talked about this. "I was going to get in the truck and drive us to town."

"Sweetheart, you've been working hard. How about I drive you around?" He starts ushering me to the shiny black BMW.

The sightseeing will be hard, but it will be nice to be a passenger princess again. "Well, okay, I guess we can take your car."

He nods, the smile on his face is genuine, I can tell by the way it makes the small creases next to his eyes stand out. He walks around to his side of the car and hops in. This isn't unusual, and before I was back, I wouldn't think much of it, but now all I can think about is how offended Weston was every time I considered grabbing my own door.

The trip to town was useful in the fact that I got my coffee, and that Josh and my grandpa got along. He met us down at the coffee shop. Gramps can be somewhat of a spitfire, and Josh can be a bit, well, judgmental, so I didn't want to show him my family home just yet. I want to ease him into this small town. I know it can be a big adjustment, because I went through the same thing, only flip-flopped. The sigh of relief I had when they started joking about football was probably audible around the world. Seeing my two guys get along is nice.

Josh looked genuinely interested in everything I showed him. It was when he started oooing and ahhhing my very small high school that my suspicions started. He's always kind to me, but never this interested in pretty much anything I have to say unless it's work-related. We're very career-driven people, so I've never put much thought into it, but now, I can't stop thinking about it. Maybe he's just missed me.

He dropped me off at my truck and is now following me as I drive to the cabin. I did try and warn him that the cabin is more on the rustic side than the one we visited in Vermont when we got engaged. He booked me a surprise getaway, and it's one of my fondest moments of our relationship. The cabin was like a five-star hotel interior meets the outdoor setting of a small-town Hallmark movie. This cabin is so far from that in its current state, it's practically in another galaxy.

When we come to a stop and step out of our vehicles, he takes in the property. I try to see it through his fresh set of eyes. The front of the cabin is very worn, and most of the wood framing will need to be restored. The two large windows on either side of the front door also need to be replaced. Years of condensation have weathered the panes, and the paint is cracked and peeling. On the bright side, there's a quaint wrap-around porch, and the cabin is surrounded by trees. It'll be the perfect oasis once we put a little TLC into it.

"So this is where you're staying?" He gives the splintered wood on the porch a dirty look as I pass by him, twisting the doorknob and pushing open the door.

"Do you not lock it?" he asks, looking horrified.

"The only neighbors I have out here are wildlife, and I'm fairly certain Bambi or Yogi the Bear will not be breaking in. I know, it's a culture shock compared to the city." This is so different from New York, where hundreds of strangers could pass our apartment building in a day.

"I guess that's fair. I just want to make sure you're safe out here. I don't really like that you're all by yourself." He looks around, as if scouting for danger.

Turning the doorknob, I stand in the doorway, blocking the space from his view, "There's not a lot of space, but it has a lot of potential, so keep an open mind." I push the door all the way open now. "The primary room is in the back. And you're pretty much looking at every-thing else. The hot water is out, so don't be shocked when your shower is cold." I fiddle with my fingers, keeping an eye on his expression. I don't know why I care so much if he likes this place. Maybe because it's become a bit of a sanctuary to me. It's quiet, and I feel like I can take a deep breath out here and actually feel refreshed.

"Wow, well it's...something. What do you think your customer base is going to be?" He walks around and runs his fingers over the old faucet and then the slightly cracked wood on the cabinets.

"People like coming out here to get away from the hustle and bustle; this is a good place for it. It'll have more amenities after construction, obviously."

He raises his perfectly manicured eyebrows as if what I am saying is completely foreign to him, and maybe it is. The city took me a long time to get used to, maybe he just needs some time out here. The quiet feels loud when you've never experienced it before.

"Well, I'm going to clean up for dinner," he says and then wipes a piece of non-existent lint off his pants.

He's already severely overdressed; if he cleans himself up anymore, he will shine brighter than a disco ball. Maybe I should have gotten him some clothes while we were in town to help him blend in.

"This is going to be a pretty laid-back dinner; you could probably dress down." He could probably step about two steps down from his down, and still be a little too clean, but that's him. And I don't want him to feel like he can't be himself.

"Oh, is that why you're still wearing that?" Dinners for us are usually a whole affair, so I get where he's coming from, but the comment still stings a little.

I was planning on changing anyway, but the comment has me quick to reassure him that I'm still me. "No, I was going to change into a dress, actually."

"Oh, great, either way you would look great." He walks over and gives my hand a squeeze. "Who is all going to be at this dinner?"

With that the warm feeling from his caring touch fizzles away quicker than it came, "Well, you've met Mabel, so her and her husband will for sure be there, outside of that, it's kind of a guess, most likely, their kids Weston and Aspen, and then the other set of kids who aren't theirs, Rhett, Mav and his wife, Ava."

"Ah, so I finally get to meet the infamous Weston." He says it like he's going to enjoy this, which makes one of us. This is my literal worst nightmare on steroids.

Chapter 11
WESTON

My mom's name pops up on my phone, and I can't help but smile. Usually, when she calls me out of the blue, it is to tell me a funny story about one of her chickens or a way Dad made her so mad she went cross-eyed. Both are very entertaining.

"Hello, mother dearest," I greet her.

"Hi, honey," she says, her voice teetering on nervousness, which is incredibly out of character for her. "Are you coming to dinner tonight?"

"If you're cooking it, I'm there," I assure her. Anytime my mom's cooking is available over mine, I'm taking it. There's only so many things you can master on the grill. And breakfast for dinner gets old and is pretty much the only thing I am good at making.

"Okay, so I might have done something that I should have asked you about first, but you know me, if someone shows up, I feel like it's my duty to feed them."

Well, now I'm a whole other level of confused. Maybe she ran into Willow. Her being at dinner wouldn't be weird, though. Mom knows she's here. Hell, she begged to stop by and visit with her, but I wasn't sure how professional we were supposed to be, so I told her to hold off for now.

"You're not making much sense, woman."

"Well, Willow's fiancé showed up to the ranch today looking for her, so I invited them to dinner." She slowly spits out the last few words like she's ripping off the metaphorical bandaid.

Making me speechless is pretty hard; I'm almost impossible to shut the fuck up, but after thirty-one years, my mom has done it.

My teeth grind at the thought of having to see Willow with another man. If I had to paint a picture of a living hell, it would be that. I thought seeing her here alone was hard, but now we get to add in Josh. Fuck that guy. It's worse because he's a total tool. I talked to him for a whopping thirty seconds and I was able to clock that.

"Honey, I am so sorry. Should I call and cancel?" she asks, her voice giving away how bad she feels. She would never intentionally do anything to hurt me, or anyone for that matter, so I try and deflect.

"No, it'll be okay, Mom. I want her to be comfortable here and it'll be nice to get to know Josh," I lie through my teeth. His name tastes like shitty cow dirt on my tongue.

"Okay, if you need to leave early or skip out, I won't be offended."

"I'm a big boy, Mom. It'll be okay."

"Okay, well, I am going to get started on cooking. I really am sorry."

"It's all good, Mom. I'll see you soon. Love you."

"Love you too, sweetheart."

The second the phone call ends, I drop the phone and run my hands through my hair. Thank God I was home for this call, because no one needs to see a grown man spiral over this type of shit. I need to man up. This whole thing is my fault; the least I could do is be a good sport.

I stand in front of my parents' door and strongly fight the urge to turn around, tuck my tail, and head home. But I'm a Taylor man, and I have to face my mistakes head-on if I want to learn anything from them.

I walk in and scan the room. Aspen is talking with Willow and the City Slicker. Aspen has her professional face on, her smile so tight and forced, it looks painful. Her eyes swing to meet mine and she widens them. The best thing about being siblings is being able to talk without saying a word. The raising of the eyebrows was code for "this guy sucks", and you know what, I couldn't agree more.

Unfortunately for Aspen and me, Willow does not share the sentiment. So, I'm going to put my best boot forward and try my best not to shove it up his ass.

My mom turns around in the kitchen, seeing me. "Just in time, honey. Dinner is ready. Everyone, come take a seat," she hollers loud enough for everyone to hear.

Like usual, my eyes snap back to Willow, knowing she will be feeling a little anxious herself. She has her hands clasped in front of her and she's fiddling with her fingers, which means she's got anxious energy she doesn't know what to do with. It's almost amusing how well I still know her, but it's not. It's sad.

My mom, ever the hostess, swoops in, ushering everyone to the table. "Here, you can take a seat. She puts her hands on the backs of the chairs she wants them to sit in and walks to the table, and my dad kisses her on the cheek before pulling out her chair. It's fucking brutal watching them, knowing that was supposed to be Willow and me. All of us in this room together feels like I'm suffocating on what could have been.

I watch Josh take a seat, not even bothering to pull out Willow's chair. This man wouldn't know how to treat a woman if someone wrote a fucking handbook and mailed it to him. So, I guess I will just do it for him.

Power walking over to the table, I pull out Willow's seat, making direct eye contact with him. "Here, let me get that for you, Sunshine."

Both of their heads whip to mine so fast, I can't help but smile. He glowers at me, and it brings me such a deep level of satisfaction that I'm worried there might be something wrong with me. But I want him to know I'm not as out of the picture as he would hope.

Willow looks between the two of us, utterly speechless, but then she pulls her lip into her mouth, trying to hide her smile, and I know I did the right thing. Maybe if anything, he will start to be self-conscious and treat her better out of fear of losing her.

She takes a seat in the chair, and I help scoot it in. When she looks away, I make sure to make eye contact with City Slicker one more time, and because I feel like being a dick, I shoot him a wink. That should make him feel about two feet tall.

I take a seat next to my sister and across from the happy couple. "Here, West," Aspen offers as she passes the bowl of mashed potatoes to me, and I plop a big glob down on my plate and hand it across the table to Josh.

"Thanks." His voice is as cold as ice. "Are these vegan by chance?"

All talks at the table cease and heads whip toward Josh.

Even Willow's face looks slightly distraught. "Since when are you vegan?"

"It's just something that I've been trying. Is that not a thing around here?" He genuinely looks confused as to why we are all slack-jawed.

"Boy, you do know this is a cattle ranch? There probably isn't an item you will eat tonight that doesn't have some sort of something beefy in it," my dad says, clearly flabbergasted by our guest.

"Actually, I can get you a salad." My mom stands from her chair, walks to the kitchen, and pulls open the fridge.

"That's very nice of you, thank you, Mavis." Josh pulls his hands from the table, leaving me holding the potatoes.

"Her name is Mabel," Willow reminds him, her cheeks flushed with rosy hues, and she offers me a small, tight smile. I hate when she forces smiles, and I hate even more that she's having to make up for his lack of people skills.

I hold no judgment that he's vegan; there are some health benefits, like a good cholesterol level, but what I can't get behind is not taking care of your woman. It takes no effort to hold the potatoes while she dishes herself some. Does he help her dish up her plate? No. Can he remember the woman's name who went above and beyond to make a nice meal? Also no.

It's now that I'm completely confident that the man in front of me is a fucking pussy.

"Right, sorry." His cheeks are now shaded a bright red, also, so at least he has the decency to be embarrassed about that.

The rest of dinner goes by without any more outbursts until Josh's phone rings. "I'm sorry, I'm going to have to step away for a second."

"No problem." Aspen sags with relief the second he's out of the room.

Willow looks around at everyone, silently moving what's left on her plate around, worrying her lip. "I'll be right back. I just need to run to the restroom."

"Let me show you where it is," I volunteer. She hasn't been in the new house before and I'd love a second alone with her.

"Oh. Yeah. Okay." She nods, and I let myself up and walk to the hallway toward the bathroom and away from my eavesdropping siblings.

"Thanks for showing me—"

I whirl and turn on her. "What the hell are you doing with a guy like that?"

Her shoulders instantly tense, rising up to her ears. "What are you talking about?"

"What am I talking about?" I encroach further in her space, caging her against the walls.

Her breathing gets quicker as she stares up at me, wild eyed.

"I'm talking about you deserving better. You deserve someone who takes care of you. Someone who cherishes you. That man does not know what he has in his hands and it's a damn shame."

"Weston—" her mouth opens, but no more words come out.

"I may not be good enough for you, but I can tell you right now, I'm better for you than that worthless excuse of a man. If you were ever to be mine again, there wouldn't be a second of the day that you would question my devotion. Now ask yourself, can you say the same thing about the man who gave you that ring?"

"You don't know what you're talking about." Her brows knit together as she stands taller. She can be mad at me, that's fine. When she gets over it, she's going to realize I'm right.

"I may not know a lot of anything else, but the one thing I know better than anything is you. We could be apart for decades and I'd still be able to read you like a book. But I'm not going to push you. When you realize I'm what you need, I'll be here. I'm never making the mistake of letting you go again."

She stares at me like she's a deer in headlights. Her throat bobs, and my fingers inch to run over it, run my thumb against the underside of her jaw. But this isn't the time for that.

I lean in and nearly close the distance between our lips. Her mouth is calling to me like I'm a man starved, because I am. For her taste, her tongue battling mine. "Bathrooms on the left," I whisper. As much as I want my lips to sear into her skin and for her to feel me hours after I've left, I pull myself away. When I claim her, she will be mine completely.

I walk down the hall, finally feeling something settle in. She may have a ring on her finger, but I can tell you right now, she ain't marrying him. The only person who's going to change her name is me. I've seen my competition and it's only a matter of time now.

Chapter 12
WILLOW

By the time Sunday morning rolls around, I need a bit of alone time. Because I am one teensy weensy complaint away from ending up on an episode of *Snapped*.

Watching Josh here and seeing how he is when he isn't in his perfectly controlled element. It was a wake-up call. I feel like someone just dumped ice on my head and I'm finally awake. Apparently, he can complain about me, and I take that just fine, but bitching about my hometown is too much for me. I'm glad I've at least distinguished the line of how much disrespect I'm willing to take.

Josh is still sleeping; he hasn't figured out that the bed is a blowup mattress, thank God. Him still sleeping is a relief because if he's sleeping, he isn't talking about how the cabin is too rustic and needs some modern amenities. Or that the birds are chirping too loud. Who the fuck complains about birds?

I quietly slip into leggings, a T-shirt, and running shoes, and slip outside because I am planning to literally run away from my problems.

Walking to the road, I take a deep breath. The fresh air and silence calming the roaring epiphany in my head.

Weston was right.

Well, maybe not about all of it, but at least about me deserving more. I don't think Josh and I have anything in common besides our love of working. If I am being completely honest with myself, I don't think we really even like each other. When I look back on it, I can't remember the last time Josh gave me a compliment. And while I've been here, I rarely felt the need to stay in contact. He's the person I agreed to marry and I didn't miss him.

The sun peeks through the tree line, and rays of light shine on my face, offering some nice warmth. I turn my face up to it and take a deep breath. Something about these wooded pines makes me feel more like myself, the one I've been suppressing. The girl who was strong but wore her heart on her sleeve. It's like I forgot having a big heart wasn't a bad thing. Sure, you might get hurt. But is being this guarded even living? I'm sure there has to be some middle ground. One where I don't marry a guy who works in finance just because he's safe.

The hardest part is knowing what to do next is scary. Starting over...again. Starting over as a grown woman who wanted to be married with kids by now. I've been down on myself for years, and I think it's due time for me to stand the fuck back up on my own two feet. Being alone is a hell of a lot better than being with the wrong person.

I think I need some time to be on my own and figure out what I want again. For myself and in a partner.

Without realizing it, I ran a mile down to the Taylors' cabin, where Weston's truck is now pulling up. He probably still eats breakfast with them on the weekends. A thud rings through the air as he closes his door and walks to the front. I don't think he has seen me. I'm mostly covered by trees, and you rarely see anyone on foot. They're usually in the pastures or on horses or four-wheelers.

My eyes stay trained on him, his every movement. The way he fixes the cowboy hat on his head. The way his arms flex when he does that. He was everything I ever wanted until he wasn't.

He bends down and pulls a weed out of his mom's grass and throws it on the gravel, dusts his hands clean of the dirt, and steps inside and out of my view. I stare at that door, wishing I could go inside and be one of them again, but does that mean a part of me wants to be his? That's a thought I haven't entertained in almost a decade. I might be able to run from my problems with Josh, but I'm scared of what will happen if I do that with West and me.

Without a shadow of a doubt, I know what I have to do. Admittedly, it's a little messed up. Waiting to break things off with someone until minutes before they leave so they can't make the situation worse is a slightly immature way to handle things, but unfortunately, I am currently engaged to a man-child who freaks out at the slightest inconvenience.

"Okay, my bag is packed. I cannot wait to get back to New York," Josh says, curling his lip as he looks over the place.

Turns out that makes two of us, I too want him back in New York. "Before you go, there is something I think we should discuss."

His face goes into business mode, and I wonder how I was ever almost married to a corporate robot. I'm not even sure if he's capable of human emotion anymore. He wasn't this bad when he first started dating, or maybe he was, and I had the blindfold tied so tight around my eyes I didn't care to see it. "Okay, what would you like to discuss?" He says discuss as if he's putting air quotes around it.

I take a deep breath to calm my racing heart before I start. "I've come to realize we are two very different people. Being back here has made me realize some things about myself, and I think I need a break from you and me. Some space to think about what I really want."

"Willow, what are you talking about? We're engaged." The tips of his ears turn a vibrant shade of red, and I know I've pissed him off.

There is no better way to make an insecure man mad than to tell him he isn't needed anymore.

"I know," I squeeze my eyes shut, I can't believe I'm actually doing this, "I'm not sure if that's what I want anymore. I'm sorry, Josh, truly, but this weekend has been eye-opening for me. I don't think we want the same things."

He scoffs and rolls his eyes, "It's that cowboy," he spits out the word as if it's filthy, "isn't it? Have you been cheating on me with him?"

My head rears back in shock. "I would never ever cheat on you, and no. It's not the cowboy. Weston is irrelevant to this decision." I can't tell if that last piece is only partially true, but he doesn't need to know that.

"Fine, call me when you get back to New York. If I find someone else, I don't want to see you pulling the infidelity card."

Him threatening to meet someone else puts the nail in the coffin. This man is not my forever. "You are free to do as you wish."

I grab his bag off the counter and hand it to him, wanting to hurry this along as quickly as possible. He rips it from my hand with a huff.

"Fucking rednecks," he mutters under his breath, and I genuinely hope the door hits him on the way out.

Once he gets in his car and drives away, I feel one hundred pounds lighter. The relief is palpable. Except for the ring left on my finger. That suddenly weighs a ton. I should take it off. Part of me wants to keep it on; it'll keep the questions at bay, and it might just serve as the willpower I need to stay away from Weston. He broke my heart once, I can't let him do it again just because things are a little different this time.

Chapter 13
WESTON

The rumble of the old truck coming up the gravel makes me stop what I am doing. Which, if I am being honest, isn't much. I've been reading the same damn invoice for the last thirty minutes. I'm lucky one of the boys isn't around to see me moping around like this; I would never hear the end of it.

I keep thinking about her and that piece of shit from the city. All weekend, I was plagued with thoughts of what they were doing. Images of them cozied up in the cabin kept playing on repeat in my mind. I was tempted to make up a work emergency just to see her, but stopped myself. I hope our chat at dinner helped her realize that she deserves better. I want to prove to her and me both that *I'm* what's better for her.

We've spent time together since she's been here, but it's never enough. I'm quickly realizing that I'm a lovesick puppy, because I keep finding reasons to talk to her when she's in this office. It's like I can't think straight when she's around, but she's all I can think about when she isn't. It's been twelve years too long since I've seen her. Now that she's back, I never want her to leave again, and I don't know what to do about that. Truth is, I can't do anything because she's with someone else now. She isn't my Willow. She's Josh's. And I fucking hate myself so much for that.

I laugh to myself, hearing just how sad I sound. Pining after a girl whose heart I broke because I didn't think this town was enough for her. I didn't think *I* was enough for her. The latter is still true, but I've learned this town can hold just about anything if you want it. I'm building something brand new here. At eighteen, my dumbass thought the only thing in this town was what was already here, but growing up has taught me to appreciate my roots.

Fiddling with the paper again, I try to retain what it says. How much do we spend on fencing materials? I swear, I spend about eighty percent of my time working on that damn fence. If the cows-

"Good morning."

Willow's sudden presence in the room causes me to jump out of my skin and let out the least manly shriek known to mankind.

Putting my hand over my chest, I feel my heart thumping rapidly behind it. "Christ, woman. Can you knock or something so I don't keel over and die before my next birthday?"

She at least has the decency to try and hide her laugh. She tongues her cheek, but the crinkles around her eyes give her away. The longer I stare at her, the harder I find it not to laugh at myself. I just screeched like a teenage girl, that'll earn me cool points for sure. Ugh.

Seconds later, the room is filled with our laughter, and God, it feels good to be laughing with her.

The laughter dies off, and I wonder if her thoughts are aligned with mine because the way she's looking at me looks awfully familiar, but I am almost scared to think there might still be a chance, that there might be a smoldering ember I can fan back to life.

She clears her throat and breaks the trance we are both in by looking down. She shakes her head, and I get a chance to look at her. Her brown hair is down, her natural waves are making an appearance, and it's on the tip of my tongue to compliment it, but I don't want to push it. The skirts have been less frequent, even better, today, she's in jeans, and damn, does she fill them out well. She was beautiful years ago, but now, she's a smoke show.

"Are we still good to go do a walkthrough of the cabins today?" She takes a few extra steps into the office and sinks into the chair opposite me. It's nice to see her getting more comfortable.

I clear my throat so I don't embarrass myself twice before the day is really over, "Yeah.""Great, I feel like I'm already really behind, so this will help give me a clearer picture for the contractors. They sent me an email a few days ago asking for the finished details, so hopefully I can get it typed up tonight and over before our final meeting with them on Friday. I need to have things finalized for them."

It's crazy to think she's already been here almost three weeks. The contractors will be working on two cabins at a time, so we should still finish on time. I know she would have preferred they start this week instead of next, but it'll work out.

I slap my hands down on my desk and get ready to stand. "Well, then let's hit the road."

I'm a man starved for her touch, without thinking, my hand lands on her lower back, guiding her out of the office. She starts to walk to my truck, but I have different plans for us today. "Where you headed?" I tilt my head and arch my brow.

She looks around, genuinely confused, before she hikes her thumb over her shoulder and points to my truck. "Uh...headed to the truck?" Her voice rises an octave at the end, and she looks at me like I'm crazy because we just talked about this.

"We'll be using a different type of horsepower today." I wink at her and my lips curve up in a smirk. Hopefully, this works out in my favor.

Her eyes go wide and she starts shaking her head. "Oh no. Immediately, no. I haven't ridden a horse in twelve years." Tilting my head to the side, I point out, "You haven't driven a stick in twelve years and you did just fine with that."Her lips purse together, and I can see her brain working overtime to find a good reason. "That's completely different.""Is it now?" I sing-song, unable to hide the smile coming to my face from satisfaction. I've got her right where I thought I would. "Elaborate."She seems flustered now, sputtering out random words and mumbles while trying to get a complete sentence or even a word out. I raise my eyebrow and tilt my head toward her, waiting for anything.

"Well, there's a lot of things." She stares at the horses, a clear bit of fear glints in her eyes.

"Well, looks like we're riding together if you don't know how to ride anymore," I challenge. If my life were a movie, I feel like this would be a good spot for an evil little laugh.

Her eyes widen, and I think she's more afraid of riding with me. My new method of winning her over is going to be forcing her to be around me more; I'll let my super charming personality do the work. It's irresistible. And I will show her she can trust me. And then maybe things can be a little bit like they used to be. Getting my hopes up for that seems like a one-way trip to heartbreak lane.

Not giving her time to think about it, I lead my horse, Buster, out of the pen and work on getting him saddled up and ready to ride. She makes mumbled, incoherent sounds that I think are supposed to be words before me, but I have the bottom leather strap going through the saddle, anchoring the saddle to the horse. Grabbing her hand, I marvel at its softness, its warmth. The way her breath hitches when I do doesn't go unnoticed. Maybe I get to her as much as she gets to me.

I lead her up to the horse; she all but digs her heels into the dirt below us.

She looks from me to the horse. "Shouldn't you go first?" "Buster isn't going to hurt you, I promise." I scooch her closer to the horse; she goes a little more willingly this time. Maybe this will end up being a good trust-building exercise, too. Two birds, one stone, if you will.

She stares at me as if she's assessing whether I am telling the truth. She must think I'm telling the truth because she turns toward the horse and puts her foot in the stirrup and grips the pommel.

I reach out to help her, but she stops me. "I do not need your help getting on this horse, keep your hands to yourself, Weston."

I put my hands up in surrender and back away, letting her do all the work. The way her brows knit together, she looks too damn cute for her own good. It's killing me.

She does the cutest round of little hops before she gets enough momentum to swing her leg over.

I follow behind and sit right behind her. The warmth of her seeps into me and fuck. I have to close my eyes and focus so I don't get ahead of myself. It's like my body remembers every piece of her and has missed her as bad as my heart has.

"I should have just ridden my own damn horse," Willow mutters as she shifts uncomfortably, and my hands shoot to her waist, stopping the movement.

"I'm going to need you to quit wiggling like that."

"Why?" I hear the sass in her tone before she realizes why.

Her perfect backside rubbing against me isn't what I had in mind with this whole horse ride. I wanted her close enough to talk, and just to have her close because it's the only time that broken piece of me feels any peace. Now, we've got a whole other problem.

"*Oh*. Oh." She clears her throat, and I have to fight from laughing at her drastic overcorrection. She now sits ramrod straight. "Uhm, sorry. I'll sit still."

"It's fine, Sunshine." Her old nickname slips off the tip of my tongue before I can stop it.

"I haven't been a ray of sunshine in a long time." Her voice has a bit of an icy edge, and I fear that my slip sent us back a few steps.

"I doubt that, you're still Willow.""The Willow you knew doesn't exist anymore. Being everyone else's ray of sunshine just left things dark and gloomy for me."

Her words are a shot to the heart. This isn't what I had planned for us, but it's better to get this shit out now, no matter how much I am dreading it. I should have told her the truth when she first got here, but I didn't think she would believe me. Even now, I don't think she will. Trying to find the right time for an impossible situation is treacherous.

"Willow...I can never say sorry enough for what I did." My voice comes out soft, but conviction is laced through every word because I mean it with every bit of my being."You mean completely turning my world upside down before I was set to move across the country on my own? That was real nice." Her tone, on the other hand, is harsh and tastes bitter as I try to swallow it down.

"I know, I'm sorry. I was eighteen and stupid and thought I was doing the right thing." More than anything, I wish that she would believe me. "Yeah, okay. Do you mean the easy thing? If you wanted to do the next step in life single, you should have done it sooner. Waiting until the last day was fucked up and you know it." Her words have a nice, sharp edge and hit their mark, cutting me deep.

"That's not what that was about at all. I'm not denying it was completely stupid, and if I knew now what I did then, I never would have done it. And I really am sorry. Losing you is the single biggest regret of my life."

"I'm sure you've done just fine. I bet you couldn't keep the ladies off you." The hint of jealousy in her tone both breaks me and gives me hope. I never want to be the reason she's stressed, but more than anything, I want her to care. To care what I do. She doesn't know how untrue the entirety of her statement is, though. I was a shell of myself for a long time after she left. Even when pieces of me came back, the most important one didn't. Her.

"I know I messed up, but I am going to earn your trust again. And not with words but through actions. I'll prove it to you, Willow. Knowing that you hate me? It kills me."

"I don't have the time or energy to hate you. But my trust, I don't know if you can ever earn that back," she says quietly, sadness lacing her tone and breaking my heart all over again. I did this and it's my job to fix it, come hell or high water.

One thing that hasn't changed about me is my desire to rise to any task she sets in front of me.

Chapter 14
WILLOW

Weston's apology rings through my ears long after we start our walkthrough. I need to get my shit together. Over my dead body am I going to let him get between me and doing this job well. It's my first solo project, and if I want to grow in the company, I'm going to have to knock this one out of the park. I should have waited until Aspen could join us, but they're short-staffed at the hospital, so I haven't seen much of her or Ava since I've been here.

"I want to keep it all rustic while still having modern amenities," Weston says as he runs his hands over the bare wood wall. It's glazed over with a preserving stain and still has a sheen. "Can you explain to me what you mean by rustic?" I've learned not everyone has the same idea as the next guy, so specific descriptions will help me better understand his vision. "Keeping the wood exposed and in this same color." He pats the honey-colored timber before looking down. "The hardwood floors need to stay but updating them would be good. Exposed beams or 4x4s across the ceiling?"

I mull over his ideas, the vision coming to life in my head. "That sounds like a good idea. If we pair that with really luxurious beds, linens, and bathrooms, I think you will attract a wide variety of guests. The more appealing we make it to the broader market, the greater success you can achieve in the long run."

"Yeah, I like all that. I just want it to be a cozy place where people can fall in love with Wyoming. It's underrated, and for a lot of my life I took it for granted." He shoves his hands into his pockets as he gazes out the window, staring at the pine trees surrounding us. His words hit their mark because I feel the same way. Being back here with all this open space and fresh air has me almost dreading going back to New York. I love my job and the hustle, but I miss this part of life. The slowdown, the scenery, the peacefulness.

"I think a lot of us did," I say without thinking.

I walk further through this cabin, wanting to fish out more ideas from him, see what he's been dreaming about. Taking note of things that definitely need work, which is basically the whole cabin, mine really is in the best shape, which is kind of sad when you think about it, but I'm glad we're about to bring them back to life and make them shine. I can almost imagine all the memories they are going to hold. Families laughing, couples exploring, or even just some single people needing some space from the real world. I can understand that.

It takes us about two hours to go through the other cabins. I take thorough notes and make sure I have all my ducks in a row for the project submission to the contractor. I'm grateful Weston was willing to splurge on two contractor teams. That's going to be my saving grace for even having a chance to finish this on time. My boss has emailed me almost every day this week, and I don't want to give him a reason to doubt me.

My cabin is closest to the main road, so our ride there is pretty quick.

"So, how long have you been at your current job?" Weston asks. His warm body presses up against me, and I have to fight from wanting to snuggle in closer, but we're not doing that. That's not what we're here for. I know better than that now.

Part of me doesn't want to be honest with him because telling him I've been at this job since college and I'm only starting to be successful feels embarrassing. He always put me up on a pedestal, thinking I was the best and was going to accomplish anything and everything because of that, so did I. Out there, I was a big fish in a little pond. I was up against people who have been in this industry much longer, people whose parents had connections, and I didn't even have parents, nevertheless connections.

"I started as an intern my senior year in college."

"Oh wow. Do you like it there?" I can feel the genuine curiosity in his tone.

That's a loaded question on my end because part of me does like it. I like the job, I like feeling busy, and I like constantly trying to be better. What I don't like is being taken for granted, and after this many years, I'm only inches away from being the office bitch. I had to work from the bottom up. It didn't matter what type of degree I earned; every opportunity given to me, I earned myself so that I'm proud of.

"Yeah. It's okay." Even I can hear the lack of enthusiasm in my voice.

"Just okay?" he questions, readjusting his grip on the reins, his elbow rubs against my ribs, and induces a shiver out of me. How pathetic that it's been this long, and a simple touch still sends me into a spiral.

Trying harder to sell it this time, I say, "Yeah, I like my job. There's always a new challenge, and I'm learning something new every day. I've learned a lot there. So better than okay." Not a lie, so it's a little easier to make it sound convincing. You can be unfulfilled while still being generally happy, right?

"I'm not sure who you're trying to convince, yourself or me, but they're lucky to have you. You've done a great job here."

I hate that he's figured me out.

"Thank you." My voice comes out soft, and accepting his praise is hard. I don't feel like I've done a whole lot here, but the beginning of projects always feels like this. Jumbled, unorganized, and a little bit chaotic, all things that I absolutely despise, but somehow find myself drawn to fixing.

When we finally make it down to my cabin, Weston shocks me when he says, "Well, at least this one won't need as much work."

Technically, he's not wrong. It has running water and is definitely a stable structure. That's about where I would end the differences between this cabin and the others.

I let out a snort. "Sure, if you say so." This man is delusional. I wonder if he's just saying all this to make himself feel better about putting me in a run-down cabin. Admittedly, I have come to love my cozy cabin.

I don't wait for his help to get off the horse. As soon as we come to a stop in front of my humble abode, I swing my leg over and drop, thankful to get some space from him and clear my mind.

"Are you okay if I head on in?" Weston says as soon as his boots hit the ground, he starts striding to the front door, and I don't stop him from going in. I knew we would be stopping by on our tour, so I made sure everything was tidied up after Josh left.

He takes a few steps in and looks around. I focus on my notes while he takes in my cabin. I've already got a laundry list of things I plan to do to this place. I guess that's one benefit of my having stayed here. I know exactly what I would want as a guest and I can implement that in all the cabins.

When I finally look at him, I realize that his face has lost all its light. His face has paled, all color drained.

He silently walks around, studying the space as he goes to the sink and turns on the water, testing the temperature with his fingers. His jaw grinds when he continues to hold it under the cold water that never heats up. "How long has the hot water been out?"

I roll my eyes at his naivety, sarcasm heavy on my tongue. "Oh, I don't know. I'm guessing the year 1984."

His voice is steel, but his control is slipping. "You mean to tell me you've been living in this cabin for almost a month with no hot water?" His usually calm eyes are wild with hurt. He uses his hand to point at the sink, and I notice the shake to it.

"I don't know why you're acting so shocked, you're the one who put me here, "I retort.

He scrubs his hands over his face and his beard, closing his eyes for a long time before looking back at me. Well, crap, now I'm feeling bad for the guy because he's clearly having some sort of revelation of sorts.

Trying to make light of the situation, I joke, "You should've seen it when I first got here. It was buried under a few inches of dust, and I almost had to sleep on a pile of clothes before I could run into town for an air mattress."

He doesn't laugh. If anything, my comment throws him deeper into his pit of despair. "You're telling me there was no bed in here, nothing?" he asks, his control is all but gone now, he isn't yelling, but the anger is clear in his voice, and I can't tell who he's mad at. Surely it can't be me. I'm having a hard time believing he didn't have at least the slightest hint that this cabin wasn't really livable.

My hand flies to my hip as I stand my ground. "And you're telling me you had no idea?" I clarify. The pain that crosses his face makes my heart skip a beat. I've been using this cabin situation as my reality check with him, and I think we both just got one.

"You seriously think I would expect you to live here knowingly?" His brows furrow, and the devastation on his face would be visible from a mile away.

This may not be intentional, but the man still has a track record. "It wouldn't be the first time you've done something without considering my feelings or well-being."

"That's not fair. You have no idea what you're talking about. I asked the boys which cabin was in the best shape, or if it was even livable, and they said this one was fine. They must not have realized how bad it's deteriorated."

My head rears back and I fold my arms across my chest. "What? Was it too much work to come check it out yourself?"

He takes a big deep breath, looking up at the ceiling, I'm guessing to try and get a hold on his emotions. Really, I should be doing the same thing. "You've got me there. I really should've come out here and checked. But you should've told me it was this bad. Never in my life would I have you living in something like this. I can't believe you think I would be okay with this." He says the last part more to himself than me, his voice barely audible, but I can hear the crack in it. He shakes his head and a vacant look fills his eyes.

Well, now I'm feeling a little guilty for lashing out. This man looks completely distraught. He takes off his hat and runs his hands through his hair. It stands up in all different directions; his eyes look like he's close to tears.

He keeps walking away and looking at things. He pulls open one of my kitchen cabinets, unfortunately, it's the broken one, and it falls off its hinge. He drops it to the ground with more force than necessary. He moves to the window to investigate the seal. He tries to open it, and no matter how hard he pulls, it doesn't budge. The anger he has is radiating off in suffocating waves. Seeing him be this worked up over this cabin, I'm one hundred percent confused about my feelings for him. The majority of my anger was toward this cabin, even after I came to somewhat enjoy it; it's not really a place you would put someone you care about. I mean, obviously, anger of the past has bled in too. But even I am having a hard time pinpointing what hurt is coming from what.

He swipes his hand over a dusty window seal before turning back to me. "Get your things, you're not staying here another night."

"My grandpa's house doesn't have a room for me, and I'm not about to impose on him. I have nowhere else to go," I state defeatedly. Kind of the whole reason I told him I needed a place to stay. He knows this.

"As long as I'm still on this earth," his hands powerfully clap against his chest as he gestures to himself, "you will always have a place to go. I don't care if it's fifty years from now and you still hate me. I will always have a place for you. Meet me outside when you're done packing." He turns to walk away toward the door.

Frustrated, I throw my hands in the air. "And where will I be staying?"

"My cabin has multiple bedrooms. You can stay with me. I can promise you it's a hell of a lot better than this, but it definitely is a bit of a man cave. I promise I'll get it cleaned up tomorrow."

My eyes all but bug out of my head. He did not just say that. "Whoa, whoa, whoa, there is no way I'm staying with you."

"You're telling me you'd rather stay here than stay with me?" Now he just looks plain insulted.

"Yeah, I'm already settled in. The cold showers really help wake me up in the mornings." And not to mention, this cabin puts a healthy amount of space between us. I'm newly single. The ring may be on, but the engagement is off. Being under the same roof takes away my safety net of space. Space I need to be able to function, because when he's around, I spend more time at war with myself than I do on my work.

"Well, it may be good enough for you," he slaps his chest, "but it's definitely not good enough for me and what I expect for you to have. You're not staying here; it's not up for discussion. Your fiancé will just have to get over us being roommates." Authority rushes out of him, and damn it, my stupid body loves it.

The good news is my brain is a hell of a lot smarter and quicker than the gooey thing inside my chest, "And who the hell do you think you are making that decision for me?"

"Someone who still gives a shit about you. You may think I don't, but you have no idea. Seriously, get your bag together." He points to the suitcase I have stashed in the corner. "I'm gonna go run my horse back and come back in my truck. If you think I won't throw your ass over my shoulder and carry you out of here, you're wrong." He turns on his heels.

The screen door on the cabin slams shut behind him, and I take a good three minutes to pick my jaw off the floor.

It's embarrassing how hot that just was. It reminds me of the man I thought I knew, the man I loved. Sometimes I wonder if that should even be in the past tense, because being here is confusing everything I thought I knew.

But over my dead body am I about to let that man tell me what to do. So, I walk across my super roomy, wonderful place and plop down on my bed. If I've survived here this long, I can finish off the summer. Even if I spend the afternoons sweating and the nights shivering.

My mind wanders, and I lose track of time before I know what I hear: truck tires on the gravel road and a door slam. I don't bother opening my eyes for my little daydream, I'm half going on.

"Why aren't you packed?" I don't even have to open my eyes to know that he's annoyed; his tone says it all.

Finally opening my eyes, I shoot him a glare. "Because I'm not leaving. I'm not just moving in with you because you say so. I can live here. I'm not above living in a little bit of inconvenience."

Weston stalks over to the bed, complete determination in his eyes. I sit up and cross my arms over my chest. I feel like a child throwing a temper tantrum, but I don't care. Apparently, neither does he, because a few seconds later, I am thrown over his shoulders and his hand is on my rear end.

"What the fuck do you think you're doing?" I try to push off him, but his grasp is firm and secure.

"It appears you didn't take me seriously, but when I said I was gonna throw your ass over my shoulder, I meant it. You're not living here, at least not while I'm six feet above."

"So you're just gonna kidnap me and force me to live in your house?" The world sways upside down as we walk across the cabin.

"Yep." His hand wraps around the back of my thigh and squeezes. Good Lord, does my whole body set a flame. A pulsing begins in my core, and I hate myself for it.

We walk out to his truck, and he effortlessly opens the door with one hand, turns me upright, and pulls me into the seat. He goes as far as to pull the seatbelt and buckle it for me. Clearly, there is no reasoning with him.

This man is going to make me live with him.

If I thought working with my ex-boyfriend would be tough, I cannot imagine living with him. I need to keep my distance and protect myself, so he can't know I'm no longer off the market. It's better for this project, and better for my heart.

Chapter 15
WESTON

After a good two hours of arguing, Willow finally gave up and conceded to my offer. Or rather, just accepted the fact that I would continue to get her until she decided she was better off at my place. She's in the spare bedroom. I tried to put her in the one closest to me, but she argued and chose the smaller room, the farthest away from me, something that was definitely not a coincidence.

Curious about where the heck her little fiancé went? The cabin showed no sign of him. He was only here for three days and is already gone. Part of me, actually, all of me, hopes I got through to her. That man isn't right for her, and even if I end up not being the "it" guy, there are better people out there.

Now that Willow's settled, I have a bone to pick with two boys I consider my brothers. I had asked them to do one job, and they fucked it up. But Willow wasn't wrong. I really should've checked things out myself. If I was worried about where she was staying, I should've laid eyes on it myself. My sister is going to have my ass when she hears about this. I already know it. She got every ounce of my mother's "I don't put up with shit" attitude, and frankly, she scares me.

When I pull up to the barn, my two favorite dipshits are standing outside. Normally, I'm part of that crew, but today, I've been promoted to leader of the dipshits. We like to take turns so that we don't all have to be responsible on the same day.

They're throwing hay to the horses in the stalls when I come up on them.

"So, uh—when was the last time either one of you checked on the cabin that you said was livable?" My hands land on my hips, and I glare at both of them.

Heaving out of breath, Maverick stabs the pitchfork into the bale of hay and says, "Oh, I don't know, probably about a year ago? I stopped in there to wash my hands. The water is cold as shit, but the place is sturdy and has running water, electricity, and a bathroom. I consider that pretty livable."

For him, that is probably livable. He spent the majority of his life on the road and on the back of the bull. I should give him some credit—he's been knocked in the head so many times he's probably got a few screws loose.

"Well, I put my ex-girlfriend in that cabin because she needed a place to stay. I took a little walk-through today and realized that that place is absolutely not livable for anybody who has any ounce of respect for."

Rhett's eyebrows shoot to the sky as he jerks his head back, "Why on God's green earth would you put a woman in one of those cabins in the first place? You know they're in shambles right now. Hence, fixing them up," he chimes in. Once again, not wrong.

I throw my hands up, feeling like a complete idiot, "Well, I was trying to be respectful of her situation and give her some distance from me, but also, give her a place to live, and dumb nuts over here said it was livable." I hitch my thumb over to Mav.

"Well, now that you know that it's not, where is she gonna be staying?" Rhett asks, leaning against his pitchfork.

Reaching my hand around to the back of my neck, I give it a scratch, a little afraid of what they're going to say when I tell them. "In my guest bedroom."

Mav let out the biggest, loudest laugh that lets me know that I am completely fucked. Once again, not wrong. A little bit tired of being wrong today.

"On a scale of one to ten, how not over her are you?" Mav squints at me with speculation.

If I had something to throw at him, I would. Instead, I just throw him the nastiest glare I can muster up. Because that's a truth that's hard to say out loud. It's hard for me to admit it some days. But now that she's here, it's like the worst decision I've ever made comes back to haunt me over and over.

He lets out a painful "ooof". "It's gonna be a long couple of months for you."

"Yeah," I say on an exhale, putting my hands back on my hips.

"Are you just gonna stand there all day or help us?" Mav asks, completely bypassing our current situation.

Not ready to let him off the hook, I snap back, "You mean like how you help me find a place for Willow to live?"

"It is not my fault you didn't give me all the information; I didn't know Willow was going to be staying there." Mav flips me the bird and starts shoveling up hay again.

"So how did the rest of the walk-through go? You know, besides the whole ordeal with Willow's cabin?" Rhett asks. He should be in charge more. He's the only one of us who really has his shit together. The older he gets, the more he settles into being the most responsible one of us. I wish I was more like him most days, instead I'm hell on boots, but I guess that's what makes us all work together as a team. We each bring something different to the table.

"Went okay, we've definitely got a lot of work to do. It's gonna be all hands on deck." Walking to the water trough, I grab a hose and turn on the Spicket to start filling it up and topping it off.

"Why do I feel like I'm gonna be spending this summer working harder than I did before I retired?" Maverick asks, sweat drips down his temple from the exertion of throwing hay.

"At least one of us can be right today," I joke.

"The good news is this will be entertaining, watching your ex-girlfriend boss you around all day. About time someone tells your ass what to do." He shoots me a shit eating grin, and I spray him with the hose.

"Hey!" Mav says, as he flings a loose bit of hay at me.

Ignoring him entirely, I get back on topic. "Rhett does a pretty good job of that most days, and on the days he takes off, my dad takes over, so I think that job is pretty well covered."

"So I take it your dad isn't handling retirement well?" Rhett asks.

"Depends on the day. I get at least a text a day reminding me of something I should be doing. But I still feel like I am walking blind here. How can I feel so...." I search for the right word because I feel a lot of things about this all at once, "ill-equipped, for something I've done the majority of my life."

"Come on, man, give yourself more credit. Helping out on the ranch and being in charge are two different things. If there is anything we can do to help, you just need to let us know," Rhett says. He pats my shoulder as he walks by, setting his pitchfork against the wall.

"I know. I'd be dead in the water if it weren't for you two. So not to get all weird and emotional, but I'm glad to be working with you guys." I don't tell them nearly enough how grateful I am for their help.

Mav shrugs. "Hey, I've got an emotionally charged pregnant wife at work. I'm getting really experienced with it."

Rhett and I both bust out in laughter.

"Let's finish this up so we can head to the house for dinner, Mom's cooking, and I'm starved."

Everyone nods in agreement, ready for a fresh cooked meal.

Chapter 16
WILLOW

I survived my first few days of being Weston's roommate, but only just. The whole house smells of his woodsy scent. I'm constantly fighting the urge to seek him out, but that's the opposite of what I'm supposed to be doing.

His home is nice; the renovations he's done on it make it the perfect family home. A nice, open living space shared by the living room and kitchen. A nice two-car attached garage, which I can imagine comes in handy during the brutal winters here. The bones are beautiful, and so similar to the dream house he and I used to dream up. Except for in my version, the couch and love seat matched, and there were rugs to protect your feet from the chilled hardwood floors. Still, for a bachelor, he's done pretty well for himself.

The more my thoughts wander to our past, the more I realize I need to get some space from this place today. There's work to do, but I just don't want to do it today; there is something else I could do. It's a good thing my favorite old man is only a short twenty-minute drive.

I stop sulking and hiding, leave my borderline empty bedroom, and dart downstairs, snatching my purse off the counter and darting for the door, suddenly feeling excited. My grandpa is my favorite person, and I am so glad that I get to do this while I'm here.

I pull into the front of my grandpa's house and immediately feel a weight come off my shoulders. Everyone in my life has left me at one point or another, but he chose me. He didn't have to raise me when my mom left. But when his daughter dropped the ball, he picked it up, no questions asked. I didn't understand what a big deal that was as a kid, but he gave up the best years of his life for me. He was financially stable and had everything going for him, and threw that under the rug to ensure I was taken care of. If I think about it too much, it brings tears to my eyes. There's a lot of things that have gone wrong in my life, but I thank God every day that he's my grandpa.

Hoping out of the old farm truck, I walk in, and my grandpa doesn't even look up from the TV. "You're here a bit early," he says as he picks up the remote and turns the TV off.

"I didn't tell you I was coming. How can I be early?" I respond as I make my way into the kitchen and set my purse down on the counter.

"Oh! Willow, what a good surprise." He turns in his recliner and his smile lights up his face.

"Are you expecting somebody else? If now is not a good time, I could head out and come back later." It'll be a bummer. I was really looking forward to spending some time with him.

"I bet my guest will be happy to see you. Do you want me to make you a cup of tea or some coffee?" he asks, the sound of him snapping back his recliner extension carrying into the kitchen along with a groan.

Maybe I should start coming over here for walks instead of on the ranch. I want my grandpa to live a long and healthy life, and if that means coming over to help him exercise, I'm happy to do it. But that's a battle for a different time, "A cup of coffee sounds amazing, thank you."

"Anything for my girl. What brings you by today?" He pats me on the shoulder as he walks to the counter and grabs coffee grounds out of the cabinet.

"Can't a girl just come visit her grandpa?" I turn in my chair to look at him.

"She can but she usually doesn't without a reason or a phone call." He turns enough to meet my gaze, his eyes saying it all. He knows something is bothering me.

I sigh, slouching into my chair. "I was having a bad day and you always make them better."

"You make my days better, too, Lo. Do you want sugar and cream?" He walks to the refrigerator and pulls out his container of cream. It's the fresh stuff, and I get a wave of excitement as he pours it into my mug.

"Yes, and don't be shy with the sugar. Who are you expecting to come by, someone I know?" I turn on the chair, folding my arms over the back of the chair, and rest my head down on it as he finishes up with the coffee.

"Yeah, from what I remember, you guys have met a time or two."

"Well, I'm glad to hear you have visitors and aren't lonely." It's one of the hardest parts about being gone, worrying about him. There's only so much I can do from across the country, but I make it a point to call him at least a few times a week.

He scoffs, "I'm not trying to be rude, sweetheart, but I have a feeling I have more of a social life than you do these days."

Uncontrollable laughter peeps out of me. "You know what, old man, you're not wrong. It's been nice being home, though, and getting to see everybody." It's like being transported back in time, almost. A different lifetime.

"Don't get so busy building that career of yours that you forget to live your life. It goes by faster than you think. It feels like just yesterday I was your age, building a family with your grandma."

My grandma passed away before I was born, but from what I hear, she and my grandpa had one hell of a love story. When I think about it, it still gives me a little bit of hope that after all these years, she's still on his mind. That's the truest form of love if you ask me.

A few words of wisdom and a couple of minutes later, I have a hot cup of coffee in front of me, and life doesn't feel so heavy anymore. I knew this was exactly what I needed. Some people go outside and touch grass. I talk to my grandpa. It's going to be so hard when I'm back in New York and won't be able to drive over when I need him. I'm seriously debating if I even want to go back at all. It's like now that I'm out of the bubble. I wonder if I want back in. My grandpa isn't wrong. I'm not getting any younger, and it feels like all I'm doing is chasing my tail in a circle.

The back door to Grandpa's house swings open, and I spit out the sip of coffee I had in my mouth. There stands the former love of my life and half the reason for my mental torment.

"What the hell are you doing here?" I look between him and my grandpa, trying to piece together the puzzle.

Weston looks just as surprised to see me as I am to see him. "What are you doing here?"

"I asked you first, and this is my grandpa's house. It's normal for me to be here. It's not normal for you to be here."

My grandpa clears his throat, and I whip my head toward him. "Actually, sweetie, it's normal for him to be here. He and I have been playing cards once a week for the last gosh, I don't know, eleven or so years?"

My head rears back in shock, and if I'm being honest, a tad bit of betrayal. He knows how badly Weston broke my heart. Grandpa dried my tears, stayed up with me on the phone, and saw what a wreck I was when he left me on that porch. "What do you mean you've been playing cards with my ex-boyfriend for the last eleven years?"

"Oh, don't act like I did some great big betrayal. You know I have your back through thick and thin, so maybe there are just some things you don't know. And you know what, I love having him around; he keeps me company."

My grandpa rarely puts me in my place, but he just did. I almost feel as if I was scolded. If there's one thing I know is true, it's my grandpa's judgment.

Well, if I thought I was confused about Weston before, it's now about a hundred times worse. There's a part of me that wants to punch him, but I also want to hug him for keeping my grandpa company. I've always worried about him being alone out here, and knowing he has Weston to keep him company brings me a sense of peace and comfort. It makes me wonder why he's visited with him all these years.

"Alright, well, fill me in. What are you guys up to when you're hanging out weekly? I ask, still feeling a bit shell-shocked that they spend time together. "Did I ever tell you that your grandpa is the biggest cheater at Rummy I've ever met?" Rummy. They play rummy together. My heart swells at the thought of him sitting here week after week.

"Son, just because you can't beat me doesn't make me a cheater. You calling me a cheater makes you a sore loser." He points to him, and it's hard to miss the mischief shining in his eyes. It's cute, really. He turns back to me. "To answer your question, I kick his butt at cards, and then he mows my lawn."

Weston snorts. "Oh, so you magically come up with the winning card every single time, huh?" He grabs a chair and takes a seat; he's clearly just as comfortable here as I am. My grandpa spreads his arms wide. "What can I say, I'm a master of rummy and the cards love me."

Listening to them bicker has me smiling. It's cute. I look over at West, and he's sporting a matching smile. His eyes are kind, and there's a contentness behind them, like being here, the three of us, brings him the same joy it does me. I hate to take Wes' side, but I happen to know my grandpa is the biggest cheat when it comes to card games and board games. He wouldn't ever let me win a damn game of Monopoly.

"How about this? Why don't we play a game of rummy right now? We'll have Willow do the dealing so we can make sure you don't cheat, and if you don't win this time, we both know why." Weston cocks his head and smiles so damn big. He knows he has my grandpa there.

"If it'll shut the two of you up about me being a cheater, I'll do it. But I don't want to hear any whining when I whip both of you." He swings his pointer finger at each of us.

Wes and I share a knowing look, and now we're officially on the same team, take down Grandpa at whatever means necessary.

Three hands, and one brooding grandpa later, we have proof that Gramps is a cheater.

"So, old man, you have any words for yourself?" West says as he gathers the cards.

"The luck just wasn't in the cards for me today. What can I say?"

West and I look at each other, eyebrows raised. The second our eyes meet, we burst into laughter.

I look at the clock hanging on the wall; I should probably get back. I need to get a few groceries from town and pick up some dinner from the diner. "Well, this has been great. I need to head back." I gather my purse off the counter.

"I should get started on the lawn. You want me to edge today or wait until next week?"

"I think it can wait until next week, son. I don't want you running late," Grandpa says as he gets up from the table, gathering our coffee cups, and walking them to the sink.

"Sounds good, I can walk you out, Willow." Nerves enter my system like a swarm of butterflies. "Okay, sounds good." I walk over to Grandpa and open my arms for a hug. He wraps me in his warm embrace, and I take a deep breath, immediately feeling calmer. "Thanks for this afternoon. I had a great time.""I'm here anytime you need, Lo." He kisses the top of my head as he gives me one last loving squeeze.

"Okay, see you later." I look up toward West, who walks over to the door and opens it up for me.

We walk out of the front steps side by side.

"Hey, so I wanted to say sorry. I hope you didn't feel bombarded." He walks forward just enough to get in front of me.

"No, actually, this was a really pleasant surprise. I appreciate you looking after him all these years."

"He looks over me just as much as I do him. He's one of the best guys I know. I've learned a lot from him. I was in a bad place for a while, and I don't think I would have made it through without him."

"He's saved me more times than I can count." I nod, smiling at the thought.

"Yeah, well, I wanted to make sure we were okay."

"We're good, I'll see you tomorrow." We're good. Maybe even friends. Something that didn't seem possible before, but it's getting harder to find reasons why I shouldn't allow him a spot at that table.

Chapter 17

WILLOW

It's been two weeks since the contractors started, and they've made quick work of demolition. There's been a few hiccups. Like all the wiring is shot, but I anticipated that, so they've arranged for an electrician to come out and make sure everything's up to code.

I've spent the last couple of weeks trying to find the best booking system that can integrate with other websites to make it as seamless as possible for them. Really, they need a property manager, but when I swung that idea by Weston, he shot it down. Just another problem for me to fix, but I love it. Having to do all the digging and research and scouring the internet to see reviews and get real-life experiences with problem-solving.

My phone starts vibrating on Weston's desk, and I see the contractor calling. Every time he calls, it's bad news. Something isn't quite right; more wood is rotten, the list goes on and on. While it's not my money being forked out, it is the money of people I care about. I don't want to see them go over budget. Poor Weston gets the nervous jitters anytime I bring up the budget or the cost of things.

"Hello, this is Willow." I put the phone up to my ear as I save the current spreadsheet I was working on.

"Willow, this is Frank. It looks like we are finding more rotted-out subfloor."

Not that I don't believe him; obviously, there can be a lot wrong. But this is the third call I am getting about rotting subfloor. I'm getting the sneaking suspicion that he's adding in extra jobs to up the labor cost. He wasn't my first pick for contracting; the company I wanted was booked, which I can understand, considering this turned out to be a last-minute project.

"Oh, really? Well, I'm in the area, so why don't I swing down there and take a peek myself? I haven't checked in for a couple of days anyway. I'm sure you have gotten a lot done."

"There's no need for that, I am happy to send pictures."

"No, really, I insist. Plus, I need a break from this office anyway." He sounds less than thrilled when we end the call, but I am not about to let them think they can pull a fast one on me. Sometimes they assume that because I am a woman, I will just take what they say and run with it. What they don't know is that my grandpa made sure I would never be taken for granted just for being a girl. So he taught me the slimy car sales tricks, he taught me to trust but verify. It looks like I'm hopping in the old truck and heading that way. Assuming I can drive without killing the engine. I'm still a bit rusty, but getting better every day.

The truck grumbles and whines as I drive up the old, wooded road. It's not so dense with trees that you feel like you'll get lost, but just enough that it feels like an oasis from busy everyday life.

I pull up to the first cabin, hoping that's where Frank will be, but with my luck, he's going to make me chase him down. I pull the key out of the ignition and shove it in my purse. My outfit today doesn't exactly scream city girl, but it isn't whispering it either. My A-line skirt fits tightly against my body. The weather's been amazing, so I have my favorite sleeveless blouse on, hoping to get a bit of color this summer.

I have a lot of opportunities to be outside with this project; I really should be taking advantage of that more.

I see a couple of guys standing at a workbench, cutting a two-by-four with a saw. I make my way over, hopeful that they'll know where their boss is.

"Hi guys, my name is Willow. I was wondering where Frank is?"

"He's inside." They nod their head in the general direction of the cabin, and I nod, seeing they aren't really the chatty type. Which I can appreciate, that means they want to work.

Walking on the dirt path up to the front door of the cabin, I slide over a loose piece of wood with my pointed heel. "Frank, are you in here?"

He audibly sighs, and my annoyance shoots through the roof. "Over here."

I walk through the space, noting how different it looks. A lot of bare bones and loose wires. "Hey, where was that rotted subfloor at?"

He heaves himself up, but not before I catch the eyeroll. I want to stomp him with the heel of my shoe right now. "Over here."

I follow behind and come to a piece of floorboard that is a shade darker than the ones surrounding it. I squat down to inspect it closer. I've learned the hard way, many times, that not everything is what it seems. When I run my hand over the discolored spot, I notice that it feels wet.

"Any idea why this one spot right here is wet and the whole rest of the subfloor is dry?" I dust off my hands as I stand up, cocking my brow up at Frank.

He mumbles out a bunch of unfinished words, variations of uhs, well, you see, and a lot of sweating going on. All of which proves my earlier suspicions that Frank made this up.

"I really don't appreciate being taken advantage of. Not only are you trying to screw me, but also the family that I hold very near and dear to my heart."

As if my words have summoned him, Weston walks in behind me.

His hands are in his pockets as he takes a look around, that lazy smile I adore on him stretches across his lips as he takes in the work being done. "Hey guys, how's it going?" he asks, oblivious to the tense conversation he just walked in on.

"What are you doing here?" I ask.

"I was in the area and wanted to pop by and see how things are going. We were trying to figure out where we're gonna drop the cows off next rotation. What's going on here?" He must now feel the tension; his smile is gone, and in its place is concern.

"Me and your little assistant here, we're just having a little disagreement," Frank chimes in.

Little assistant. I may have been raised in small-town Wyoming, but I spent the last twelve years of my life in New York. And this bitch is about to see the inner East Coast badass me unleash.

Weston gets to putting him in his place before I do. "Excuse me? What did you just call her?" His voice comes out in calm, cool, collected rage.

"Come on, West, we both know she's basically a glorified assistant."

Not that there's anything wrong with being an assistant, I was one for years. I had to fight and claw my way up, but the way he's saying it is absolutely derogatory.

"That woman happens to actually be your boss. She's calling the shots here, not me. Since you decided to put me in charge, you're fired."

The fire of my rage gets put out by the ice bucket of panic now washing over me. We don't have time to find a new contractor. This isn't the first time a contractor, or a man in general, has tried to pull a fast one on me; definitely won't be the last time.

"Weston, can I speak to you outside, please?" I interrupt.

He has a puzzled look on his face, but nods his head yes and walks out, which should be at the front door, but it's currently just a bunch of tarp.

Grabbing him by the arm, I drag him farther away. "What the hell do you think you're doing? We cannot fire him."

His jaw briefly drops before he chimes in, "He deserves to be fired. He's disrespecting you."

Closing my eyes, I put my thumb and index finger on my head. Frustration is getting the better of me, and I feel like I'm the only one here who cares if we finish on time. "You do know you're on a very tight timeline, correct?"

Clearly unaffected by me, he says, "It doesn't matter. He talked down to you and he's out of here."

"He's far from the last man who is going to take advantage of me because I'm a woman. He's also not the last man who's ever going to disrespect me because he doesn't think a woman should be in charge of this job. You can't fire everyone who's a kind of an ass."

"You're right, I don't want to fire everyone who is kind of an ass, I just want to fire the ones that are kind of an ass to *you*."

That's a hard sentiment to be mad at. The inner part of me who loved this side of Weston, who was hell bent on defending me, is melting at this. I rake over memories of the last few years, trying to scrape up a time someone stood up for me like this.

"I appreciate you defending me right now, but I really can't do this. If you want to fire him, you're going to have to find a new contractor that can be here in the next forty-eight hours."

He folds his arms over his chest and shrugs. "Done."

Okay, that's it. I'm going to lose it, and Frank won't be the only one getting fired today because I am going to kill Weston. "You can't be serious. There's no way you will find somebody. Not only that, when you come in here, and you take over a situation like that, you make it seem like I can't handle it, and I can."

His face falls when my words sink in. "Shit, Willow, that wasn't what I was trying to do at all."

"Unfortunately, I don't have a set of balls hanging between my legs, so men tend not to take me seriously. You know what does make them take me seriously? Standing on business and reminding them who's boss. I can't do that when you come in and take over. I appreciate you wanting them to respect me, but I can earn their respect on my own merit."

He nods with a remorseful look on his face. "Okay, from here on out, I'll stay out of it unless you loop me in. I wasn't trying to step on your toes. It's hard for me to watch someone being an ass to you and do nothing about it."

My anger is short-lived because, as much as I hate it, he's only trying to be kind. "I'll make you a deal, as long as they aren't working for me, you can come to my defense anytime. But at work, you need to let me handle my business."

West puts his hands up and surrenders. "It won't happen again. But I really think we need to fire Frank. I don't know what was going on between you two, but chances are, he's not the type of person we want working on this project anyway. I'll find somebody by the end of the day, I promise."

"Don't make promises you can't keep." Her statement is a harsh reminder of the past promises he made about never leaving or hurting me, only to do both and provide me the deepest cut of my life.

"I've let you down in the past. I'm never going to do that again. That's a promise I know I can keep. Now I'm gonna go and find Frank's replacement."

Weston stalks off toward his truck, and I stare at his large frame. And I can't help but notice how damn good he looks in those wranglers. As annoyed as I am with him right now, a part of me is glowering. That man, right there, saw a problem and solved it for me, no questions asked. And not to prove he's some sort of man's man. He did that just for me. I've spent twelve years missing someone I didn't think existed, but as I watch the dirt kick up under his tires, I wonder if I've had it all wrong.

Chapter 18
WESTON

Family dinner is exactly what I needed after a stressful few days. Somehow, I was able to magically pull a reliable and honest contractor out of my ass. My dad has connections with just about everyone and was able to help me find someone in a hurry. Willow was beside herself, but anything I can do to make that girl believe that she can count on me, I'm going to do it. I'll show up one hundred and ten percent every day of the year if I have to.

Laughter sounds off from around the table, shaking me from my thoughts. I take a good, hard look at the faces sitting around it and get a sudden wave of appreciation. While not everything in my life is perfect or has gone to plan, this group has been with me through it all. I'll never take my family for granted. My dad stands behind my mom's chair, his arms gently draped over her shoulders. Aspen's at work, and Rhett is out of town, but everyone else is here. It's not often that we all get free time to shoot the shit, but today things are calm, and we're actually caught up.

I pull out my phone and check the time; I've got a standing meeting I can't miss.

"Alright, I've got to head out. You making dinner tomorrow night, Mom, or are you forcing me to scrounge up food on my own?"

She rolls her eyes. "Sweetie, you're thirty-one. I know good and well you can make your own meals. You're on your own, your dad and I are going to do a long weekend in Cheyenne, and we're heading up tonight."

"Why can't your 'weekly meeting' make you dinner. I'm sure she would be more than happy to," Mav jokes.

Cocking my head to the side, I look over to his wife. "Ava, did you just hear that Mav wants to cook dinner for the rest of the week?" I ask.

"I'm so glad I'm not the only one who heard that. Steak sounds great with mashed potatoes. Oooh, and some gravy." She turns to Mav and holds on to his arm as she paints the picture of her perfect dinner, which I admit, is making my mouth water, too.

"Are you ever going to introduce us to this girl?" my mom asks.

"No, because you all are delusional and I'm not seeing anyone." I stand up from my chair and push it back under the table,

"We know you're full of shit. Or is it a different girl each week? We know you like to play the field," Ava says, no longer on my team, apparently.

"Keep that up and you're going to have to find someone else to gang up on Maverick with." I point to her and shake my head.

"No, you do it so well," she whines.

"That's what I thought. Now, have a good night. I'll see you tomorrow," I say, looking toward Mav.

"Have fun with your mystery date," he says as I walk to the door.

I don't grace any of them with a response. If my mother wasn't sitting there, I'd flip off the whole table.

They have no clue how wrong they are. I haven't gone on a date in years. Finding someone new absolutely fires no interest in me.

I hop in my truck and drive with the windows down through town. Afternoon is my favorite time of day; things slow down, it's not too hot, and you get a chance just to breathe. I need to do more of that. Relax. It's been hard to do that since taking over, and even harder since I decided to renovate the cabins and restructure the backend of the business.

I have a hard time asking the boys for any more help because they already work from sunup to sundown for me. I can't ask them for more if I can't give them more. Someday, hopefully, I can give bonuses. But for now, Maverick is footing the bill on the remodels. It'll work out, I know it in my gut. I just have to remind my overactive head of that every so often.

I pull into the same driveway that I do every Thursday at three and walk up the back porch steps. I haven't knocked to enter this house since I was twelve. I thought that would change when his granddaughter and I broke up, but it didn't. He still welcomed me into his home as he always had.

I walk into the kitchen and see that he already has the cards set out and ready, a good sign that he has rigged his hand to beat me, but I don't care. Time with him isn't about that. At first, it was because being around him made me miss Willow a little less. Being in this house let me pretend for a while that she wasn't gone and that she still loved me. But then it turned into me not wanting him to be lonely. Genuinely, I enjoy his company. The man is wiser than his years, which is saying something, because he's getting up there.

"Good afternoon, son. How was ranch work today?" He sets down a steaming cup of coffee.

"It was a good day. We actually didn't have a whole lot to do, and today seemed like a good day to give everyone a little bit of a break before the next shit show pops up," I say.

"You shouldn't have said that out loud, you just set yourself up for a shit show tomorrow." He shakes his finger at me.

He would know, too. He worked for us for years as a ferrier. He was the best damn one we've ever had. No one took greater pride in their work than he did. It's no wonder Willow is the way she is; she learned work ethic and accountability from the best.

"How's our girl doing?" he asks, catching me by surprise.

When I raise my eyebrows, he gives me a look.

"You think I haven't been able to tell you've still got it bad for her all these years? You ask about her every time, hanging on to every word that has anything to do with her."

I want to deny it, but it's no use. He's right. To me, she will always be mine. "She's doing really well. She's too hard on herself. She blew through the back end of the work in a couple of weeks, all while arranging contractors. She's got it in her mind that she's behind."

"Sounds like her. Must say, it's easier to sleep at night knowing she's back around these neck of the woods. Part of me hopes she won't go back."

"That makes two of us." Maybe then we could try again, as these grown-up versions of ourselves.

"Well, enough with being all sappy. Let's play cards. I hope you don't mind, I dealt the first hand."

"You try and deal every hand," I level with him.

"Well, if you could shuffle worth a shit, I'd let you do it, but half the cards end up on the floor. We'd spend half of the hour I get with you picking them back up and trying again." He scoots his chair in closer, not caring that he just roasted the shit out of me.

"Thanks for that, Vern, you really know how to build a man's confidence." I shake my head as I grin.

"You've got plenty of that to go around. Someone needs to keep you humble. When Willow decides she still loves you, I'll let her take over."

"You really think she still loves me?" I ask, taking us out of the lighthearted moment.

"I have no doubt in my mind."

Not knowing what to do with that, I pick up the hand I was dealt, realizing I don't like it at all. I look up over my cards and see him snickering in his seat.

"Whatcha laughing at, old man?"

"How pathetic you are." He snickers some more, holding his cards in front of his face.

"Ouch. And you're a liar. But let's get started. I'm going to need a miracle to come back from this hand."

Looking at my hand, I have ten cards, and no matches. So I choose to discard my first turn, hoping to unload some of this crap.

Vern lays down a match, and I already know how this game is going to go. "So, do you have a plan for winning her back?"

"No, she's barely been tolerant of me thus far. Maybe we should wait and see if she even likes me."

"She's just being mean to protect her heart. Her mom was the same way before. Well, when her mom was still her."

"I did what I did for her, and I don't think she will believe me. It's not like I have a way to prove it."

"Actions speak louder than words. Be the man she needs without her having to ask. It should come naturally to you anyway."

He takes his turn and lays down his matching set of cards. I'm going to get my ass whooped in this game. I take a sip of coffee, and the warmth slides down my throat. He makes his coffee so strong it'll put some hair on your chest. But it does help wake me up, almost as much as his comment about winning back his granddaughter.

More than anything, I want that girl to be mine. I don't know how yet, but I'm going to win her back, and this time, she's not leaving Windy Peaks without me.

Chapter 19
WILLOW

"Yes, I understand the severity of the timeline. The contractors are certain they can finish on schedule." I leave out the part where I am absolutely certain we will not finish in time.

"To make sure you're staying on track. I'd like for you to send out an email of your weekly tasks and their status," Tony says, and it's in such a tone that it makes me feel about two inches tall.

I should've known that when I was assigned my own project, he would micromanage me. It'd be nice if the company I've busted my ass for could trust me with this. Even if it does end up going over the budget and timeline, I wouldn't be the first person to have that happen to. But unfortunately, those thoughts have to stay inside my little brain because I don't feel like being fired today.

"I can do that, but I do want you to know that I have complete confidence in this project and would appreciate you reciprocating that." Being firm like this feels abrasive, but it's a tactic I've had to learn the hard way if I ever wanted to be taken seriously.

"Sure, but trust has to be earned. I know it's frustrating to have eyes on your project, but if this is a success, you'll have a lot more freedom." I can hear the squeak of his chair on the other end of the line, and it adds to the simmering fury I have. I can just picture him comfortably reclining in his chair, having the gall to lecture me from the comfort of his big office with a view.

I've been at the company for twelve years. You think that would earn me a little bit of trust-induced freedom, but you know, beggars can't be choosers; at least I got a project.

"I plan to knock this project out of the park," I say through tight lips. My tone could use some work on being more convincing, but at least I didn't mouth off.

"I'm sure you will. Listen, Willow, I've got a call coming on the other line. Send me that email by the end of the week, thanks." The line goes dead, and I debate chucking my phone across the room.

The phone call leaves me with restless energy. I feel frustrated by the lack of autonomy I have over the project, but also anxious that I've overpromised what I can deliver. I need to get this energy out, and the only way I can think to do that is a nice long run.

It takes twenty minutes to dig through my half-unpacked bag and fling all my stuff haphazardly around the room to find my running shoes. When Weston insisted I stay with him, he took on the task of helping me pack, and his way of organizing was to throw everything in as quickly as possible. The fact that I have yet to unpack is further proof I'm living in a state of denial that I'm newly *secretly* single and residing just a few doors down from the man that still has the power to make my heart flutter.

Since I don't feel like being eaten by a bear today, running on the gravel road instead of through the woods will be my safest bet. Plus, with my sense of direction, I'd probably end up getting lost, and that doesn't sound like a pleasant way to go. There's no GPS, and even if there was, the cellphone coverage up here is terrible.

With every step of my feet hitting the gravel, I feel a bit of relief. I've always loved the clear head running gives me. I get to think through all my thoughts in every single possible scenario. It's like my own little movie in my head. My best planning for projects is always done on runs.

I make a mental list of all the things I need to get done at the cabins, like finding a booking system that will be user-friendly for the family but also supports long-term growth for the business. Then I need to really get started on making a mood board for the decor and seeing if Weston agrees. Better yet, I should loop his style-loving sister in.

It would be a good reason to see her. She's been working long hours at the hospital since I've been back, and I miss her. I've missed her the entire time I was gone. She was always the little sister I didn't have, and I'm bummed we haven't had the opportunity to spend much time together while I've been here.

Pulling my headphones out of my ears, I take a step into Weston's cabin. My new home for the next couple of months. I'm seriously missing my rustic cabin right now, even though Weston's home is really nice. My room, even for a spare room quite spacious. It has a whole bedroom set, a nice quilt, and even an extra throw blanket, which I'm pretty sure had something to do with either Aspen or Mabel, but I'll give him credit for it at least being there. The bathroom I was in even had soap that wasn't a bar.

It's clear to see that Weston has put a lot of time and effort into his home. Maybe that's why it's so hard being here. He's literally everywhere. He's in the pictures hung by the TV with Maverick and Rhett next to him. His cowboy hats are hung near the front door and his scent lingers in every room. Sometimes it's hard to remember that I was a piece of this family, and I'm not anymore. Being here is a cruel reminder of that. Not being with Weston was hard, but losing his family felt like I was losing my own, especially since all I have left is my grandpa.

Weston's parents have a knack for making everyone feel like one of their own, but when Weston left me, they distanced themselves. At least I know why now, can't say the same for my dear old dad.

You would think that, after people keep walking out on me, I would be numb to it all. And I try to be, if I don't think about it, and I just shove it really far down. It doesn't hurt as bad, but being in this house makes it impossible to shove into that tiny little box in my heart. It makes it raw and real and something I have to deal with. Maybe that's why life brought me here, so I can deal with all the things I've avoided for years.

For once, I want somebody to pick me. Make me a priority even when it's hard, or the future is uncertain. I realize just how sad that is, but you know what, I pick me, and for today, that's good enough.

Walking into the kitchen. I grab a glass of water and take a few big chugs. A few drops escape my bottom lip and trail down to my chest as Weston walks through the garage entrance to the house.

His eyes immediately meet mine. They slide down my body, perusing it, and I feel a sudden rush of heat. I know that look in his eye. I've seen it many times before. He used to make me feel like the most powerful woman in the world when he would look at me with pure hunger.

His mouth quirks up on the side as he starts to kick off his boots. "Glad to see you still like running."

"Glad to see you still like staring." My retort was purely instinctual.

He laughs a little bit, no shame in his game at all.

He looks me dead in the eyes as he says, "Believe me, if I stared at you as much as I wanted to, you would be serving me a restraining order."

Having spent the last twelve years of my life in New York, I'm used to people being bold. But I'm not used to this. I'm not used to it coming from Weston and I'm not used to it coming from someone I'm supposed to be having a professional relationship with right now.

Clearing my throat, I try to move past the moment because I feel awkward even though he clearly doesn't. He's still sporting that stupid sexy smirk. Part of me wants to throw my glass of water at it to wipe it right off, but really, he hasn't done anything besides make me feel utterly discombobulated and stand up for me.

That's what makes it so difficult not to let my walls down again. He hasn't done anything, aside from completely turning my world upside down years ago, and it would make things a hell of a lot easier to hate him if he did. It'd be easier to want to stay away if he did, but no, he shows up like a perfect gentleman and does all the right things and says all the right things all the time. Disgusting, really.

Steering the conversation back to professional grounds, I say, "The new contractor will start on Monday. They somehow were able to start right away, and I genuinely cannot believe it. Or the fact that they have a shorter turnaround time than the last group. We might just finish these cabins in time, after all."

"That's great. What sounds good for dinner tonight?" He walks into the kitchen and swings open the refrigerator.

"I wasn't under the impression we'd be eating meals together," I respond, setting my glass down and leaning against the kitchen counter. I've been here a few days, and this is the first time he's approached this particular topic.

"I think it'd be a waste for both of us to be cooking in this kitchen. Last time I checked, we were trying the whole friends thing out, remember? I'm pretty sure they eat dinner together sometimes." *Friends.* Why does that sound like a taunt? And why do I feel like he's using it against me?

After that run, I am absolutely famished, so I'm not going to argue with him. "How do you feel about grilling some burgers?" I suggest.

"Whatever you want, Sunshine."

My heart does a little flip-flop at the sound of my nickname coming off his tongue. I used to have dreams where we were still together, and that was the only time I'd hear his voice, the only time I'd hear that nickname. I miss it. So as much as I want to tell him to stop calling me that, I don't have the heart to, or my heart doesn't have the strength to. It's almost like it lets me pretend for just a second that that moment twelve years ago never happened.

So for now, I am going to play pretend. Pretending that twelve years ago didn't happen and that I haven't spent every single day thinking about Weston.

Chapter 20
WILLOW

"You're going," Aspen says, yelling outside of Weston's front door, which is currently my front door, too.

"Oh, no, I am not," I sing-song to her through the door, "but you're welcome to hang out here with me while I work."

The lock on the door clicks and in walks Aspen. I throw my head back and ask the Lord what I did to deserve this.

"Wipe that sorry look off your face, we're going to the fair. It only comes once a year, and Ava is pregnant, so she can't have the type of fun with me that I'm looking for. But we do have a ride home." I feel like we shouldn't bother the pregnant woman to drive us home, being that she's busy growing a whole human, but sure.

Aspen struts in and makes herself at home by dramatically flopping down on the couch next to me.

Crossing my arms, I sigh, "Aspen, I love you, but I have a million things to do."

She sits straight up, "It's Saturday night, enough work. Whatever you don't have done will be there tomorrow, or better yet, Monday. I've been working my ass off, and I want to go shove my face full of turkey legs, funnel cakes, and beer, and you're going to do it with me."

The idea of going to the fair is not the worst. I used to look forward to it every year since we moved to Windy Peaks when I was in elementary school. I just know this will be a mini high school reunion, and the thought of seeing everyone after all this time gives my stomach a solid drop into overwhelming anxiety. What would they think of me? Are they going to question why I am hanging out with my ex-boyfriend's little sister? And what happens if one of them knows I'm living with Weston?

It's stupid to let these things stop me from going out and having a good time. I've wanted to see Aspen more, and now I have the chance. She's stopped by more since I've been here, but it's only a few minutes on her way home. Really, my boss can wait to have his list of weekly accomplishments. Maybe I'll just forget altogether and send him an imaginative middle finger. Being babysat like a child is really grating on my last nerve. I'm really starting to wonder if corporate life is for me. I thought having my own projects would give me the freedom I crave, but it's felt utterly constricting.

"Fine, but you owe me a beer every time I run into someone I went to high school with." I stand up and make my way to my bedroom. If I am going to be seeing people from high school, I'm at least going to look hot while doing it.

"Great, I'll get you drunk, and maybe you'll remember that you love the fair."

We pull up to the county fair around eight at night. The bright lights from the rides and light towers shine all around. Our usual sleepy little town is alive tonight.

"Come on, the boys have been here for like an hour." Aspen grips onto my hand and drags me to the entrance gates. Digging my heels in, I stop in my place. "What do you mean, the boys are here?"

The other benefit of being here was that I got some extra space from Weston. Being around him so much is confusing me. I can't keep my eyes off him when he's in the room, and I can't keep my mind off him when he's not. I don't want to want him, but my brain and my heart seem to be on very different pages. Luckily for once, my head is stronger than my heart.

"Duh, it's just like old times." She winks at me, and her brown hair sways around her shoulders as she turns and starts pulling me forward. I have a terrible feeling that she's going to enjoy this, and that she may have even left that little piece of information on purpose.

"You're officially buying my beers all night," I mutter.

"Guess it's a good thing I've been working extra then, huh?" She turns around and manages to do a backward skip while doing it. She has grown up to be such a beautiful and confident woman. I'm sure Weston hates that. Not the confidence, but the beautiful part. I'm sure he's been busy chasing the boys away.

We pull up to the group, and my eyes immediately find Weston. They always do. They do, however, take a second to take in the long, leggy blonde hanging off him. My heart drops, and it feels as if it may have just shattered on the floor.

"Hey guys, sorry we're late," Aspen says as she steps between Rhett and Weston.

Rhett smirks as he looks down at her. "If we wanted you here on time, we would have told you to be here an hour ago."

She rolls her eyes, but the edges of her lips quirk up as she crosses her arms and bumps into him with her side. His smirk morphs into a full smile and his gaze stays locked on her.

Mine, however, fights not to look in Weston's direction. I want to know what he's doing, but I can't stand to see him with someone else. I didn't think I would; in fact, I had hoped he had moved on, so that it wouldn't complicate things, but after weeks of not seeing him with anyone else, I thought I was safe. I should know better than to feel safe.

I almost completely miss Mav and Ava while I'm wallowing in my thoughts, but Ava steps forward to greet me.

"Hey, I'm glad you made it out. I was hoping to get to see more of you before this summer was over!" She pulls me into a hug, or tries to, but her bump mostly gets in the way now. "Ugh, sorry, I'm still getting used to walking around with a basketball in my shirt."

"Don't be. It's great to see you. How are you feeling?" We stay with arms locked, and I can't help but feel a little better with some familiar faces around. "Hungry, tired, and then hungry again," she says.

The forced tight smile on her face makes it hard not to laugh. She's not super far along, but I think she's starting to tiptoe toward the more complex phase of pregnancy. Not that I would know, but the girls who have all had babies in the office have said plenty.

"Well, let's remedy the hungry part," Mav says as he throws his arm around her shoulder and presses his lips to her forehead. She waves as he drags her off toward the line of food trucks.

They're so disgustingly cute that I feel a pang of jealousy shoot through me.

I want that.

I haven't let myself admit that I want that in a long time, but it's hard to fight the thought when it's all around you. With Josh, I was just there, co-existing, but that's not love. I know, because I've had that kind of love before. The kind that hums through you like a familiar song, both comforting and intoxicating. It's the best thing I've ever experienced, the heartbreak I experienced after, on the other hand... Gut-wrenching.

My eyes drift to Weston, and I find his eyes are already on me. Watching intently as the girl next to him talks his ear off. I shouldn't feel happy that he looks like he's paying more attention to me than her, but here I am feeling relieved. And I know that makes me petty and awful, and I will deal with the guilt of that tomorrow.

"Surprised Aspen drug you out of the house," he says, interrupting my thoughts. His gaze is like a soft caress, and damn it, I hate it. I hate the way goosebumps appear on my arms, and I especially hate the way my heart pitter-patters around him.

"She bribed me with food and beer." I shrug my shoulders, trying to hide the war inside my head. "Speaking of, let's go make good on that deal, yeah?" I raise my eyebrows to Aspen, hoping she's listening.

She turns from her conversation with Rhett and looks over, "You got it, let's get you a beer."

"Or five," I mutter under my breath as I start walking to the beer garden.

"Heard that," Aspen says as she loops her arm through mine. "Tell me, what's making you want to drink five beers?" She asks it like she already knows the answer, and I'm sure she does.

"I'm just thirsty," I respond simply, not wanting to dive into the myriad of thoughts spiraling in my mind.

"For my brother or for beer? I could probably help you with both of those things, but one will be much easier to obtain." She checks me with her hip, and I can't help but smile despite her calling me out.

"Beer," I say, completely unconvincingly.

"That's too bad, the brother thing would be a lot easier." She shrugs.

We come to a stop at the back of the line. Apparently, I am not the only one who is having a hankering for a crisp beer. "What does that mean? It looks like he's pretty well entertained tonight."

"Willow Rae, is that jealousy I am sensing?" She unlinks her arm only to grab onto my arm. There is way too much excitement shining in those eyes.

"What? No. He can do whatever he wants. I was merely stating a fact," I say as I step back

"If you want anyone besides me to believe that you are not drowning in jealousy right now, you are going to want to work on the delivery of that. Zero out of five on the convincing scale." She holds her hand up in a zero and looks at me through the center of it.

"If he believes you and Rhett are just friends, I'm sure he'll believe that I'm not jealous." If she wants to speak my truth, I'll speak hers too.

She darts her gaze from my eyes to the dirt beneath our boots. "I have no clue what you're talking about."

"Great, so then we're on the same page. You're not doing God knows what with Rhett, your brother's best friend, and I'm not pathetically jealous over seeing Goldilocks touch your brother as she owns him, deal?" I cock my head to the side.

"Deal. Also, don't worry about her," she waves her hand, "she's been fawning after him for years. He's never entertained her."

"Looks like she's being entertained tonight." I fight the urge to turn around to see what they're doing. See if she's still hanging on to him, stars in her eyes.

"Willow, looks can be deceiving," Aspen reassures me. "It doesn't matter either way, I'm not going to do anything about it." I can't. My time here will be up soon anyway. "Doesn't mean he won't." It's her turn to sing-song to me, and I realize just how annoying it is. We take a few steps forward in line.

"What does that mean?"

My question is interrupted by us being next in line. I don't order five beers, but I do order two.

I want to re-ask my question, but I fear that it is too far on the pathetic side even for me. I shouldn't be hopeful that he wants me. It can't happen for a multitude of reasons, one of them being that I know how it ends. We've done it before, and it ended with my heart broken. But that doesn't keep me from wanting it, even just a little bit.

When we rejoin the group, a few more people have joined. Some I recognize from school, some I don't.

"Willow! It's great to see you. I heard you were in town!" Holly says. She was always so nice in school. It's good to see that time hasn't changed some things.

"Same. Yeah, I'm here until the end of summer. How have you been?" She gives me a little rundown of her life, and I feel a bit relieved that she doesn't ask any questions about mine. In fact, this almost feels nice. Catching up with old friends, having people who know you, and you know them.

When she turns away from me, I muster up the courage to hand off my extra beer, "Here. Got you this." I hand the extra beer in my hand to Weston, and his eyebrows shoot up in surprise.

"Thanks, that was nice of you." He smiles at me, and I don't miss the glare I get from Goldilocks.

It might be time to introduce myself to her. "Hi, I'm Willow. I don't think we've met." I shoot out my free hand for her to shake.

"Brittany. We haven't." She gives my hand the most pitiful shake, and I have to fight rolling my eyes. My grandpa always said you can tell a man by his handshake, and while we aren't men, the concept still stands.

Aspen hides her laugh behind a sip of her beer. I meet her eyes and find myself doing the same. At least I know she's in my corner.

"Weston, what do you say we get out of here?" Brittany runs her finger up Weston's bicep, and I think the world stops spinning. The sensation running through me is so visceral that it knocks the wind out of me. The moment of joy I was having leaves just as quickly as it came. Suddenly, the thoughts of him with her in bed makes tears spring to my eyes. The thoughts of him with anyone feels like a shard of glass slowly shredding my heart.

"Excuse me," I quietly murmur and back away, quickly turning on my heels. I want to get as much space between me and them as possible. The thought of having to be in the same house as him and another woman? Now that just might be enough to make me quit, corporate ladder be damned.

"Willow, wait." Weston's voice comes from behind me. I keep my head down and pick up my pace. I have no clue where I'm going or even what direction leads to the exit, but I can't let him see me, not like this.

I feel a hand come around my bicep. I quickly bat the tears that have been threatening to fall away.

"Willow, stop. Please. Talk to me." His voice is a desperate plea.

I stop, but I don't turn because I know he will see it, my eyes red and tears staining my cheeks. Not to mention the fact that I haven't come up with a believable excuse for why I'm upset yet.

Taking a deep breath, I swallow the emotion down before turning to face him. "What?" I ask, my voice cracking at the end.

"It's not what it looks like," he says, hitching his thumb over his shoulder in the direction of the group.

"It doesn't matter, you can do what you want," I assure him, doing my best to sound as unaffected as possible. I cross my arms, hoping it will help shield my heart.

His eyes snag on my ringless finger. It's felt wrong lately putting it on, even if it's to protect myself from the man standing in front of me. "If I could do what I want, it wouldn't be *that*," he replies with conviction, staring me in the eyes so reverently. It feels like he can see directly into the depths of my soul. It doesn't matter that I want to close him out; he's had the key to my heart all along.

"Then what would it be? Because you looked pretty cozy back there." A touch of anger laces my voice.

"I don't think you're ready to hear that quite yet." He brushes a piece of my hair behind my ear, the movement so soft and so gentle that I have to fight the urge to turn my face into his palm.

I look away from his gaze and nod my head because he might just be right. I've been running from this feeling since the second I got to town, and it doesn't seem like I can run fast enough. It's constantly nipping at my heels. My heart *still* beats for him.

Weston grabs one of my arms and pulls me into his chest. We haven't really touched outside the horse ride since I've been to town.

His strong arms come around me, and my head perfectly tucks under his chin. My arms uncross and I grip his shirt. It's not quite hugging him back, but it is holding on for dear life. Because for this one second, it feels so good and so right. My heart feels at peace and so does everything else. I sink my weight against him, and I feel his lips touch my forehead.

"How about you and I go on a ride? Like old times?" he murmurs into the top of my head.

"Okay," I whisper.

He places his hand on my lower back, and we walk toward the rides, the lights leading our way. I might regret this tomorrow. But for right now, I don't want to fight this fire between us.

Chapter 21
WESTON

My hand stays firmly planted on her lower back, not wanting to sever the connection. My gaze keeps going to her hand, where her ring should be but isn't. She'd never forgotten it before her fiancé came to town. It's just the sign I needed. I didn't really give a fuck about her piece of shit fiancé, but I do care about her. If the ring is off, she's fair game, and I'm coming for what's mine.

"What do you want to do first? We can ride the Ferris wheel or the tilt-o-whirl. I'm not sure what else is around here." I look around, taking note of the bright neon lightbulbs on the edge of the rides.

"I'm not sure, I haven't been to one of these things in years. Do they still give away goldfish for prizes?" she asks, looking down the row of games we're coming up on.

"Please tell me you're not going to come home with a goldfish tonight?" I ask, amused.

She wrinkles her nose. "Absolutely not, I think I've got enough on my plate at the moment and don't need to add on keeping something else alive, right now."

"Mmmm, good call. Is there anything I can do to help you with what's on your plate? If you're overwhelmed or anything, I'm always here to support."She lets out an amused chuckle. "You have a whole ranch to run; I think you're busy enough."

"I'm never too busy for you, Sunshine. Don't ever forget it."

She looks up from the flashing lights of the games and over at me, her face soft, and if I'm not mistaken, there's a bit of a smile there. "Okay. But no, thank you. I'm a bit of a control freak. I'm still untangling the last mess a Taylor man left me." She playfully bumps into me, hinting at my dad's lovely filing work.

"Fair enough." I sink my hands into the front of my jeans as we walk, not wanting to scare her off with too much touch. "Do you want to play any of these games?" There's a whole slew of them here. Ring Toss, Whac-a-Mole, basketball, pretty much all the standard carnival games.

She looks around. "Actually, can we grab a snack? I didn't eat dinner when your sister came and kidnapped me." As her face tilts up to meet my gaze, I can't help but notice she did her makeup differently today, the edges of the liner flicked out on the ends, which makes her green eyes look like they're practically glowing.

"Whatever you want, Sunshine, something sweet, or something salty?" I smile at a passerby. This year's fair is even busier than normal.

"How about some cotton candy and then maybe the Ferris wheel?" she suggests, and I wonder if she remembers why that specific ride is my favorite. But at this point, I don't really care; I'm just glad to get this time with her.

"Sounds perfect, let's head that way." My hand slides to her back as I steer her away, glad I lasted three whole minutes without touching her. Part of me is terrified of touching her, like she's a wild horse and one wrong move will scare her off, and the other, the other feels like I'm dying every second she's not in contact. It's a dangerous game I'm playing.

"Do you think we should go get Aspen?" She turns out of my touch, looking around. The breeze comes by us, and I get a whiff of her perfume: sweet, almost like honey.

I love my sister, I really do, but having her here, when I feel like Willow is finally opening up, is the last thing I want. "How about for the rest of the night it's just you and me?" I brush a stray lock of hair out of her face and drop my hands to my side before I do something stupid, like lean in and kiss her. Even though that's all my body wants right now.

Her cheeks redden at my touch, but there's a small smile peeking through. "Okay." She tucks her head.

Being braver than I feel, I wrap my arm around her shoulders as I say, "Now, let's go get you that cotton candy." My excitement is anything but forced. I never thought I would get to do this again, enjoy a night out in our favorite little town together, but it seems like maybe just maybe, my hope isn't futile. That hope explodes as she wraps her arm around my back and leans into me, nestling her arm into the crook of my chest and armpit.

We got through the cotton candy line with only a few wandering stares. This town is small, and everyone knows who we are, who her grandpa is, and who my parents are. So, they know our story, because gossip travels faster than a wildfire during a drought in a windstorm here. Seeing her tucked into me, probably will have some questions stirred up on Monday.

When we get in line for the Ferris wheel, she's content as she eats her bag of cotton candy, and as for me, well, I'm thinking about how utterly fucked I am. I am so enamored of her that it's terrifying. But I don't care, even if this winds up to be nothing, this brief bit of happiness I get with her will be worth the fallout.

We move up the line, and the worker asks, "Tickets?"

Willow's eyes go wide. I am guessing she wasn't really planning on riding rides. But I had hoped this would happen when Aspen said she was going to try to convince her to come, so I bought the tickets. In fact, I bought enough for us to ride this damn thing all night. I'd do it too, if it meant I got more time with her.

Our tickets get collected, and we sit side by side, the worker putting the bar over us. The ride jolts to life, and we start our ascent to the top.

"You gonna share some cotton candy?" I look over with raised brows as she drops another bit of cotton candy in her mouth.

"No, I think I will keep it all to myself, thank you." She drops another piece of cotton candy into her mouth; the act in itself shouldn't be hot, but watching her lick her fingers clean. It's borderline erotic.

I reach over and snag the bag from her hands. "I'll decide." And shove a piece into my own mouth. Its sweetness melts over my tongue, and I can't help but wish it was Willow I was tasting.

She huffs, playfully slapping my arm. "Hey, that was mine! You didn't want any."

"That was before I saw you eating it." I wink at her as I take another bite. I don't really want this cotton candy, but toying with her like this makes it feel like old times. My heart feels like it could soar every time I hear her laugh.

"Oh, what now you wanna taste?" She rolls her eyes, completely oblivious to how true that statement is.

I want a taste of something that's for fucking sure. I cannot help but think of how sweet her lips will be right now with the lingering taste of cotton candy on them.

She goes to snag the bag back, and I shield it from her just as the ride takes off.

I take more than my fair share of bites of the cotton candy just to rile her up.

"Are you gonna let me have a bite?"

"Sure, you can have a bite." I grab some with my fingers and offer it to her.

She shocks the hell out of me when she leans in, her plump lips coming around my fingers, taking the cotton candy from me. The act in itself is hot as fuck, but she looks at me the whole time. I may have turned this cotton candy thing into a game, but she's playing dirty.

My breath shudders as she licks the remnants off her lips, my eyes staying glued on them; I couldn't look away if I tried. She is so magnetic, every bit of her. A show I could watch for the rest of my fucking life.

"Thanks for sharing." She's now the one doing the winking, taking back complete control.

Fuck, all of this is far too familiar. This exact ride holds memories for us, too. I cock my head. "Do you know why this ride is my favorite?"

Her eyes flash, and I just know she's replaying the same memory. We were fifteen, and she had begged me for an hour to ride the damn Ferris wheel. I had been avoiding it because being next to her, even then, was too damn tempting. Things were changing between us, and I knew if I kissed her, that would be it; we would be more than friends. She was my best friend, and the thought was terrifying because I didn't want that to go away.

"I might have an idea." Her eyes drop to my lips.

"It was you and me, just like this. We went on that ride as friends, but I walked off it a completely different person. It was the best day of my life as a kid; it still is now."

"It was a pretty good day." Her gaze still lingers on mine, both of us lost in our own little bubble. I feel us making our way to the top of the ride, the stars surrounding us.

"I kissed you for the very first time that day." My arm wraps around her, bringing her closer. I want to feel that again, that rush I felt when I kissed her. It was like a jolt of lightning went through me, shocking me to my core and branding my heart as hers.

"Weston," she whispers, meeting me in the middle, our faces so close now, I can smell the cotton candy on her breath.

The ride jolts to a stop, shaking the seats we are in. Willow blinks rapidly, as if the fog of the haze of the memory is gone. She looks at me and takes a shuddering breath before scooting away ever so slightly.

I was so fucking close to having her lips on mine again. So close to bridging this gap between us, for one second, it felt like we were one small jump away.

Not wanting to push her before she's ready, I offer her a peace offering in the form of spun sugar. "Want a bite?"

She snags the bag from my hands. "Yes, I do want a bite of *my* cotton candy, thank you very much." She smiles, and I feel a bit of relief.

The moment may have passed, but the next time it comes around, I'm seizing it. I'm going to fix what I broke and make it shine again. In time, there will be no fighting about the fact that she was always going to be a Taylor.

Chapter 22
WESTON

Sweat drips down my forehead as I hop off the horse, leading it into the barn. It was a hot son of a bitch out there today. Shit always hits the fan when the sun is at its hottest. We had one of our best bulls get stuck on the wash bank of the river, took everything we had to get him out. We'll keep him at the barn for the next couple of days to make sure there aren't any injuries we didn't notice.

"Next time you need help wrangling up an escaping cow, call Maverick," Rhett says as he takes his saddle off his horse. He runs his hand up and down her neck before giving her a couple pats.

A breeze comes by and brushes against my sweaty exterior, cooling me down. "Where the hell was this breeze when we were out there sweating our balls off?"

"I think you've shit talked Mother Nature a few too many times for her to want to do you any favors." Rhett levels me with a look.

I have cursed her a few times. Too much rain. Not enough rain. Too much snow. Not enough snow. Honestly, I'm a bit high maintenance when it comes to the weather.

"Well, at least we get to head off to Mom and Pop's for dinner." The one thing I had pulling me through today was the thought of a good meal and an ice-cold beer. And seeing Willow. That might just be the best part about her living with me. I get to see her at least once a day.

"No, we don't, she and your dad headed out of town, don't you remember?" He picks his saddle up off the ground and starts carrying it into the barn from the stalls.

"Son of a bitch, I forgot about that. Well, sandwiches are sounding mighty fine tonight." They sound awful, actually, but I'm beat and don't have it in me to whip something up or drive to town.

"You mean to tell me you can't wrestle your pretty little roommate into helping you with dinner?" he asks.

I scratch the back of my neck, feeling a little bit awkward because she's far more than a little bit pretty, and I don't really know where we stand. "I don't think I'm in any position to be asking her to do a damn thing for me. She's finally coming around, and I don't want to push her too far."

"Well, you know, you don't want to be too complacent either. I know you don't want to talk about wanting her back, but if you do, you're going to have to do something about it. You can't just expect her to come to you when she's ready. You're gonna have to fight for her."

I know in my gut that he's right. I pushed her away all those years ago and it was the biggest mistake of my life.

Rhett puts a saddle away before walking next to me, slapping my shoulder a couple times. "It'll work out, bud. You just gotta give it time and some effort."

Somehow, this man always has the answers. He's wise beyond his years, and I can't understand how the hell he's still single. "You know, man. I'm kind of surprised you haven't gotten married yet."

He stills, stopping his stride. "What makes you say that?"

"I don't know, you seem to have it all together. Most of us still act like we're teenagers, and you've always been an old soul. I've heard girls like the whole emotional stability thing." Wouldn't know because I'm still trying to figure out how not to be a total idiotic jackass. Those are my sister's words, but honestly, she's not entirely wrong. My heart's in the right place, but good Lord, could my head just work for one minute? Things would be a lot easier.

"Well, I'm glad you think so, man. I don't know. That's just not in the cards for me, I don't think," he says, a heaviness to his voice.

Wanting to lighten whatever is weighing on him, I respond, "If it makes you feel better, I had the perfect hand dealt to me and then screwed it all up."

"Don't lose faith. She still loves you. She's just not ready to admit to herself yet."

With those final words of wisdom, he steps out of the barn, and I'm feeling even more tired than I was when we got back. This whole living with the love of my life but not being together is exhausting.

The drive home is short, but not short enough because my stomach is rumbling. All I've had today is a half-melted protein bar and a peanut butter and jelly sandwich I packed for myself. And I ate that at ten am. It's now almost eight-thirty pm. The sun is already making its descent behind the mountain. Painting the sky the prettiest shades of orange. A good old-fashioned Wyoming sunset is hard to beat.

In these moments, I have to remember to take in the good times. It keeps me grounded. Remembering to be thankful for what I have, not what I'm missing out on, is the only reason I've been able to stay positive even in times when I've struggled.

I park my truck in the garage and head into the kitchen through the connecting door.

What I see before me makes me stop in my tracks.

Willow rubs her hands on her jeans, dusting off whatever remains are left on them. "Sorry, I was hoping to be done by the time you got here. I came home and saw that you weren't here, and I waited around a little bit, but then you still weren't here, so I figured you'd be hungry when you got home, but then I looked in the cabinets and they we're kind of running low of basically everything so I just ran to the store and went grocery shopping." She says in a rush before adding. "I just realized I am rambling like an idiot." She shakes her head and smiles at me, but it seems a little forced and a little bit awkward and completely adorable on her.

"You were right, I would in fact love dinner. It was a really long day and I'm starved." Both for food and more time with her.

"Well, don't get too excited. It's gonna be nothing like your mom's cooking. My kitchen in New York is like 3' x 3', so I don't have a lot of experience cooking. But I was able to pan-roast some chicken and make some mashed potatoes and gravy. And green beans! If I'm gonna be on my grandpa about eating better, then we're going to live by that as well."

I feel that bloom of hope I've been feeling take root, become tangible. It feels warm and all-consuming. Kind of like the way I feel about her. The beautiful woman standing in my kitchen cooking me dinner after a long day. This is what I dreamed of. This exact thing right here. It may not be perfect, and she may not be mine, but I've decided it's not over till you say it's over.

"It smells incredible, so I'm sure it will be perfect," I say, setting my hat on the counter and emptying my pockets. "Thanks for making my day a little bit easier. Is there anything around the house you need help with?"

"Not that I can think of, you can go clean up, and I'll have dinner ready when you're done."

I stare at her for a long while. She gazes back, and I feel like I'm memorizing her all over again. The slope of her nose. Freckles that line the apples of her cheeks, which are more prominent now that it's summer and she's been in the sun. The way her hair sits messily on the top of her head, a few tendrils framing her stunning face. I'm so hopelessly in love with her. It's almost painful.

She's the first one to look away, and I glance down at my work boots. Quickly, I take them off and head up to my shower, but not before catching another glance of Willow. She's turned back to the stove now, giving me a perfect view of that tight little ass of hers. My heart isn't the only part of me that misses her. Just one glance of her like this has me going crazy. My fingers itch to touch her. To come behind her while she's cooking on the stove, circle her in my arms, and brush my fingertips against her bare stomach as I reach around. My lips would kiss down on the curve of her neck, and she would whimper, making my cock harden.

I quickly shake my head, letting go of that image before I have a whole other problem to deal with.

My fork scrapes against the plate as I bring a bite of food to my mouth. She was downplaying how good she was at cooking. This meal is incredible.

"Not only did she get the order wrong. Instead of commenting in our side chat, she accidentally sent it in our meeting chat, where the boss caught her talking shit. Which was all very accurate and totally justified, but that was her last day as the office assistant." Her body shakes with laughter as she brings a glass of wine to her lips. Her cheeks are flushed from the alcohol and her lips are stained the perfect shade of red from her wine.

"I really think you should be able to complain or even give direct feedback to your boss without getting fired. I can't tell you how many times I told my pops he was being a jackass. He never fired me, but I did have to shuck cow shit out of stalls for a month straight."

She wrinkles her nose up in disgust, and it's the cutest thing I've ever seen. *God fucking I'm pathetic.*

I literally can't look at this girl without daydreaming and getting lost in the thoughts of her. I'm supposed to be a man's man. But when it comes to her, I just want to be her man.

Finishing my dinner, I wipe off my mouth with my napkin and throw it onto the plate.

Willow gets up and reaches over to take my plate. "Here, let me take your plate to the sink."

"Nope," I bat her away and shake my head, "you cooked dinner, I got cleanup duty. If you're not too tired, we could watch a movie or a TV show."

She nods her head, yes, before replying, "That sounds nice."

"Great, well if you want to pick something to watch, I'll clean up and do the dishes, and I'll meet you on the couch."

She hops off to the living room; her shoulders seem lighter, and she has a pep in her step. This version of Willow was exactly how I remember her, just a little bit more grown-up and a hell of a lot more mature. She has a lightness to her that was missing when she first got here. I knew it was still in there somewhere. I could see it in her eyes, but I think there's something about New York that is weighing her down. Something about the past, maybe? That's something I can relate to.

When I sit down next to her on the couch, I leave enough space not to be touching, but not so far away that I can't subtly slide my arm across the back of the couch, you know, for comfort. Not because I'm a pathetic thirty-one-year-old man too scared to tell the woman living in his house that he still loves her, so he'll slowly convince her that he does with his actions.

"What are we watching?" I ask as I set my feet up on the ottoman.

"50 first dates." She looks over to me with a touch of glee in her gaze.

"Good pick," I say as I snag the blanket from the back of the couch and throw it over our legs.

We get more comfortable on the couch, and the urge to touch her and be closer becomes overwhelming. I dare to slide my arm across the back of the couch, my fingertips just barely touch her shoulder, her silky strands intermingle with my fingers.

She leans in, ever so slightly, but I feel her warmth seep into me. "This is my favorite part." I turn to look at her, more enraptured by her than by the movie.

I turn my head just in time to see Drew Barrymore beat the crap out of Rob Schneider's character. Willow throws her head back in laughter, and I can't help but join her. "Okay, this might be my favorite, too."

She looks over to me, her eyes bright from the laughter. "You have to pick your own favorite scene. This one is mine." She winks and snuggles in a little closer, her head resting on my shoulder. "Is this okay? If you want space–"

"It's fine, Sunshine. Get comfy." Space is the last thing I want from her. I want her skin on mine. But this, this will do."

Her hand lands on my torso, and I, a grown man, feel fucking butterflies. It feels like we're kids again, dancing around wanting to be more, but not really knowing how. My hand rests on her waist as she sinks in further.

Within a few minutes, her breathing levels out, and when I look down, her eyes are closed, and she's completely relaxed. Fuck me. This is what I want, every single night. Her asleep in my arms.

I haven't felt this at peace in years. When I close my eyes, savoring the moment, it becomes harder and harder to try and open them, so I don't. I sink into a deep sleep. Hopefully, my dreams are full of her, too.

Chapter 23
weston

My brain feels foggy as I try to figure out how the hell we got here, but Willow dragging her index finger up and down my chest makes it difficult to really give a shit about the hows and whys of the moment. She goes a little lower, each pass, until it becomes impossible to ignore the heat thrumming in my veins.

"Sunshine, what are you doing?" My voice comes out rough from sleep and arousal. Each drag of her finger is like another match being struck, sparks flying everywhere.

"I had a dream about you and it got me thinking..." Her finger toys with the buckle of my belt.

Fuck. Me.

My breath starts turning into pants. "That maybe, being careful isn't worth it. You miss me, you miss us, right?"

When my head turns and our eyes meet, there is nothing but pure heat there. Desire so fucking hot, it feels like my skin is burning. "More than anything." She gives me a saccharine smile at that. "Can I touch you?" Her finger skates down one last time before she starts pulling apart my belt buckle.

Touching me is the one thing I want her never to stop doing. "You never have to ask if you can touch me; my mind, body, and soul are yours to take." I make sure my voice carries the truth of my words.

She kicks off the blanket from our legs, and sinks to the floor in front of me, my cock stands at attention behind my jeans. Fuck I cannot believe this is happening. I've dreamed about this. I've stroked my cock until it was almost raw at the thought of her, now having her here, down on her knees, wanting me again, it's like a dream come true.

"You sure you want this?" I ask. More than anything, I don't want her to regret this, because I know I won't.

The soft light from the TV behind her makes her glow. "I wanted you for so long, West. I've loved you for as long as I can remember. I'm tired of fighting it. I want us back. Let me show you." She runs her hands up my thighs, making my whole body shudder in anticipation.

This feels too fucking good to be true, but I can't bring myself to care. We can figure the rest out in the morning, but for right now, it's going to be her and me.

"I love you too, Sunshine, so fucking much."

Instead of responding, she answers by working my belt apart, and I lift my hips as she tugs off the top of my jeans.

I should be the one on my knees for her. I've made it my new life mission to worship the woman. "Willow, I think I should be the one to show you how much I missed you, how fucking sorry I am."

"Oh, you will," she winks, "but I had a particular dream about this, and I need it, West, please." She looks at me doe-eyed, and I've never been able to resist her, but much less now.

I nod, unable to speak, and she slides off my boxers, my cock springing free. It feels as heavy and as hard as lead. A bead of precum already sits at the tip, just from the anticipation of it all.

Her eyes don't leave mine as she leans in, dragging her tongue up the length of my cock. It twitches with the sensation. My eyes fight rolling back. I don't want to miss this. I want to keep my eyes on her. Watch her lick my cock like it's goddamn candy.

She pulls back. "I'm pretty sure I still remember how you like this done." Her hand grabs the base of my cock, working it up and down in slow strokes as she wets her lips. With our eyes locked, she inches my cock between her pretty puckered lips.

Even if she didn't, there's nothing she can do right now that would be wrong. She leans back down, taking me all the way till my cock hits the back of her throat. I have to fight coming already. It's too much. It's everything I've ever wanted. My ability to make this last left the window the second she dropped to her knees.

"You suck my cock so good, baby." I throw my head back, losing the fight to keep my eyes on hers as my hips buck. My hands fist at my sides as I savor the feeling. Her mouth on my cock is utter heaven.

She rewards my praise by lapping her tongue around the tip of my cock as she sucks. My hands unclench and seek her out; they sink into her silky strands, unable to keep them off her. I help guide her motion up and down my cock. She never takes her eyes off me, moaning the faster we go.

"Baby, if you keep this up, I'm gonna come right now, and I don't wanna come in your mouth. I want to fill your pussy up." It's a primal need I've unlocked, the desire I have to watch my come drip out of her pussy.

My filthy words have her moaning again; the sound is erotic, but the vibration of it on my cock has my mouth drooling.

Desperately, I ask, "Can I fuck you, baby, please?"

"You think you deserve to fuck me?" She arches a brow. Looking way too sexy for her own good. It doesn't help my situation at all; it just further spurs my need to sink my cock into her. "No, but I'll be spending the rest of my life trying to deserve it." It's borderline begging. "If you need me to drop to my knees and beg for it, I will. I'm not too proud to beg, baby."

"As fun as that sounds, sucking you off has me so fucking wet for you, West. I think you can take care of that for me," she says as she strips her shirt off over her head. Making a whole show of it. I can't help but stare at her beautiful tits right there, looking like pillows I want to sink my teeth into.

Her pants hit the floor next. I expect her panties to follow, but what she does is so much fucking better.

Pulling her panties to the side, she moves to hover over me, straddling me. "I'm gonna fuck this cock. Is that okay with you?"

My hands instantly find her ass, gripping each cheek as if my life depended on it. "Fuck yes, it is, sit on my cock, baby, ride me."

The smell of her perfume permeates through and sends a new ripple of desire through me. Her scent is like a calling card to me. Whatever pheromones she's got coursing through her were made for me. Everything about her was made for me. She fits too damn good in my hands for there to be any other explanation.

My hands move from her ass to her tits, which are perfectly bouncing in my face. I grip them hard enough that she moans; the sound is fucking music to my ears. I bring my mouth down to one nipple and suck. Her pussy clenches around me at the sensation.

Her pussy inches over my cock, taking in the head.

My eyes fly open. I blink slowly, coming out of the lust-filled haze I'm in. You have got to be fucking kidding me. It was a damn dream. Not the first I've had, but disappointing nonetheless. Willow's here, but she's sound asleep in my arms. She snores lightly. It's so fucking cute. I forgot how much I missed the sound. I will my arousal out of my body trying to enjoy the moment that we have. I may want her in my bed, but I want her in my life permanently so much more. So, I can be a man and shove this desire down.

This woman is mine; she's been mine for as long as we've known each other. After this, there will be no going back.

Chapter 24
WILLOW

The old farm truck rattles down the road. This thing has to be getting close to its deathbed with the way it clinks. As I pull into the front drive of Weston's house, my jaw hits the floor. I finish parking, turn the truck off, and hop out, my body moving on its own accord.

The sight before me could have been conjured during a wet dream, because Weston is in a skin-tight white T-shirt, sweaty, and sporting a backward ballcap. It's like the universe wants me to be miserable.

As I step closer, I see what he's doing. The air whooshes out of my lungs and I stand frozen. A mere nineteen hours ago, I had brought up to Weston that the front of his house would look better with some color, and here he is, in ninety-degree heat, planting flowers when he could be out working on the ranch.

My steps slowly drag forward as I continue to stare. "Weston," I say to gain his attention. "What are you doing?"

If I thought I felt breathless before, it's nothing in comparison to how I feel when he looks at me, the sun beating perfectly on his face. He's so damn beautiful it hurts. My heart aches with the need to be closer to him, not just physically, but it feels like my heart is tethered to his.

His smile annihilates me in the best way possible. "Hey, Sunshine, planting some flowers. Are tulips still your favorite?" He looks down to his spread, rubbing his dirty hands against his wranglers.

The fact that this man still remembers my favorite flowers all these years later is almost as special as him planting them in front of his home for me. Tears threaten to fall, but will them away as quickly as they came. "Yes, they are so beautiful," I say, glancing around at all the shades he selected from orange to pink, red, and yellow. "I can't believe you're planting flowers." "Well, I think it's the least I could do to make you feel more at home here. If there's any other flowers you want, I can run back to town. I think the Potted Leaf is still open." He goes to stand, and I walk over to him.

Laying my hand on his shoulder, I give it a squeeze. "No, this, this is more than enough. Thank you, West. This is…" words fail me, because this little act is everything. All of his little acts, knitted together, are starting to feel like a tidal wave, coming to wash away the wrongs of our past.

"Really, it's nothing. Hey, are you busy tonight?" His eyes squint, trying to hide the sun from them. The urge to turn his hat around is strong, but he looks too damn good with a backward cap on.

"No, I'll just be here."

He smiles. "Good, I'm making us dinner. I thought it would be nice if we sat down, enjoyed a home-cooked meal together, and talked."

"We talk and eat together every day." Almost always about work, though.

"Yeah, I'm thinking maybe tonight we talk about everything but work." Normally, I would fight him for the sake of protecting myself, but I'm starting to question what I'm even protecting myself from. Someone who hears me and fixes the issue immediately, no matter how trivial. Stands up for me when I'm being disrespected? The more I think about it, the easier my answer comes.

"Yeah, that sounds nice. Six?"

"Six." He nods. His smile is so broad that the warmth from it sinks into me like a caress.

Six rolls around, and I stare at myself in the mirror, probably a little more done up than necessary, but this dinner feels different. I look down at my ring. I've been wearing it to keep him away, but it's starting to feel all wrong. I've skipped wearing it here and there because it's serving a purpose I no longer want. The longer I stare at it, the more it feels like a chain, and I don't want that anymore. I don't want to keep my heart in a protected box, because that isn't living.

My hands shake ever so slightly, but I slide the ring off, and I know in my heart it will be for the last time. It may change nothing for Weston, but it's the first step for me in trying to be brave again.

When I make my way downstairs, I see the usually bare kitchen table draped in a cloth with a candle burning in the center of it. The smell drifting from the kitchen is heavenly, and I'm suddenly grateful that he inherited Mabel's ability to cook.

Weston turns on from the stove, dressed up pretty dang nice for a dinner at home. His baby-blue shirt has a fancy pearly snap button and is tucked into starched wranglers. His hair is freshly cut.

My smile stretches wide; this feels almost like a date.

When his eyes meet mine, he smiles broadly. "Hey, Sunshine, dinner is about ready." He walks over to the table and pulls out my chair, gesturing for me to take a seat. "Wine okay? And before you ask, yes, it's the sweet stuff."

I dip my head to hide my elation. "Yes, that's great."

He runs around, filling our plates and cups before finally making it back to the table and ready to dive in.

"This is a mighty nice dinner, West," I say as I bring my glass of wine to my lips.

"I think it's the least I could do after everything," He shrugs and looks at me sheepishly.

I roll my eyes, "I'm over the cabin ordeal, it's okay, really." In fact, in the long run, it was probably better; I got great ideas for our project.

"I think I owe you an apology and an explanation for a whole lot more than the cabin. I've made some pretty massive mistakes."My hands start to shake with that statement. "What do you mean?"

"I've been really wanting to talk to you about that night. I wasn't quite honest all those years ago when I left you on the doorstep." His finger drags up and down his fork. Confusion washes over me and my face pinches.

He looks at me, stares into the depths of my soul, straight down the pieces he shattered. "The reason I broke up with you was that I thought you staying in this town was going to hold you back. I thought that I needed to put you first and that meant putting us last. Now that I'm older and definitely a lot more mature, I realize how stupid that was."

My breath catches, and a million emotions flood my system all at once, overwhelming me. Breathing suddenly feels impossible. I've wondered for years why he left me, and that is why. "You seriously expect me to believe that you dumped me to make my life better?"

"I swear my life on it, Willow. It never was because I didn't love you. It was because I did, I wanted to see you shine, and I didn't think you could do that here." His voice shakes with emotion, his eyes shining.

If I didn't know the man so damn well, I would think he was lying. But he means it. My hands fist on the table as I try to get a hold of my anger. "That wasn't your decision to make, Weston. That was mine. I get to decide what is or isn't enough," hurt and anger intermingle in my tone.

He wants to reach for me, I can tell by the way his hands keep inching closer. "I didn't want to hold you back, Sunshine. You're so much bigger than this small town and I didn't want you to be stuck here."

My voice cracks as my control starts to wane. "You didn't think maybe looping me in on that thought process would be a good idea?" I say, cocking my head to the side, letting anger take the forefront here.

He blinks up at the ceiling, taking a deep breath. "At the time, no. I knew that you would disagree. And I really wanted you to give you a fair shot. I thought that I was putting you first. I was eighteen and self-deprecating." The way he looks at me right now, shifts something, I can't tell if it's in the right direction, "I loved you so fucking much that I wanted you to have better than me and this town. Believe me when I say I regretted it every single day you've been away. I've grown up and I realize that you can chase every dream you want and still live within the county lines. Even more, I could've gone with you. I just thought that I was doing the right thing."

I hate this. I hate that this is the reason why we fell apart. We should have been so much more; we should have been endgame. But instead,

I got a broken heart and trust issues. "Did you know that I almost failed out of my first semester of college because I was so depressed? You never even called to check on me." My voice teeters on a full sob, admitting what I've never told anyone.

He rubs at his chest, like it hurts the same way mine does right now. This was supposed to be a fun dinner, but this, this is brutal. "That's not quite true. I mean, I didn't call, but I did check on you.

Taken aback, I ask, "You never came to see me, you never called, you didn't check in on me."

He sits too still for my liking. "I came to New York. I got your address from your grandpa. It was about a year after you left. I asked your grandpa about you every single time I saw him. He finally convinced me to go talk to you, but I wanted to do it face-to-face. When I got there, you were walking into your apartment with a guy. You were smiling and laughing," he pauses for a second, the pain in his heart glints in his eyes, "and I thought that maybe my plan had worked out and that you were thriving."

For the second time tonight, I feel like I can't get a hold of reality. They say the truth can set you free, but this? This feels suffocating, like I'm drowning in what could have been if he had just talked to me. I squeeze my eyes shut, feeling the tear leak out the side. "I don't know what you expect me to do with this West."

"Honestly, I'm not sure either, but I wanted you to have all the facts before you end up married to the wrong guy." His eyes glisten with tears as the full weight of what his decisions have come to settle on him.

Unable to take this anymore, I stand up. "Well, next time you decide to make a life-altering decision for me, maybe consider respecting me and my thoughts enough to have a conversation," I point at him, "because you ruined everything for no good reason. You broke my heart that day. And I've been fighting every single day to put it back together, and now you tell me this?" My hands drop off the back of the chair as I step away. "I think I need to go. I can't do this." I sob, as my tears steadily track down my face.

The sound of Weston's chair scratching against the floor fills the room. "Willow, wait, please talk to me." He reaches out, gently wrapping his hand around mine.

Wiping my tears, I pull my hand out of his. "The time for talking was twelve years ago. This is too much. I need some space from you right now." This dinner has suddenly become another scrape on my heart. I rush to the stairs, wanting a wall and as much space between us.

"Willow, wait." His hand gently stops me as I stride up the first few stairs. My temper is fully boiling now, I whirl around to find him eye to eye with me. He leans in close, the scent of him wrapping me up; it's almost like a balm over my scuffed-up heart, turning my anger to a dull simmer. After all this time, even when he's the one who's the reason my heart is broken, it still yearns for him.

With his face so close to mine, we are eye to eye. God he's so close, if I moved just an inch forward my lips could be on his. And I hate that I want that. I shouldn't. I know it was twelve years ago, and he was young and dumb, but he's had years to fix it.

"I have something I really need you to know." He wets his lips and my eyes track the movement.

Breathlessly, I ask, "What?" What could he possibly need to say this close to me?

His own eyes catch on my lips before he looks at me again. "I'm gonna make you trust me again, Willow. I'll put in the work every single day to show you that I am the man for you. I spent the last twelve years obsessing over you, missing you, and wishing you were here for me to love, and now that you are here, I'm gonna win you back," he says with finality. "I'm pretty sure I have quite a big say in that," I say, holding my head, squaring off with him.

"Yeah, but when your head catches up with your heart, there's gonna be no denying that you were made for me. And I'm not letting you go this time." He says it with such conviction and passion that I have no choice but to believe him. "I made that mistake once and I'm never making it again. You're gonna be mine again, Willow, just watch and see." He grabs my hand, squeezing it before starting down the few stairs he climbed, "I'm sorry for ruining dinner. I can leave so you can eat?" he asks.

"I just want to go to bed." My voice sounds as breathless as I feel. Without looking back, I rush to my room. Once the door is closed, I sink to the floor. A guttural sob crawls up my throat. Half because of his confession, half because I miss him, and I miss us. There's no denying it anymore. I feel so incredibly lost in this chaos that he created.

I stay there, getting my bearings and letting myself feel the things I've been refusing. If there is going to be any moving forward, any chance of me coming back from this, I can't shove it down.

A gentle rap at the door startles me; I don't get up right away. I wipe away my tears, steeling my nerves for whatever he has to say. When I swing open the door, he's nowhere to be found. But my plate of dinner is sitting there, alongside a steaming brownie and "I'm sorry," written on the back of an envelope in his messy scrawl.

My hand comes to my mouth as I bite back more tears; no more crying for tonight. I know he's trying to fix things, but I wish they could be fixed without me having to be broken all over again.

Chapter 25
WILLOW

My alarm goes off, and I've never dreaded the sound more in my entire life. I tossed and turned so many times last night that the blankets are a knotted mess. A reflection of my mental state right now.

Weston's words replayed in my mind all night. Part of me is relieved, and part of me is utterly gutted. How could he do that? I know he was young and dumb, but when he realized it was a mistake, he never came for me. I spent half the night wrestling demons inside my head, telling me to go and knock on his door. I don't know what I'm expecting him to tell me or what that's even going to do, but I want to talk to him because no matter what he says, I still can't make sense of it. There were a million options out there, and he thought leaving me was the best one, even if it was for my sake, which I'm not entirely sure I believe he didn't even care enough to loop me into the conversation.

Being mad at him when I thought he completely deserted me for no real reason was easier. Now, I have to deal with the fact that he left me because he thought it was the best thing for me. But it wasn't. I almost failed out of school because of how heartbroken I was. The amount of shitty dating decisions I made after him is insane.

I tried so hard to love every single person I came into contact with, thinking that if I loved them, I wouldn't love him anymore, and if I didn't love him anymore, I wouldn't hurt. And maybe I'd find someone who'd want to stay. The only thing that taught me was to depend only on myself, because people are characteristically unreliable. So I learned to rely on myself.

I sit on the edge of my bed, swinging my legs over the side while rubbing my eyes. I thought seeing West on all the other days was hard. I don't even want to think about what today's going to be like.

Begrudgingly, I get ready, and I put on my favorite clothes. Because if I feel good on the outside, it may help with the inner turmoil. When you look good, you feel good, and when you feel good, it's easier to handle the chaotic disaster that is my life. At least that's what I'm going to tell myself.

I crack my door open and peek around like I'm some sort of teenager trying to sneak out. This is ridiculous. I am a grown ass woman. I live here, and just because things are about as clear as mud between us right now, doesn't mean that I cannot walk down the hall normally.

Wanting to get it over with, I walk down the hall and down the stairs. The smell of bacon hangs in the air. Weston is nowhere in sight, but my coffee sits on the corner of the counter like always. I walk to it and see the note.

Breakfast is ready in the oven, should still be warm for you -West

Walking over to the oven, I pop it open and see all the fixings for breakfast in there: bacon, scrambled eggs, and some toast. Closing it, I look around. Maybe he's left already. I'll have to see if his truck is in the garage.

Walking over, I swing open the door and peek my head inside. What I find are years' worth of memories that I thought were gone forever, sitting on the shelves inside his garage. The old truck he had in high school still sits there.

I hear rolling, and Weston pops up from under the truck. He has a shop towel he uses to wipe his hands, and grease stains on his shirt and jeans. "Good morning, did you find the breakfast?"

"Yeah, but what's this?" I look to the truck; every single memory we've had in that truck plays through my mind.

"You said you missed it. I tracked down the guy I sold it to and got it back." He shrugs like it's no big deal. He looks back to me, where I stand speechless, he takes a deep breath and seems to debate his next words. "I got rid of it because it reminded me of you. I couldn't look at it, but now that you're here, it felt...wrong not having it. So I got it back."

This truck was his baby in high school; it never had less than half a tank of gas, it was always clean. I was shocked to hear he had gotten rid of it. Now that I know why, my heart breaks for him. It breaks for us. We are in such a fickle spot, I don't know how to move forward, or what forward would even look like.

He continuously shows me that I can trust him and pushes me to the edge of falling for him. There's only so much digging my heels in I can do before I'm thrown from the ledge. Last time, it hurt, but what would this time look like? I'm too scared to think about it.

All the anger I had felt is gone, a bit of melancholy and forgiveness linger instead. I'm not over it, I'm not even sure I've fully processed it all, but today, I think I need to try something new. Try to do what I would have done years ago: lead with kindness.

"Are you at a stopping point? I was just going to eat breakfast," I offer. It's the world's shortest olive branch, but it's all I have right now.

"Yeah, I can be. Are you sure you want me to eat with you? I get it if you need space."

He's so God damn respectful of me, it's equally annoying and sweet. "I'm okay. Let's eat."

He smiles, tender and soft, and inside, I feel the ice fall from my heart. My armor is gone; what comes next will be up to him. "Okay, Sunshine." He finishes wiping his hand clean and throws the rag in the garbage. He nods to the door, to start heading that way, and places his hand on my lower back, guiding me inside.

Trying to ignore how utterly aware of him I am, I ask, "What do you guys have going on at the ranch today?"

"Well, we have to separate the calves from their moms, so most likely I'm gonna get my ass kicked. That'll be fun." The mental image that flashes through my brain, and I feel guilty for the bit of joy it brings.

"Funny enough, my schedule just opened up. It looks like I'm free for the show." I laugh as I say it.

He steps in front of me, leveling me with a look as he sweeps past me to open the oven. "Ha, ha, very funny. You know you're always welcome to tag along with me whenever you want. If the office and cabins start to make you crazy, some fresh air and cows might help."

Those things are all lovely, but the thing that grounds me the most is him, but I get the feeling he knows that already. "Actually, I love the work I've been doing; my boss is a bit annoying, but it's my first project, so micromanaging is to be expected."

He brings the tray of food to the table, laying it down on the center. The cloth and runner are still on it, a harsh reminder of last night. "Do you need me to talk to him?"

I groan, "Did we not learn our lesson with the contractor?"

He holds his hands up. "You're right, you can handle your business."

He gets my plate and serves me a plate while I watch him. Weston doesn't do anything half assed. If he's going to care for you, you're going to feel pampered. Which is exactly how I feel when he sets my food and coffee down in front of me.

"Please accept my 'I'm sorry I was an idiot breakfast peace offering'," he says as he sits across from me.

"I'll accept it only because I know being an idiot comes so naturally to you," I say with a wink. Weston is far from an idiot; he's kindhearted and selfless. He was just a kid who made a dumb decision that blew our love into smithereens.

He feigns being hurt by my words and places a hand over his injured heart. "Did anyone tell you you're kind of mean in the morning?"

"That's because I haven't had my coffee yet," I say, blowing into the hot mug.

"You mean your creamer with a splash of coffee," he challenges with a raised brow.

"Yes, I do," I sass back with a smirk.

He shakes his head, laughs, and brings a bite of food to his mouth. This is nice. Starting my day with him. Teasing, laughing. My eyes linger on him, thinking about whether this is what I want.

"So, what have you got going on today?" he asks as he takes a sip of his own coffee.

"Well, I need to take pictures of progress to email to my boss because apparently my word is no longer good enough. Then I'm going to continue to work on the bookkeeping. And then I need to call your sister and see what she wants to do for interior decorating."

"Why do you need to call Aspen? I can help you with that. "You're good at man caves, but I think you might want to go for a little bit more of a homey feeling, and I think Aspen has the perfect eye for cozy rustic that will make this a success." In reality, this is a really nice cabin, and it's not as bachelor pad as I was expecting. The flowers up front are already sprucing it up. If I could talk him into matching furniture, we'd really be on a roll.

"Yeah, I'm gonna need you to drink that coffee faster before I need an ice pack for the burns that you are delivering to me." His smile is devilish.

I chuckle and I hate myself for it. I love giving him a hard time. It used to be our favorite pastime. But mostly, I teased him. He never really gave it back to me; in fact, if you dare to ever insult me, even to this day, he comes running to my rescue, apparently.

"I'm sorry that was kind of mean. Your cabin is really, really nice, but I think your sister will be the perfect person to help make each cabin special for your future guests."

"That she does. I guess I can hand the reins over to her when it comes to interior decorating. Will you show me what you come up with?" he asks, hope in his eyes.

"Sure, I can CC you on the email proposal I sent to my boss." I angrily stab my pancake with my fork as I think about that.

"Yeah, or you can just show me when you get home?"

I take a moment to look at him, really look, and I can see he's trying. He's giving me full reign of the project, and I see the remorse that's still in his eyes, and I decide to give him this win. "Okay," I agree as I finish up with what's left on my plate and go to take it to the sink.

"I can get that for you, don't worry about it." Weston stands, grabbing my plate and empty mug.

I sigh, "West, I know you're sorry, but I promise I can clean up after myself."

"Yeah, and I promise I don't mind helping you out. I'm going to take my plate in a second anyway."

"Okay, that's sweet of you. Thanks."

"Willow, are you going to be able to forgive me?" Weston asks, his voice low and his back turned to me.

The sudden shift in conversation throws me off.

"I do forgive you, but what does that mean for us? I don't know yet." The roaring voice inside my head wants me to run into his arms right now, but the smarter part of me wants to take a breath and think it through. I don't want to hurt him, so I tack on, "You're still the best guy I know, West."

My feet carry me up the stairs, and my thoughts are going in circles, practically making me dizzy. What do I do when the only person I want is him?

Chapter 26
WESTON

R hett clinks his beer with mine, and I bring it to my lips. It was a long week. Plus, it's good to drown out the nerves. Aspen and Willow have been hanging out a little bit more this week. She called me earlier this afternoon to let me know that she and Willow would be joining us tonight.

I feel nervous, and it's ridiculous, considering that we live together. She's everywhere, in my office, around the property and in my home. I see Willow every single day. In fact, it smells more like her these days, and it does me, but I love it. Sometimes I follow into rooms after she leaves just to take a deep inhale of her vanilla scent.

The truth is out about why I left her on that porch all those years ago, and I've made it good and clear where I stand. Or rather, where I want to stand, right by her. At her side for the rest of our lives. I know it'll take time. It feels like every step forward we take, something sends us two steps back. We're better than we were when she got here, friends even.

Never in my life did I think friends would taste so bitter on my tongue. But I hate it. I don't want to be her friend. I want to be so much more and I thought telling her the truth would help. Maybe it did, but we're teetering on the edge, and I don't know if she's going to let herself fall.

For now, I'll be counting my blessings that she allows me in her presence. When she first got here, I wasn't sure if we'd even get to that point. She acted as if we had never known each other. God, but I know every inch of her. I know exactly the way her curves feel under my hands. Sometimes I find myself reaching out, wanting just to touch her.

I've gone as far as thinking of ways to sabotage this project to make her stay out here longer. The longer she's here, the longer shot I have of earning her heart back. It's wishful thinking, but it's the only hope I've got, especially now that I've had her back in my life. I can't stand to have her out of it.

Coming back to reality, I spot Maverick as he spins Ava around on the dance floor and it brings me back to the conversation he and I had right here in this very spot. Little did I know that a year later I would need to take my own advice. That if you want something, you have to take the risk. I didn't realize how scary it can be to put yourself out there when your heart is on the line. I don't know if I can handle losing her again.

Willow and Aspen sit at the table next to us, laughing as they sip their drinks. Every day that she's here, I see a bit more of the old Willow come out, the one who was carefree but driven. Kind but strong. I think all of her has been in there the whole time, but what I did to her was the last straw. She buried all the parts of her that made her soft, that made her vulnerable, and damn it, I hate myself for it. Those were always the very best parts. I thought I did the right thing years ago, but it's become the biggest regret of my life. I wish I could take it back.

I want to play it cool and not push her, but I'm as far from cool as I can get. I am a man undone by my love for her, and it's eating at me a little more every day.

Aspen breaks my trance, sighing deeply. "I want to dance, and you're all being boring."

Rhett gets up, a smile on his face. "Well, we can't have that, now can we?"

Aspen does an excited squeal and bounces on her toes as she grabs Rhett's hands and drags him to the dance floor. At least she's dancing with him and not one of these trashy horndogs in here. My boys protect her like she's one of their own, and I thank God for that. I don't have enough time to be chasing boys that don't deserve her away.

Willow sits next to me, fidgeting with her hands in her lap. Things have still been a little off since our dinner a couple of days ago.

Just ask her to dance, you idiot.

Taking a deep breath, I stand up, wiping my palms against my jeans. I'm so fucking nervous I feel like I'm fifteen again and going to ask her to be my girlfriend.

I move to stand in front of her. She looks up from her hands in her lap, our gazes catching.

"So, what do you say we go join them out there?" I keep my smile small as I hitch my thumb over my shoulder, pointing to the dance floor.

Her eyes nervously shift from me to Aspen and Rhett spinning on the dance floor. I can hear my sisters' laughter over the music, and I want to feel that. That little bit of joy, and the person who can bring it to me, is right in front of me.

"Come on, dance with me, Sunshine." I reach down and gently grab her hands, not giving her the chance to say no, cause if I can get a chance, I won't blow it this time.

"I don't know if this is a good idea," She slightly pulls against me, but not enough to make me think she doesn't want this.

"Well, I think it's the best idea I've had in a long time." A smile tugs at the corner of my lips. Having her close tends to do that.

"Well, good ideas come so few and far between for you, we shouldn't waste it." The little twinkle in her eye makes my chest feel like it's going to explode. She's flirting with me.

"No, we shouldn't. Plus, I could tell you wanted to dance with me but were too scared to ask, so I figured I should be a gentleman." I shrug nonchalantly.

I spin her in a circle the second we hit the dance floor, and she laughs and ends up looking right at me.

"Ha! If that's what you need to tell yourself, I'll play along." Her eyes have a sparkle in them that wasn't there when she first got here. It's like Windy Peaks brought her back to life. This town has that effect on people.

"So, you going to play cards with Grandpa and me this week? I think the only way he can't cheat is if he has all of our eyes on him." My hand moves to her waist as we move around the floor.

She shakes her head and squeezes my hand. "I still can't believe you two have been hanging out behind my back all these years."

"Well, now that you know, you're welcome to join us. He's missed you. I haven't seen him this happy in years."

Her grandpa has always been the one constant in her life; the bond they share is special. "It's been so nice being able to be with him again, even if you show up and crash our party." She jokes. The tempo of the music changes, and the band transitions to playing as a slow song. Willow looks to me. "That's our cue." She goes to step off the dance floor, but I grab her by the hand, stopping her.

"Come on, at least give me one full dance," I plead with her to stay with me, just a few more seconds of having her in my arms.

She looks at me for so long that I start to get nervous that she's going to leave me hanging. "Okay, but only one more."

My hands slide around her waist like it's the most natural thing in the world and her hands go up behind my neck as we sway side to side.

"It's been really nice having you back here, Sunshine." I stare down and get lost in her eyes. She must be as nervous as I am, but she doesn't shy away from my gaze. "I missed you like you wouldn't believe." I'm grateful for the slow dance and the chance to talk face-to-face.

"I've had a really hard time fighting the fact that I've missed you, too. But it has been nice. I forgot what it was like having someone you could count on." She speaks so softly now, it would be hard to hear if I wasn't hanging on to every word she says.

It's on the tip of my tongue to ask why she can't count on her jackass of a fiancé, but I don't want to talk about him; in my world, he doesn't exist. I wonder if he still exists in hers, because the ring is still off. I haven't seen her wear it in days. "I'll always be in your corner, Sunshine, here, or in New York. If you call, I come running."

She laughs, breaking the seriousness that has built up. "I think I can use that to my advantage. Next time I have a midnight hankering for some ice cream, I'll be waking your ass up."

I wince. "Maybe I should have been more specific; the come running only applies to emergencies."

"Craving ice cream and not having any is an emergency, West." She looks at me with such severity that my laugh comes out on its own accord.

"Whatever you say, Sunshine." Realistically, I know that it doesn't matter. Because in my heart, she's still my girl, and my girl gets what my girl wants.

"Good boy. Since you so nicely agreed with me, I will help you take down my grandpa in his quest you cheat at cards next week." Her hand slips into my hair, ever so slightly as she speaks, making it hard to focus on her words. How can something so small feel monumental? But I feel it, I've felt it, the shift with us. It's like her body and heart want to give in, but her brain won't let her.

"Perfect, you and me, we make a pretty good team, don't we?" I ask not just about card games, but about life. How well we've worked together on the cabins is living proof.

"We do, don't we?" Her face turns pensive, as if her thoughts are going down the same road mine has been.

"The best. Now are you ready for the big finale?" I ask as I raise my brows in excitement.

"The what?" Her brow furrows, clearly confused.

But as the fiddle winds down, ending the song, I spin her into a dip, her hands still clasped at my neck, my hands holding her waist, keeping her from falling. "I just wanted to prove to you that the next time you fall, I'll be catching you."

I bring her back to her feet, and she stands breathless, with warmed cheeks. My hand reaches out and puts her hair back in place. "Thanks for the dance, Sunshine." My thumb rubs her cheek tenderly for half a second before I drop my hand and escort us off the dance floor.

Chapter 27
WILLOW

My music plays through the AirPods in my ears as my feet pound on the gravel below me. I keep replaying the conversations I've had with Weston, unable to shake the fire it has stirred in me. He's made it well known that he's going to win my heart back, and the longer I'm around him, the more I want to let him. I've gotten a taste of what we've been missing, and I think I want more.

I come up around the curve and see Weston's cabin come into view. It's exactly the home I would have wanted. I wonder if he thought of me while he was fixing it up. The tulips in the front add a nice splash of color. His place has the perfect bones for a forever home. It's a perfect mix between rustic and modern, and I really love it. The interior just needs some warmth. Nice rugs, throw pillows, you know, the things men don't think matter but make all the difference in the way a room feels.

I give the last little bit of this run all I've got, trying to burn off all this anxious and slightly pissed off energy. As I walk up the steps to the front door, sweat pours into my eyes. I'm definitely going to need a shower.

Walking into the house, I immediately head for the kitchen. I need a tall glass of ice-cold water. After a few chugs, I feel a little bit less like I just spent the summer in the Sahara. Humming along to my favorite song that is bumping in my headphones, I walk up to the bathroom. I should probably grab my clothes, but Weston's at work, so it doesn't matter anyway, plus catching me covered in a towel is probably inevitable while we live together.

I pull my phone out and press pause as I push through the door and hear my name being called.

Through the frosted glass of the shower door, I can see the side of Weston's naked, wet frame. Time has been kind to him because, good Lord, does that man look amazing. He was a relatively scrawny eighteen-year-old boy last time I saw him naked. Even then, he got me hot and bothered, but now with his filled-out frame, wide shoulders, and muscles that definitely were not there last time.

Holy shit.

It's clear he hasn't noticed me come in, or if he has, he has no shame. He strokes his hand up and down his hard length, and I feel a fire bloom within me.

"Fuck, Willow, just like that," he growls as he works his length. Water drips from his hand as it flexes around the head of his cock.

Heat blasts through me.

He said my name.

My name.

I should leave. I need to leave before he sees me, but it's like I'm frozen in place. My body feels like an inferno. My legs rub together to ease some of the throbbing in my core. If I can just build up enough pressure, it might relieve some of the ache I've had building up.

Closing my eyes, I take in the way his grunts and low moans sound. My back is plastered to the door, and I really need to get out of here before I get caught. There's no way in hell I can explain this.

"Fuck me, Willow. Just like that." The hand propping against the wall squeezes into a fist. How I wish that hand was on me. In my hair, rubbing down my body.

Maybe I can slide my hand down and relieve some tension. Clearly, he thinks of me when he does it, so this can't be wrong.

I go to slide my phone in my pocket and music starts blaring through the speaker.

Fuck, fuck, fuck.

I fumble with my phone and end up dropping it. Son of a bitch. You have got to be kidding me. I try to pick it up, but it's harder than you'd think with shaky hands.

"Uhm, not that I mind your company, but what are you doing in here?" Weston asks as I snatch my phone off the ground.

I stand ramrod straight, Diva by Beyoncé still blaring on my phone. Fuck that song. I am never listening to it again.

"Well, I.. I, uhm. I went for a run and I needed a shower."

"And you thought that watching me shower would make you feel cleaner?" He stands with his hands over his crotch; they're doing a terrible job of covering it up. So I turn around and face the wall. It's less embarrassing this way.

I watched him do a lot more than shower, but that's a need-to-know situation, and he does not need to know that I watched him jerk off to the thought of me.

"You're never in here. You're usually in your own shower."

"Correct, but I just recalked the shower so it needs a few hours to dry."

"Well, that would have been good to know," I seethe.

"But then you wouldn't have got to see me naked? Did you like the sound of your name coming off my lips?" His voice has an edge to it, brought on by his desire.

My cheeks flood with heat from the embarrassment. I am never going to live this down. The only solution is to change my name and flee the country. "I have no clue what you are talking about."

"You think I didn't see you come in? I heard the door open and figured you would leave when you saw it was occupied."

"Well, I'm going to go ahead and do that now." I should have done it three minutes ago when I thought about it.

"I think you wanted to watch, to see what you do to me," he taunts as he turns half toward me, giving me the perfect view of his cock as he continues to stroke it unabashedly. I can see pieces of ink wrapping around his ribs; that's new.

"It was an accid--" I blurt out, but he cuts me off before I can finish.

"Maybe it was an *accident*," he says, water dripping down his abs in the most distracting way. "But if that was the case, you would have left, and you have yet to do so. Therefore, I think you want to watch, and baby, I'd love nothing more than to give you a show."

I stand there, jaw slack and completely at a loss for words.

"Unless of course, you want to join me?" He proposes with a cocky grin. "There's plenty of room. Although I'd much prefer dirtying you up with my cum than cleaning you up."

"Fuck." The mouth on this man. My thighs rub together of their own accord. My clit pulsing beneath my panties.

"The things I'd do to you, Willow. I've had twelve long years to imagine all the ways I could ruin your perfect body. All the ways I could make you come with my tongue, my cock," he says, shuddering, "and my fingers."

His hand starts to work his length again as he speaks out his fantasy, "Every time I see you in one of those pencil skirts, I have to fight the urge of pulling it up to your waist and fucking you over the desk."

My hands slip down the front of my shorts, unable to stand the ache between my thighs. I want to come more than I want to breathe right now. I close my eyes, imagining the scene he's painting.

"Would you like that baby? To be fucked raw over your desk? Just my hard cock stretching that tight little pussy out. I want you to drench my cock as I fuck you." My eyes open, and I look over to see him looking straight at me. The hunger there makes me pick up my pace on my clit.

Weston's eyes are locked on the movement beneath my shorts, his pace quickening. I watch him, the room filled with the sounds of the water running and our parallel play. I feel the crest of my orgasm come, and I lean against the wall as my legs get shaky.

"Are you going to be a good girl and come for me? Be sure to moan extra loud for me. I want to see you come undone."

That does it for me; my eyes flutter shut. "Oh fuck, Weston. I'm coming."

When my eyes open, I see him coming against the shower wall. "Yes, Willow."

He braces himself against the wall, catching his breath, when he turns his head, the water runs perfectly over his hair, dripping down his face.

"I hope you enjoyed this, baby. But the next time you come thinking of me, it's going to be on my cock."

I bite my lip, the mental image of that stirring up another round of desire, before I do something stupid, like join him, I slip out of the bathroom. My back lands against the door as I close it. After that debacle, there's going to be no denying that I want him, too.

Chapter 28
WILLOW

When I walk into the construction zone that is cabin B, we've had to name them due to us agreeing to meet, and then showing up at the wrong one. I can hardly believe my eyes. It's like a completely different place. It holds all the charm you expect from a cabin, but it's starting to feel way more of this century and less like the 1800s. There's still a lot to do with wiring, lighting, and flooring choices, but we're getting somewhere. This is the first time I've walked in here and not wanted to go cry in a closet somewhere. For my first big girl project, I feel like I'm doing a pretty damn good job.

Terri, the contractor that Weston hired to lead the job, walks in.

"Hey there, Willow, how are you today?" His ballcap is covered in white dust. He wipes his hands on his jeans, which probably doesn't do much good since they are covered in gunk.

"I'm great, thank you, even better after seeing all the progress you're making." My eyes roam over what a few weeks ago were the bones of the cabin; now it's starting to look like it's going to be a livable space.

"I'm glad you're happy with it. Want me to show you around so I can talk you through some of our next steps?"

"Yes, I'd love that, thank you," I say as I step alongside him.

He spends the next twenty minutes walking me through the cabin, showing me the ins and outs of his plans and vision for the place.

"Weston is going to be so happy, it really sounds like you're nailing his vision." The exposed beams on the ceiling add height to the small space, making it seem even bigger. They expanded the windows, adding more natural light. I can see it already. It's going to be beautiful.

"Well, I'm glad to hear that. Speaking of Weston, I'm supposed to grab the first check from him, but he got busy. Do you by chance have a way to get that to me today?"

"I'm sure I can find a way to work that out. Let me get with him and I'll get back to you by the end of the day. How does that sound?"

"That works perfectly for me, dear. I'm going to get back to work and make sure my guys are working hard," he says before making his way toward the back of the cabin, where some workers are installing new plumbing in the bathroom.

I walk back to the truck and get it started. The AC unit is shoddy at best, but it's better than nothing. The summer heat has really ramped up.

Pulling out my phone, I dial West's number. He answers on the second ring. "*Yes*, Sunshine." He draws out the yes in a sing-song manner.

His greeting brings a smile to my face. It's getting harder and harder to deny my growing feelings for him. "Hey, Terri needs a check from you today. Is there any way I can come grab it from you and bring it to him?"

"Shoot, I totally forgot about that. I'm so sorry, yeah, it's in the top right drawer of my desk. You're gonna need a key to get in there."

"And where can that key be found, or are you gonna make me go on a wild goose chase?" I'm sure he would love that.

"As fun as that sounds, I'm living with you and would prefer to go to bed without being smothered by a pillow, so it's in an envelope in the left drawer all the way to the back."

The key is really only one drawer away? "That's really the best you could do to hide that key?"

"Listen, if I made it any more complicated, there's a ninety-nine percent chance I'd forget where I put it, and then everybody's screwed. I like to work smarter, not harder these days."

And now I'm smiling so hard my cheeks hurt. "I think you have a lot more work to do on the smarter side, West."

"Somebody's feeling a little feisty today."

"Some call it feisty, some call it honest."

"If you keep this up, I'm gonna have to hire HR and turn you in for bullying."

"Okay, I've had enough of you for now. I'll call you back if I can't figure out where the hell you put the key."

"Sounds good. See you for dinner."

If I try hard enough, I can almost pretend that this is more than it is. What our life would look like if he hadn't left me on my doorstep years ago. I know why he did it now. But it doesn't take back all the pain I felt since then. All the abandonment issues I brought back up. It's like he stitched me together, just ripped me back open. It sucks when the person who broke your heart is the only one who can put it back together the right way.

I did a pretty darn good job by myself putting it back together, but there's a piece of me that has always belonged to him. I can feel it now that I'm back here. That piece of me that's been missing. He always said I was his sunshine, but really, he was mine. I lost it the day he walked out of my life, the light, the joy, and my spark. I became quiet, cold, and withdrawn. The longer I'm here, the more I can feel myself slipping back into who I used to be, who I really am.

I let these thoughts carry away as I drive back to the barn and office. Realistically, I'm daydreaming about my life with him. What it would have looked like, maybe even could have if I could figure out a way to forgive him. If I can figure out a way to trust him with my heart again.

Walking into his office, I sit down in his chair and go to the left drawer. "Okay, we're looking for an envelope; it can't be that hard," I talk out loud to myself.

It's exactly where he said it would be. I fumble with the key and unlock the drawer. I probably should've asked him exactly where this check was in here because it seems like this is a catch-all drawer. I pick up a lockbox and find the check underneath it.

I really shouldn't care what's in this lockbox. And I really should probably respect his privacy. But the curiosity is yelling at me. What in the hell does he have a lockbox for, and how hard is the sucker to open?

I fidget with it and find that it's not at all hard to open when the top springs open. I almost drop it when I see what's inside. It's the movie ticket from our very first date, but we were only kids. There's a corsage in here from prom. A Polaroid picture of us from when we were sixteen and he first got his license. We spent that whole summer driving around in his truck. Did a lot more than driving in that truck. It held a lot of memories. I fell in love for the first time in the front seat, right next to him.

When I fumble through layers of stuff and make it to the bottom, I see the bracelet I made him when we were maybe twelve. I can't believe he kept this. This bracelet right here started everything. He said he liked my bracelet on my first day of school. My grandpa and I had to move him a few times, and it got harder every time, starting over. When I sat down in my first class, he said he liked my bracelet. I was desperate to make a friend, so I came to school the next day with one for him, and I walked out with a best friend. It's crazy to me how much has changed since then. How much more he became to me than just a friend, even now calling him a friend seems wrong. Not enough, he's so much more to me than a friend. I was wondering whether he really felt the way he said he did.

God, I can't believe he kept all this stuff, it's like a shrine to what we used to be. Tears start to stream down my face as I look at our relationship condensed to a little box. I loved him so much. I loved him at every single phase, as a kid and as a teenager. If I'm being honest, I still love him now. I've loved him every single day since I was twelve years old. I hold the picture of us to my chest and let out a silent sob. I don't know what to do. There's an ache in my chest, and there's only one way to make it better. But if I do it and it goes wrong, I don't think I'll be able to stitch myself back together this time, and that's terrifying.

I try to put everything back exactly how it was in here, preserving it. I don't want him to know that I went through this, but now that I've seen it, I fear I won't be able to look at him the same. Because I think he was telling the truth, he did what he thought was right for me. There's no way he kept all the stuff and didn't truly love me. Maybe that's why it's hidden and locked away.

I put everything back nice and neat. I close the drawer, lock it up, and head back to my truck. Going back to work after such a revelation feels frivolous. God, I wish I had someone to talk to. I think I need a girls' night or something. I know Aspen's going to be a little bit biased, but right now, I don't think I really care because my options are him and my grandpa, and I already know my grandpa's going to take his side. At least I know Aspen thinks he's a bit of a dumb ass. Have that going for me.

After dropping off the check, I text Aspen and see if she can meet me for a quick drink. Shock fills me when her response is almost instant. There's one thing about that girl. She's always down for a good time. But I also know the side of her that's down for just about anything, and that includes the heavy stuff. She was so much younger than I, but even then, she had a heart of gold. The little sister I never had.

We agree to meet at the local bar. She's already sitting at a table when I get there. George Strait plays on the overhead speaker system.

"Thanks for coming to hang out with me." I smile at her. She's already got two drinks sitting on the table.

"Thanks for inviting me. How's your day going?" She sits, looking so happy to be here and I know I made the right call. Even if she can't offer me any advice, her company will make me feel better.

"Uhm." I'm not really sure how to answer her, because overall my day is fine, but my head, my head is a tangled mess.

"It's my brother, isn't it?" I look up to see her narrowing her eyes, as if she's trying to fit pieces of a puzzle together.

She's quite possibly the most intuitive person I've ever met. I groan, "If I want to talk to you about your brother, is it possible for you to be on my side?"

"As much as I love him, I love opposing him so much more. I think it's the little sister in me." She smiles before taking a sip of her drink.

"Did he ever tell you why he broke up with me?" I toy with the rim of my glass, skating my finger around the rim.

She slaps her hands down on the table, making me look up at her. "No, and I have been pestering him about that since you left town."

"Okay, well, I didn't really know either, until the other night that is." My brows knit together as I relive our conversation, the pain I felt then bubbling back up.

Aspen reaches across the table, grabbing my hand, "When I said you could talk to me, I meant it. I know that it's hard because he's my brother, but I'm still your friend."

I nod, I know I can talk to her. "That's why I called. I just don't really know how to put this into words."

She gives my hand a reassuring squeeze before saying, "Don't over-think it, just tell me what you are thinking."

I dive into the whole story of why he broke up with me. Going into detail about what happened at dinner the night he confessed why he left me.

"What a total dumbass. I wish I had been old enough to set him straight before he did something like that." She shakes her head at her brother's actions.

"I didn't really know what to do with it, and honestly, I thought he was lying. But today I had to go into his office and into a secret little drawer, and I found a little lockbox, and it literally holds every single big major memory we have together. What do you think that means?" I ask, feeling completely exasperated.

"If I had to guess, it means my brother is still hopelessly in love with you." Her gaze is soft, and I know she's right.

"Did he ever date anybody after me?" I don't really know if I even want to know the answer. I've obviously dated, so I can't hold it against him. But the thought of him being with somebody else feels like a knife through my chest.

"He's never brought anybody home, talked about anyone. This is a small town; if there had been something going on, it would have gone through the rumor mill."

"Would it be crazy if I still had feelings for him?"

"No. It would be crazy if you didn't, you guys are Weston and Willow. I don't think there's ever been a more famous couple from this town. Everyone thought you guys were it for each other."

"I'm not sure I can truly forgive him; he broke my heart. t. How do I get over that?"

"I'd love to be able to answer that for you, babe. I will tell you this, I don't think he'd make the same mistake twice."

Weston has alluded to the same thing himself, and I believe him. More than that, I want to be his again. I want him to be mine. More than all of that, I want this ache in my heart to stop, and the only person who can do that is the person who broke it in the first place.

Chapter 29
WILLOW

I stare blankly at my computer this morning, thinking over the conversation I had with Aspen yesterday, when my phone rings, I pick it up, and see a number I don't recognize.

Answering, I bring it to my ear, "This is Willow."

"Hi Willow, I am a nurse here at the hospital in Windy Peaks. Your grandfather, Vern, is here. You were one of his emergency contacts, and we were wondering if you were in the area and if you could head this way?" The woman's voice is calm, the polar opposite of what her words have done to me.

"Yeah, I can be right there. Is he okay?" I stand up from the chair, grabbing my purse.

"He's being evaluated right now; it's looking like he potentially had a heart attack. We should know more upon your arrival."

"Okay, I will be right there." The second the call ends, I run to the truck as fast as my legs will let me. My hands shake as I fumble with the key, trying to put it in the ignition, tears blurring my vision.

I won't believe he's okay until I see it with my own eyes. He's all I have left in this world. The only person who has ever chosen me, and the thought of him not being okay, makes my heart feel like it's being torn apart.

When I turned the key over in the ignition, the engine made a rumbling sound. This truck is older than I am; hell, it's probably older than Jack, and sometimes it takes a few times to get going. I try again and again and again, no luck, no sound of the engine roaring to life.

"Fuck, fuck, fuck. Why today?" I say, as I angrily slap my hand against the steering wheel, my breath coming in quick, heavy pants.

My head sinks into my hands as tears stream down my face. I can feel the panic taking over, all sense of logic and rational thinking is out the window.

Reaching over the cab, I pull my phone out of my purse and search for Aspen's contact. I click on the call option and press it to my ear. Aspen's voice comes over the speaker, but unfortunately, it's her voicemail. Why today of all days is this woman not answering her phone? She's supposed to be off work today.

I go back to my contacts and click on Weston's contact. He picks up after the first ring. "Are you on your way to the hospital?" He spits the words out so quickly, I have to take a second to process them.

"No, the stupid truck won't start, and I couldn't get a hold of Aspen, and I really need to get there, West." My voice cracks as emotion floods through me.

"Okay, I was already on my way to you. I'll be there in about three minutes."

"Thank you, I'm sorry." I feel bad for taking more time out of his day. He's constantly having to switch things up for me.

"Don't be. I was on my way to you the second I got the call."

Confusion halts my panic attack, and I'm grateful, but so very lost. "How did you know he was there? I just got the call."

"Well, when you moved away, he needed a new emergency contact that could, you know, be local, so he put me down." He says the words slowly, as if he's walking on eggshells.

An overwhelming feeling blooms in my chest. "You've been my grandpa's emergency contact while I've been away?"

A wave of emotion runs through my body. Gratitude. Longing. Thankful, but most importantly, forgiveness. I've been trying to edge him out the entire time I've been here. Scared that he's going to let me down and hurt me again, but I don't think that he will. I've been suppressing my feelings for him since the second I pulled back into town, but I can't anymore, not after this.

"Are you mad?" He has his voice sounding tender and soft.

Throwing my head back against the seat, I let out a huge breath, mostly of relief, relief that I can finally let go of this resentment and darkness that has been clouding over me. "I've never been more grateful for you in my life. Thank you, West. I will never be able to thank you enough for being there for him when I couldn't be."

The difference is I could be there. I could've been here this whole time, but instead I chose to chase a dream in New York, a dream that never panned out; that's all New York was. If I had any question in my mind if I was thinking about heading back, this absolutely seals the deal. I'm going to finish this project, and that'll be my last day working for them. I think it's time I come home for good.

"There's no reason to thank me, Sunshine. I'm happy to fill your shoes when you can't be here, as best I can."

I didn't think it was possible to smile in a time like this, but somehow he has managed to brighten a dark situation. "You're one of the best people I know, West. I'm sure you filled my shoes just fine."

He's quiet on the other end of the line, and I wonder if maybe I said something wrong, but he clears his throat and says, "That means a lot hearing it come from you. There's not a lot of people's opinion I care about, but yours, yours matters."

Not knowing what to say to that, I stay quiet. "Please stay on the phone with me till you get here. I'm scared."

"I know, baby, he'll be fine. He's a hell of a lot tougher than people give him credit for."

His words help calm my racing heart, but the anxiety of losing the only family I have left stays on my mind. "I know I just can't lose him. He's my only family. Well, my only family who actually wants me, I should say."

"Anyone who doesn't want to be in your life is a fucking idiot, take it from somebody who thought letting you go was the right thing to do. It wasn't." There is no hesitation in his words.

"You mean that?" My voice comes out softer than I want it to. A whisper of hope, and maybe the start of something new.

"With every ounce of my being. Where are you at? I'm pulling into the ranch right now."

"I'm in your office." Really, I could work from anywhere. But being in his space has been the only hidden way I could feel close to him.

Weston's truck comes into view, and I let out a sigh of relief. It's like my body knows that when he's near, I'm safe and everything's going to be ok. That I can breathe, break down if I need to, and someone will be there to put me back together. It's funny how quickly my trust in him came back. Maybe I'll regret it, but I think I might regret not letting it go more.

His truck comes to a stop beside me, and he flies out of his driver's door, running over to me.

His hands come up and cradle my face, his thumb swipes under my eyes, wiping away the tears that won't stop falling. "The doctor said he's okay. I know it's scary, but he's gonna be fine. Come here."

He drags me to his chest and wraps his big, muscled arms around me, and I swear I've never felt safer in my life. A sob rocks through me. I know he's probably fine, but hearing that he had a heart attack made my heart drop. Because he's fine this time, but what about next? What if I don't get to make up for any other time I wasted?

Weston's hand wraps around the back of my head, smoothing my hair down as he tries to calm me down.

"I know I'm being ridiculous, that call just scared me."

"You're not being ridiculous, being scared for someone you love is absolutely justifiable. Let's get you to the hospital so you can lay eyes on him yourself."

"Okay." I pull away from his chest and nod.

Weston takes my head back into his hands. "Everything is going to be okay. I promise. Take a deep breath." He doesn't let my face go until he watches me take a deep breath, which does help.

He laces his fingers with mine when we walk to the truck, not letting go until I get into the truck.

He hops back in, backing out far enough until he can turn around and get back on the main drive to get on the road.

Right about now, I wish he would have driven the old truck, the one where I could sit in the middle seat and still be close to him. That's all I want right now. There are one billion people on this planet, and I think he's the only one who makes me feel okay when my world is crashing down. I wish I could ask him to hold my hand, but I don't know how. It feels scary to bridge that gap.

It's almost like this man can read my mind, because his hand comes over the center console and grabs the hand I was toying with. He gives it a squeeze, and I look over to him and give him a small smile of reassurance.

When we pull up to the hospital, we park in the ER parking lot. It takes everything in me not to full-out sprint inside.

I get out of the truck and wipe my tears from my eyes. But it's no use. My mascara has streaked halfway down my face, and my hair is a mess from me running my hands through it so many times, and my distress, in short, I'm a hot mess.

The walk to the sliding glass doors is short and the walk to the waiting room and check-in desk is even shorter.

"Hi, I'm Willow, and my grandpa Vern is here. I was wondering if we could get back there to see him." The receptionist must be in her late sixties, lowers her glasses to get a look at Weston and me, with a knowing grin, she says, "He said you guys would be on your way. Let me take you back." She waves her hand for us to follow.

Weston comes up behind me and places a reassuring hand on my lower back as we walk into the treatment bay area.

When my grandpa comes into view, my hand flies to my chest. He's connected to all sorts of wires and has an oxygen hose up to his nose. I hate seeing him like this.

I rush to his side. "Grandpa, how are you feeling?"

"Oh, Lolo, I'm doing fine. There's no need for all those tears. Weston, what are you doing here?" But he says it sarcastically enough that I'm pretty sure he somehow knew we would be together when we arrived.

"I told you to lay off the bacon." My voice is full of authority. "And he's with me. I needed a ride out here." Because my luck with vehicles since I've been here has been downright terrible.

"Hm. Well, it looks like my health crisis might've done some good after all." He wags his eyebrows at me.

My eyes roll. "Yeah, yeah. Did they say what the plan is?" Clearly, he's doing pretty darn well. He's back to his meddling.

"Well, looks like I'm gonna need a stent. I think they're gonna have me stay here tonight and transfer me out in the morning to a facility with a cardiologist to do the stent. But you know, doctors and all their medical mumbo-jumbo, who knows. But I do know they said I'm gonna be all right and that they caught it in time."

I pull up a chair to sit beside him and grab his hand. His skin feels warm, and when he gives me a little squeeze, he still feels strong, which gives me more reassurance that he's feeling strong too. Weston comes up beside me and places a hand on my shoulder, grounding me as always.

After about twenty minutes of chit-chatting, the doctor walks in and extends his hand to me. "You must be Willow, the granddaughter."

"That would be me. I'm hoping you can give me more information than this old man can."

"Your grandpa has coronary artery disease and will need a stent as of right now. I don't believe he's in any major danger. We have an accepting facility that we will ambulance him to in the morning, and he has surgery scheduled for eleven am tomorrow. We're going to keep him overnight for observation. I have no reason to believe he's not going to make a full recovery."

Hearing it come from the doctor's mouth himself has me finally believing that he's really okay. Well, mostly, apart from the coronary artery disease, but realistically, that's relatively common in people his age. But I'm definitely going through his fridge while he's in the hospital and restocking it with healthier foods. I want this man around as long as humanly possible.

We stay and visit, the nurse even has a deck of cards, so we challenged Grandpa to a game of rummy. With no sleeves, Grandpa couldn't cheat, so he only won one of the games.

He lets out a big yawn. "You two should get out of here. It's getting late and I already know you're gonna be following me around tomorrow."

"You scared me so bad that I'm probably gonna be following you around for the rest of your life." He's probably never going to be allowed out of my sight again.

He widens his eyes as he looks over to Weston for help. "Looks like I'll be changing the locks at the house."

"Grandpa!" I scold him as I stand up out of my chair.

"I'm only joking. Weston, you take care of my girl tonight. Make sure she gets something to eat."

Weston nods as he slips his hands into his pockets, a lazy smile on his face. "I can do that."

Judging by the smile on his face, I think he's all too happy to be taking care of me. And judging by the way my heart is racing right now, I think I'm a little too happy, too.

Chapter 30
WESTON

The whole walk to my truck is spent fighting the urge to take her hand in mine. It was easy to justify when she needed comfort, but she seems calmer now that she's laid eyes on her grandpa. My own heart dropped when I got the call, so I can't imagine how she felt.

We make our way to the truck, and I open her door, and she hops into the cab. I pause before shutting the door. The way she looks at me right now has my heart feeling like it could soar.

A piece of hair falls into her face, and I tuck it behind her ear. "Are you feeling better?"

She puts her hand up against mine and holds it against her face. "Better, thank you for being there with me, it meant...everything."

"I know I let you down in the past, but I won't ever again. I mean that," I say, holding eye contact.

"I know." Her gaze moves from my eyes down to my lips as she pulls the corner of hers between her teeth. Her beautiful eyes land back on mine, and in the softest voice ever, she murmurs my name, "West..."

"Yeah, Sunshine?" I ask, leaning ever so slightly closer to her.

"I...I...I think I need you to kiss me."

I've longed to hear those words for so long, but I want to make sure she's in the right state of mind. I don't want this to be because she's vulnerable right now.

"Willow, believe me, I want that more than anything, but I'm not sure now is the right time. And you've got a fiancé." I look at her bare finger; it's been bare for weeks now. I have hope in what that means, but I know better than to get my hopes up. She squeezes my hand. "No, I don't actually. He wasn't right for me. He wasn't...you." She says, looking at me like I hung the moon. Me wanting this has nothing to do with me being wrung out emotionally. It has everything to do with needing you. So, please."

The relief that courses through my body could knock me on my ass. I've hated that ring on her finger, I've hated that she was someone else's.

Please. That one word shatters every sense of resolve I had.

Not waiting another second, I lean in close and softly touch my lips against hers. My hand grips the back of her hair, holding her closer to me. My other hand slides around her waist, and I feel her melt against me. I want to make up for all the time we lost not doing this, not kissing. Not being together. Not being Weston and Willow. It was always supposed to be us.

We spend far too long in that position; it feels like forever since we've come up for air. I don't care if it makes me the most pathetic man in the world. I don't need air, I just need her.

She pulls back just far enough to press her forehead against mine while we both catch our breath. "I've missed you, West. I've missed you so damn much and I've been trying to fight the fact that I need you. But I don't want to anymore, it's exhausting.""Well, I haven't spent any time at all fighting it, but I've spent years wanting this. Wanting you. I've been yours since I saw you for the first time, and it's the only thing I want to be."She leans in, pressing her lips against mine again for a quick peck. "Glad we are on the same page, but can we move this party back home?"

"Yeah, baby, we can go home." I lean in and give her one last peck on the lips before making my way back to the driver's seat.

Now that I have her in my house, I don't want to let her go. I want this to be our house. And if she doesn't want this here, I'll go there with her. New York can't be that bad if she's there. Besides, she's my home. My heart lives with her, now and always.

We get on the road, and my head decides to drive away with my thoughts. What's going to happen now? I guess I should be happy that we are both on the same page, finally.

"I wish you could have driven the old truck, our truck," Willow says, her head leaning into the headrest as she looks over at me.

"Why's that?" I question.

"I used to be able to sit right next to you; now this big ole thing is in the way." She taps her hand against my center console, which, in her defense, is rather big. This truck, in general, is so much bigger than my high school truck.

"I almost forgot all about that." I look over to her, and take her hand, my other on the wheel. "You're right, I'll drive the other truck as soon as it's running again."

We drive the rest of the drive home in silence, and I wonder if her mind is running as wild as mine. We have a few things to figure out, but we've got time. She's still here for at least another month.

I hop out of the truck and run to her side to get her door. She barely has it cracked open when I finally get to her.

"I can get my own door," she assures me, but the smile on her face tells me she enjoys the sentiment. She's worth the effort.

"Yeah, well, you're going to have to get used to it." I lean into the cab and bring her lips to mine. She melts into me and brings her hand up behind my neck, her fingers just barely in my hair, but enough to send goosebumps over my body.

God, I love her touch. There's nothing in the world like it. She gently tugs at my hair, and I let out a groan into her mouth. Fuck.

"Something wrong, West?" she murmurs over my lips, her own turning up in a smile.

"Yeah, there's this girl. She drives me fucking crazy."

"Hmm, she sounds like quite the gal."

"Mhmm, I think I need to get her inside." Because we have a lot of wasted time to make up, and I'd prefer to do it without any clothes on.

"Okay." She unbuckles her seatbelt and hops out of the truck.

I can't believe this is really happening. I'm almost scared even to ask that this is. But she said it, she's tired of fighting it, and I thank God for that because I can't go another second without her in my life. She's my whole world.

I no more than step inside the house and she's on me, her mouth is against mine, and now that I know this is what's on her mind, I can take the lead.

My kiss is ravenous. Every kiss brings my fire for her to new heights. My cock feels like solid lead beneath my zipper; it's been far too long since we've done this.

I scoop my hands under her ass and bring her legs up around my waist, carrying her to the couch.

"Fuck, West. I want you so bad. I missed you. I missed this," she says as I sit down on the couch. Her hips roll against me as she moves her mouth to my neck.

The pressure builds within me, and I fight the urge to meet the next roll of her hips.

"You're going to need to stop that, baby. It's been a while, and you've got me fucking burning."

"Oh, really?" she asks, flipping her hair over to one side as she grinds her hips against me. God damn. Dry humping is going to send me over the edge.

"Willow, God." My hand flexes around the curve of her. Needing more skin, I grab the hem of her shirt and pull it over her head. Her perfect breasts sit high in her bra right in front of my face. She's filled out since the last time I saw her; her curves are perfect against my hand.

"God, these tits, baby. They're fucking perfect." My hands roam up her sides, my palms push up the bottom of her tits, and I give a little squeeze.

"That feels so good, West." She throws her head back in ecstasy, moaning as she wiggles across my rock-hard cock.

She increases her pace, grinding back and forth, faster and faster. I can feel my balls start to tighten as she drags her covered pussy across my cock. God, I want these clothes off, want to be buried inside her.

She puts her hands over mine and squeezes, making me put more pressure on her perfect little tits, and I lose it. I lose what little control I had.

"Oh fuck, fuck. Yes. No." My brain tries to make sense of what happens as my cock erupts inside my jeans, spilling out. I can feel the spot get wet instantly.

"Weston Taylor, did you just come in your pants?" "Yeah, well, it's been twelve years since I've touched anyone. Since I've touched you, really, I'm kind of surprised I didn't come the second you laid your lips on mine."

She rears back in shock. "West, are you telling me you haven't been with anyone since we broke up?" I can't find the words, so I shake my head no. I couldn't. It's not like I didn't try to move on. Every time I did, I was reminded of how wrong it was. I hated it, every second of it. The second a girl even touched me, it felt revolting, which wasn't fair to them. So eventually, I stopped trying and started praying she would come home to me. Prayed that she would be mine again.

"*West.*" Her voice comes out half broken.

"It's okay. I'm glad. You're it for me, Willow. I never stopped loving you, not even for a second. Your hands are the only ones I want on me." I lean in and kiss her; this time, it's much slower. The raging fire in our veins before has now simmered down to a smolder, something sustainable. We aren't going to burn out this time.

"I love you, Weston. You're it for me, too. Now, how about you take me to bed and we make up for some lost time."

"I thought you'd never ask."

Chapter 31
WILLOW

He hasn't been with anyone since me? How is that possible? It's been twelve years. Over a decade without having sex? God, that's punishment enough for what he did. All at once, I feel every bit of animosity I had toward him vanish. He waited for me to come back, and now that I'm here, I'll never let this slip away again.

"Are you sure you want this?" Weston says, his breath heavy against my lips as he lays me down on his bed.

"Yes. More than sure. Please, Weston." I need his hands on me like I need air in my lungs. There is something different about being with someone you love. Someone who knows every inch of your body.

"I want to take my time. It's been a while, and I want to learn what makes you scream my name so loud it bounces off the mountainside." His lips press to my neck, his breath skittering across my bare skin, making my whole body tingle.

"Something tells me you won't have any problem with that," I say on a gasp as he lightly bites down my neck. He drives me wild in a way that I didn't think was completely possible.

"Yeah, you know. I don't think so either. But I think we need to establish some ground rules." Weston crawls back and stands at the end of the bed. He starts slowly unbuttoning his shirt.

"Oh, and what are those?"

My eyes catch on the way each finger meticulously works the button, wishing they were working me with that rapt of attention.

"First. I call the shots. You can take charge anywhere else, but here, when my hands are on you, I take the lead," he says, his voice like gravel. "Oh really, cause I'm pretty sure I just made you come in your pants in, what was that, two minutes?" I cock an eyebrow up in defiance, knowing good and well I am playing with fire.

"Oh, you're going to regret that, brat. There might be a few times I get carried away, but just remember I love you and respect you. But I'm going to fuck you like I don't."

Good God. This should probably scare me, but it doesn't. It causes a fresh wave of desire to engulf me, and I think I might get off on his rough words alone. Weston has always been good about being in control, but I can only imagine how that's grown.

"I'm going to hold you to it." There's way too much excitement in my voice. I should be fighting him, but I've spent enough time doing that.

"I've spent years planning the first time I get to lay my hands on you again."

He tosses his shirt to the side, and I see it. The willow tree tattooed across the whole left side of his torso. My hands immediately go to it, running my hands over the ink. "West, what is this?"

"I couldn't have you here, but I needed you with me in some way. So, I tattooed you on me, that way in some shape or form, I could keep you forever." The look in his eyes is enthralling.

"I'm here to stay now," I manage to get out, overtaken with emotion.

He leans down and cages me in with his strong arms, forcing me to look straight up at him. "Good. I'm going to make up for lost time, so I hope you weren't planning on getting any sleep."

He immediately starts working on my jeans and pulling them off my hips. I reach for him and am met with a sharp look.

"Uh-uh, baby. I'm going to need you to put your hands up until I tell you to move them." He grabs my hand and puts them above my head. Slowly, he moves down and gently brings his lips down my body until he reaches my unbuttoned pants.

His hot breath is so close to where I wish his mouth was. My body feels on edge, knowing it's waiting for something good, something great even. Maybe I'm crazy for liking this, but his control of the situation forces me to let go. Forces me to trust him.

My hips buck up, eagerly searching for something. A kiss, a touch, literally anything.

"Keep still, I promise I'm gonna take care of you, but only if you're a good girl and can listen to instructions. You want me to fuck you? Don't you?"

I eagerly nod my head, because that's what I want more than any-thing right now. I can feel myself getting wetter by the second at his words, causing my body to come alive.

"Say it for me." He works his belt now, slowly sliding off his pants. Why is he taking so long? This is borderline torture.

As much as I want to, my brain is having a hard time forming a single comprehensible thought. "Please," is what my brain comes up with, close, but I already know this bastard is going to make me do exactly what he asked.

"I don't think that's what I wanted to hear, pretty girl."

"Ugh, I want you to fuck me, West."

A saccharine grin stretches across his face. "That's good, 'cause I want to fuck you too. But first, I want to have a little fun."

A shiver runs through my body at the thought of what fun could possibly mean; hopefully, it has something to do with his hands all over me.

His fingers brush against the lace of my panties, putting just enough pressure for it to feel good. I have to fight the urge to lift my hips to get more pressure; it's so close to being enough, but yet nowhere near enough.

He runs his fingers up and down my covered slit. "Oh, baby, I love how wet you are for me. This pussy is practically begging for my cock to fill it up, isn't it?"

I nod my head, because yes, that is exactly what my pussy wants.

He takes his hand away. "What was that? I couldn't hear you." Son of a bitch. My frustration rises alongside my desire. How something can be so hot and so damn infuriating at the same time is a mystery. "Yes, that's what I want."

He nods his head in approval as his hand starts to work my pussy again. He slides the panties to the side, and my breath starts to turn ragged. I struggle to find a reasonable pace of breathing behind all the arousal. I can't think straight when I'm strung this tightly. A coiled rope that is seconds away from snapping. All I need for him to do is... His finger slides into my pussy, *yes*. That's what I needed.

An unrecognizable moan claws its way out of my throat as I feel the first bit of friction.

"If you sound like that with just my finger, I can't wait to hear you scream when my cock fills you up."

"You could find out faster, you know." I try to smile, but he hooks his finger right against my G-spot, and I feel my jaw drop open as a silent plea escapes me instead.

"Oh no, I am not near done playing with you. In fact, I think I might be in the mood to be reminded of what this perfect pussy tastes like."

Fuck, if there is one thing I remember about this man, it's how damn good he was with his mouth. He's witty and a spitfire at baseline, but when that man goes to work on you? He does a damn good job.

"Please, West."

"God, I love it when you ask so nicely. I need you to go face down ass up, baby, but keep those hands under you. I want to see this sexy little ass while you come on my face."

I roll over and arch my back up as quickly as I can, not wanting to wait a single second more for his mouth to be on me.

When his tongue slides over my pussy I feel my whole body spasm. My back arches farther, wanting to give him as much of me as my body will allow.

"Look how sexy you look with that ass up in the air like that. You arch it so good for me."

Those are his last words before he goes to work, making good on his promise. His tongue glides through me, and I can feel my pussy start to drip down my thighs. I don't think I've ever been quite this turned on. My body feels like molten lava.

Within seconds, my hands are gripping the blanket covering the bed as I scream his name, my pussy spasming as he fucks me with his tongue. His hands reach up and grip my ass as I ride out the rest of my orgasm. It feels never-ending. So good it almost hurts.

I don't have any time to recover before Weston is filling me up from behind, stretching me out. "Oh my God."

"That's funny. I'm pretty sure that's not my name. Maybe I need to fuck you a little harder for you to remember."

He immediately picks up his pace, and I wonder how the fuck he went twelve years without any of this. Because one time with him again reminds me just how great he is. Our bodies work together in perfect tandem. My body comes alive for him like he's its lifeline. Probably because he's my lifeline.

"Fuck baby, this pussy is so tight. It's gripping my cock." His hands travel up my arched back until they land on my waist. He grips on and pumps harder into me. "I need you to reach around and play with your clit for me. I want to feel you come on my cock."

My hands immediately follow his command, desperate for another round of release, as my fingers start rubbing circles across my clit. The tension quickly builds in me. Hearing Weston's groans of pleasure behind me adds fuel to the fire, turning me on with every sound that comes out of him. It makes me feel so damn good to know it feels like this for him, too. Too good, too fucking good to ever miss out on again.

"I need you to come for me, squeeze my cock with that perfect little pussy. And please, tell me I can fill you up."

"Yes. We're protected." Even though my birth control has been pretty much useless this last year, I've never been so happy to be prepared.

"Good, cause I want to see how good you look with my come leaking out of that tight little pussy of yours."

His filthy words are all I need to be thrown off the edge into the abyss. My body coils tightly around him as I let go.

"Fuck, yes. Squeeze my cock." Weston's words sound grated and strained. The groan that comes out of him tells me he wasn't that far behind me. He comes with a guttural moan.

He slowly pulls his cock out of me, and I feel almost hollow without him there. My breathing is ragged and uneven as I try and catch my breath after that...experience. There is no other word for it besides that.

I feel his fingers drag up my pussy, "Look at how well you took my come, baby. Such a good little cum slut for me. Come around and sit on the edge of the bed."

Having been fucked into complete submission, I follow his task without a smartass remark, but my brain feels oddly quiet. At peace even.

"Open," he commands as he taps his fingers against my lips. Once I do, his fingers glide into my mouth. "Suck."

At this point, I would probably do anything this man said, so I do. I relish the taste of our mixed arousal.

"Do you like tasting how much I fucking love that pussy of yours?"

I nod my head yes because the salty flavor coating my tongue is somehow the best thing I've ever tasted.

He surprises me by leaning forward, and his lips meet mine. When his tongue sweeps against my lips, I open for him. His kiss is all-consuming. He slows, and against my lips he murmurs, "Me too."

I chuckle against his lips and I feel them stretch out in a smile. He leans back, and I come up for air for the first time. Feeling like a new woman.

"Was that okay? If it's too much, just let me know. I want to make sure you're taken care of."

Just like that, he's back, and I love it. Having two sides. He's rough with me where I need him to be, but still my soft place to land.

"It was perfect. Don't change a thing.""Good. Now let's get you cleaned up and get some food in you.""West, I know that we have a lot to figure out and talk about. But I want you to know I forgive you. And I ... I don't know. Thank you for today."

"For the orgasms?" He cocks his head, but the stupid smile on his face says it all; he knows exactly what I meant.

I slap his arm. "Yes, that exactly. Thank you for the penis, it was wonderful. I'll leave you a glowing Yelp review first thing in the morning."

"Anytime, now go get cleaned up, and I'll get you some food."

I look at him for a second, and it finally hits me that this is real. That this could really be our second chance. The future we were supposed to have all along.

"How about you come with me, and we cook together."

"Whatever you say, Sunshine." He lands another kiss on my lips, and I start to wonder if I will ever feel like I've had enough of him.

Chapter 32
WILLOW

My heart pounds so hard behind my chest that it feels like it's about to break out. I know that I'm being ridiculous. I've eaten dinner at this house a million times, and the last time I did, I was someone else's fiancé. West and I are happy; the best I can hope for is that they're happy for us.

Maybe I'm overthinking because of all the stress I've had lately, but Grandpa is fine now. He's set up with a cardiologist who he will hopefully listen to better than he listens to me.

"You about ready to go?" Weston asks as he pokes his head into the bathroom. He takes me in, head to toe, before smirking at me. "You look beautiful, by the way."

My heart sputters a little bit. I look from him to myself in the mirror. "I'm as ready as I'll ever be."

"So you're a little nervous, I take it?" Weston's arms come around me, pulling me to his chest.

I look at him through the mirror and sigh. "A little would be the understatement of the century."

His brows furrow. "Why?"

"To be honest, I can't really put my finger on it, but I'm nervous about whether they won't like me anymore." I'm not blind to the fact that I'm not the same girl that left, and sometimes I don't like the version of me I became after leaving. What if they decide they don't like who I am now?

He shakes his head at the thought, softly bringing his lips to my neck, kissing my fluttering pulse before looking back up to me. "You are aware you've been around them multiple times since you've been here, and everyone still loves you the same as they did twelve years ago."

But that was before I was his girlfriend again, before we became us again. "I know that, I want them to still like me, you know? Your family was my second family for as long as I can remember, and then they weren't anymore, and I don't know how it's going to be today. Is it gonna be like old times, or are we starting over?" I shake my head; even I can see I am diving way too deep into this. "I'm overthinking it. I know. It's just the first time since, you know." Since we fell apart all those years ago.

He nods in understanding. "I'm sure you'll find it as soon as we sit down for dinner. My family is as dysfunctional as it always has been."

His family is the opposite of dysfunctional. They're kind, they love each other fiercely, and they have some of the best senses of humor I've ever seen. His family is literally a dream. When I was a kid, I always wanted a family like his. Siblings to fight with, parents who loved me and put me first, and a big kitchen table where we can eat dinner at the end of the day and talk about everything. I'm really grateful for my grandpa, but sometimes I wish I had a traditional family. It was both heartbreaking and freeing when I realized I was going to have to create that myself someday to have it.

When we walk up the steps, Weston gives my hand a little reassuring squeeze before opening the door and ushering me inside.

"Weston, you live like five seconds away. How are you late for dinner every single week?" Aspen says, cocking her hip out and pointing to the clock hanging on the wall.

I can almost hear his eyes roll, and I can't help but laugh at their spat. "Aspen, I really don't think you want to be talking about running late. I think the last time you ran on time was the day you were born."

"I'm not late. I'm just running on my own time. It's my world, and y'all are just living in it," Aspen replies with perfect amount of attitude. I look around the room and see Mabel heave out a deep sigh and shake her head. She's been dealing with their shenanigans forever.

Weston looks over to his mom. "I'm not sure what you did wrong, but Aspen didn't quite turn out right."

"Sweetie, I'm not sure if you really want to start comparing things." Mabel jokes from the kitchen.

It's been twelve years, but things are exactly the same, and I've never felt such a huge relief. Me being here wasn't some big shock.

"Glad to see you're back at family dinner with us, Miss Willow. Would you like a beer, wine, or some water?" Mabel asks.

"If I'm gonna have to listen to these two bicker all night, I'm gonna need some liquor in me. Surprise me with the beer or wine, please."

"God, I would kill for a couple glasses of wine," Ava says as she leans back in her chair, her arms folded over her pregnant belly.

"If this one over here is leading you to drink, you just need to tell me. I'm pretty sure I could scare him back into a straight line." Mabel shakes her spatula in Mav's direction, and I see him shiver from fear.

"No, he's been quite the gentleman. Probably deserves a prize for dealing with my hormonal ass. I even get on my own nerves some days."

"You're not that bad, baby," Mav says, running his hand over the back of her head. "I've only feared for my life like three times."

"Sounds like she's taking it easy on you, son," Jack chimes in, and I swear I see a smile behind that graying mustache.

"I told him it could be worse. He didn't believe me," Ava jokes.

I can't help but laugh at the interaction. Ava wasn't here last time I was, and I haven't got to spend a whole lot of time with her, but I am quickly regretting that. She's hilarious, and I love her. She's the perfect match for Mav. Everything I loved about this family is exactly the same except for it's growing. I take a minute to soak in the feeling of gratitude. How lucky am I to get to be a part of something like this?

It doesn't take long for Mable to finish up dinner and for us all to head to the table. Weston pulls out the chair beside him, and I scoot in.

"So, how's work on the cabins going?" Mav asks.

Weston looks to me and lets me answer, "I feel like it's going really well. The construction crews are moving really quickly." I have to admit the construction crew Weston found was even better than the one I found. They work faster, and their boss isn't a raging asshole.

"You know what I was thinking, we really might look into hiring someone full-time for property management, not just for the cabins, but maybe to run our books with us expanding and growing, and everyone's lives getting busier, it might be a good idea," Rhett says. He's always the logical one. That has been my concern this whole time, too.

"Do you know who that would be perfect for that job for?" Aspen asks, looking directly at me.

Everyone at the table says my name unanimously.

"Oh, that would be a wonderful idea," Mabel says with way too much excitement in her eyes.

Aspen starts to laugh, and Weston is immediately suspicious. "What're you laughing at?"

She takes a sip of her wine before selling herself out. "Just watching my plan perfectly into place. It's such a beautiful thing to see." She pinches her face in a smile and brings her shoulders up.

"What do you mean?" Mabel asks cautiously.

Aspen quirks up one brow, still holding her wine glass. "You don't seriously think I found some random ass company in New York to do this job, do you?"

"Well, I thought it was a little weird, but I know better than to criticize your choices," Weston says.

"I knew where she worked, so I reached out to her company and hired her, knowing that if I got you two together, there's no way in hell you'd be able to stay apart."

"Aspen Marie Taylor!" Mabel says.

"There is no way in hell I'm about to apologize when it worked out this well. Weston's finally happy, Willow's finally home, and the ranch is running smoothly from the way I'm looking at it. You all owe me a thank you," she says, taking a sip of her drink.

Okay, so maybe this family is a little bit dysfunctional, but I like it. All my fears about things being different are gone. She wanted me back so bad. She was willing to manipulate not only me and her brother, but my career so I could be here. Sure, I could be mad, but I'm not. A family that wants me that badly can have me.

Chapter 33
WESTON

Willow's hand holds her head up as she talks on the phone. Without even seeing her face, I can tell she's had a long day. She then slumps back in the chair, miming stabbing herself with the pen at the desk. My chest shakes with laughter at the motion. She hasn't even seen me yet, but I can tell I need to get my girl some fresh air.

"Rough day, Sunshine?" I inquire.

Her look says it all, but mostly, *no shit, Sherlock.* "Well, the floor we had picked out is no longer in stock, so we're gonna have to figure something else out, and the windows are two weeks delayed. I really need something to go right today. Or ever for that matter."

I walk up behind her and lean down and wrap my arms around her chest, pulling her closer to me as I kiss her forehead from behind. "How about you and me get out of here for a little bit?"

"As amazing as that sounds, I have so much to do, West." Even though her words are saying she needs to work, she grips onto my forearms, leaning her head into the crack of my elbow.

"And you know what? All that work will be here when we get back. You work all the time, nonstop. I love your dedication, but let's go outside."

"Are you trying to gently tell me I need to go outside and touch some grass?" Her tone is filled with faux attitude.

That wasn't really where I was going with that, but she probably could've benefited. "I'm saying you need some sunshine and I miss my girl. So, let's get away for a while." I let her go and spin her chair around so she's looking at me. I put my arms on each side of the office chair, leaning down while getting face-to-face. I lightly press my lips to hers. "Please."

She lets out a groan as she throws her head back. "You know I can't resist you when you ask like that."

"I have no idea what you're talking about." I beam at her, knowing exactly how to get what I want. To be fair, I'd do the same with her. She says jump, I jump.

"You play dirty, Weston Taylor. Real dirty." She shakes her head at me, squinting her eyes. Even I can see the relief on her face because she's getting a break

"When it comes to you, I don't think I ever play dirty enough." I wink at her. It's true, though, there's twelve years of missed time to make up for. She rolls her eyes. "Okay, you pervert, get me out of here." She lifts her arms, and I pull her out of the chair and into my embrace.

"Okay, but we're gonna stop by the house first. You need to change into something comfortable." I tap her ass a couple of times before letting her go and linking our hands together.

"You sure are bossy today."

"Well, I take taking care of my girl very seriously. And it appears I've been slacking so I need to make up for it." I give her hand a quick squeeze.

"You know what you're right, pamper me, Weston." She beams up at me, and fuck, I love it. The only thing I wake up wanting to do anymore is put a smile on her face and make her laugh.

"Not sure who told you pampering is done on the back of a horse, but you might want to have a conversation with them," she says from behind me, her arm wrapped around my torso.

My body shakes with laughter. "You're the one who brought up pampering. I just mentioned getting the hell out of that office."

She pokes me in the rib from behind, causing me to fold in on myself. "I'll make sure to ask more questions next time."

"Speaking of asking questions, I have a game for us to play. Twenty questions. You've got a lot to learn about each other and catch up on. I think this would be a good way to do it."

"Oh, good, horseback ride and an interrogation," she says with a mischievous smirk.

She may say this isn't fun, but I know her; she loves being on the back of the horse with the fresh air blowing through your hair. It's one of the best parts of having all this land. "Don't lie, I know you love being on the back of the horse."

"You're right. It is nice being back out here, and I am feeling much better now that I'm not in that office."

I see my need to start putting the pieces of the past together. "Speaking of office, what's the favorite part of your job?"

"Starting the questions off with a bang, huh? I love watching things all come together. Even when they seem like they won't, and you've got a million different balls bouncing in different courts, somehow things always work out. It's fun managing the chaos. Do I get asked questions too?"

"Sure, we can make up the rules as we go."

"Are you liking taking over the ranch?"

I consider her question not because I don't enjoy it but because I want to answer it honestly. "Yes. But I'm also terrified. I don't want to be the generation that loses the ranch. And I also want to set it up so that my kids will never have to worry about losing it."

"I've seen the numbers. You guys aren't in any trouble."

"Yeah, I know that, but things can get quick. Equipment is expensive. Fires can happen, droughts, all sorts of things. I have a really hard time letting go of the things I can't control."

Not being able to let go of things I can't control got me into this position. I thought I could control her future and make sure she was on a good path, and the only thing that did was break both of our hearts. Guess you could say I learned the lesson the hard way.

"Half the fun is learning how to roll with the punches. You were made to run this ranch. You do it with such joy. I was concerned you would hate it when we were in high school. You didn't seem to love it here, but something must've changed."

I consider her input, because she wasn't wrong. In high school, I thought Windy Peaks had nothing to offer. "I can't say if something really changed or if I learned to find the beauty in the little things and realize life doesn't have to be all big and grand to be great. Okay, time for my next question. Who is your best friend in New York?"

She stays quiet for a beat longer than normal, and I wonder if I struck a nerve. Maybe I shouldn't have asked this question. "This is gonna sound really pathetic, but I don't have one. I have friends, but they're all surface-level. People I have met in the office who have kept in contact with me after they moved on, and people I met in college.

Honestly, the person I'm closest to is my seventy-year-old neighbor," she says with a self-deprecating laugh. "God, I live a sad life."

My heart cracks at this revelation. I thought she would have a big friend group, knowing how she is. Willow is kind and funny. She would do anything for anybody. It doesn't make sense to me that she doesn't have a whole entourage of friends. It also gives me a more realistic picture of what I set her up for in New York.

"Are people in New York that hard to get along with?" I probe.

"No, I think that there's a part of me that doesn't jive well with New York. You know, I'm different there. Not to bring up the past, but when I got to New York, I wasn't the happiest person, and I think that really set the tone. I was a shell of myself for a long time, and when I finally came out of that depression, I didn't really have it in me to try and make friends or at least friends like I had here. Maybe I was a little afraid of losing them, too. Like the fewer people I let in, the less I could be disappointed."

This was supposed to be an adventure to make her feel better, and I feel like I'm weighing it down. I feel terrible knowing she didn't have the support she could have had here. I'm glad she's behind me and can't see the tears in my eyes, like guilt is bubbling up on me and has nowhere to go.

"Willow, I'm so sorry."

She wraps her arms around me from behind in an embrace, like she's trying to comfort me after all that I have done. That is my Willow, my girl. The one with a heart so big you can break hers, and she will still be more worried about you. I wonder how I will ever move on from this guilt. It's soul-crushing. But I don't want to carry that with us. We're getting to try again, and I want to make it last.

"I forgive you. And you know what, I actually think this needed to happen. I think both of us needed to see that life was really better together, and if we had never been apart, we wouldn't have ever really known we've grown a lot since then."

I can appreciate the sentiment, but we didn't need time apart to know that maybe she's just telling herself that, or maybe she's saying it to make me feel better, which I love her for. But I don't think either one of us would've ever taken each other for granted.

"My turn for a question," she says, clearly trying to shift the conversation. "What do you see your life like in five years?"

"Would it scare you if I said I saw you and me?" That's all I see now that she's in my sights again. A full life with her. I don't just see the next five years. I see our whole life. Kids, careers, rocking chairs on the front porch when we're eighty. The rest of my life will be spent devoted to her.

"It would scare me more if you didn't."

My heart soars at her admission. "Good, then I see you and me. And hopefully, a little girl with your spunky attitude and kind heart. You know the world means more sunshine, like you."

"I love you, West." She leans her head against my back and for the first time in years everything feels perfect. The oceans have settled, and I can finally take a deep breath. A fresh breath of her is all I needed to ground myself.

"I love you most, Sunshine."

We continue our game of questions. Our hearts at the core are the same as they were years ago, more mature now, more settled, but that spark that brought us together is shining just like it always has. Things have happened that have changed us into who we are now, and it's good to know that about each other. We've got a lot to catch up on. How lucky am I to meet the love of my life twice?

The sun beats down on me as we come to a corner with a clear view of the river, and I get an idea. I guide the horse toward the water. There's a little patch of short grass and tree coverage to stop at. It makes the perfect beach spot.

"What are we stopping for?" She looks around at our surroundings. It's nothing but the trail, a thick covering of pines and aspens out here. Wild grass and flowers grow in sporadic patches. There's not another soul for miles.

"Well, I don't know about you, but it's hot as hell, so I think I'm gonna go cool off." I slide off the horse and tie it to a low-lying branch.

"I didn't bring my swimsuit, West." She looks a little panicked, but after our little chat, I know that country-loving girl is still in there. So I'm going to coax her all the way out.

"Wouldn't be the first time we skinny dipped in this river."

"But we were teenagers then. I'm not trying to catch an indecent exposure charge."

I look around for dramatic effect. "Sunshine, this land is ours, nobody's going to come and give us a ticket for being naked on our own land."

"You're serious?" She still sits atop the horse, staring down at me. Both figuratively and physically.

I don't answer. I drop my drawers and strip my shirt over my head. "Are you too chicken to get in, baby?"

There's one thing about her that hasn't changed. It's her love to prove a point.

"I know you didn't just call me a chicken." She kicks her leg over the horse and drops to the dirt like she's been doing it for years, and goddamit if it doesn't turn this sad sap on.

"I'm kind of surprised I haven't heard you bock from all your chickeness." I wink at her, knowing good and well I'm playing with fire now.

"First of all, you're dumb. Second of all, fine. I will get naked and swim with you."

"Let's not pretend like it's such a chore. You love to see me naked. It was you who watched me shower and stroke my cock to the thought of you, wasn't it?"

If I thought her face was pink from the sun, it turns a whole new shade of red at that.

"No need to be embarrassed. I like seeing you naked too, baby. Now strip for me."

"You know, I'm so tired from work. I think I might need a hand."

I don't need a second to think about what I'm going to do. I strut up to her. And grab the hem of her T-shirt and pull it over her head. My fingers glide down her silhouette, roaming over her curves. Her breath hitches as my fingers move to the button of her pants, unbuttoning them. I pull them down until she stands for me in nothing but her bra and her sexy little lace thong. Good God, this woman was made for me.

My hands skate across her ribs as I move to the latch of her bra. "Have I told you lately how sexy you are?"

"No, you've been really holding out on me." Her smile is devious, and fuck if it doesn't make my cock even harder.

"Mmm, I think I need to fix that." My lips move to her neck, gently kissing upward as I pull off her bra. My hand finds her breast, pinching her nipple between my fingers, and she gasps into my mouth.

My cock turns into lead just by touching her. I wouldn't even need a touch, just laying eyes on the woman has my blood boiling. I'm so fucking hot for her. It feels like I'm going to burn from the inside out.

Her hands slide into my hair as I make my way up to her mouth. I slide my tongue in as she moans against me. I press my cock deeper into her abdomen, wanting her to feel how hard she makes me. "You feel that, baby? This is what you do to me, you drive me fucking crazy."

"Do you want to feel what you do to me?"

I nod my head yes, and she grabs my hand and slips underneath her panties. I slide down her flesh until my fingers meet her wet heat. She's so fucking soaked for me right now just from one kiss.

She takes control by grabbing my hand and guiding my fingers into her pussy as she spreads her legs wider. I grab one leg and heave it across my waist, giving me easier access to her center.

I've been completely in charge every other time we've gotten busy; it's equally as hot to see her take charge now. She guides my fingers in and out of her slick little cunt, and my cock feels like it's ready to explode.

I go to pull my hands out, but she stops me and says, "No, I want you to feel how bad I want your cock." She guides my fingers to my lips, and I suck, relishing the taste of her.

My control snaps in an instant. I grab her other leg and hitch it around my waist and back up to the poplar tree. "You're gonna want to hold on nice and tight, baby."

I spent so many years thinking about the ways I could fuck this woman, so many fantasies. When you've spent twelve years fucking your fist to the thought of a specific woman, when she's finally in your hands in front of you, it's hard to keep control. So I think there's going to be a lot of making up for time in our future.

I pull her panties to the side and glide my cock to her slick entrance. It takes nothing for me to sink into her, both of us moaning as my cock stretches out her little pussy. The way it grips me as I slide out and pump back into her is euphoric. I throw my head back and close my eyes so I can concentrate on how good this tight little cunt is.

"That's what you brought me out here for, fucking me in the woods?" She pulls at my hair, making me look at her. She's beautifully undone, her hair is a mess from my hands, her cheeks are rosy, and her eyes are wild. Just the way I like her.

I lean in and kiss her, nipping at her bottom lip before replying, "I've got a lot of fantasies of places I want to fuck you, and this is only the beginning."

"Thank God for that. Fuck me, baby." Her hands grip my hair to the point it almost hurts, making goosebumps break out over my flesh.

If she says jump, I'll do it. So, if she's telling me to fuck her, I'm going to do it like my life is depending on it. My cock pumps in and out of her as I brace her against the tree. Her legs squeeze tighter around my waist as we get closer and closer to our climax. I feel like a fucking teenager unable to last three minutes when I'm deep inside her tight little cunt. I can't help it.

"I'm close, baby," I tell her, biting my lip to cause just enough pain to keep me from spilling over the edge.

She moves her hand down between us and starts little circles around her clit as I thrust in and out of her. I look down to where our bodies meet and watch her pussy grip my cock as I slide out. Watching makes the sensation so much stronger.

If I thought that was hot as fuck, it has nothing on what comes next. Her pussy squirts, drenching my cock, drowning it. "Yes, baby, that's it." It takes mere seconds before I feel her tight little pussy spasm around me. Fucking her is like a drug. There's no other way to word it. She leans her head back as she screams my name for all the mountain to hear.

"That's a good girl, come for me, baby scream my name." My hand wraps around the back of her neck as my other arm holds tight to her legs.

Unable to hold back anymore, knowing that my girl got what she needed, I spill into her, filling her up. She looks so good when she's full of my cock.

Her legs shake around me as I catch my breath. "Well, I don't know about you, but I feel a lot less stressed," she says.

There's my sunshine, the girl who knows how to adjust enough lightness to a mood. The girl who keeps me laughing at all times, the girl for me.

"That makes two of us," I kiss her softly, "now how about I take you for that swim?"

She nods her head, and I carry us into the river, washing away the day and all our regrets from our past.

Chapter 34
WILLOW

For once, I open my emails with a smile. My boss's usual passive-aggressive email no longer brings my mood down; in fact, it almost brings it up. Knowing that I only have a few more weeks, and I'll be closing out my first and last project with them.

I'm staying in Windy Peaks. I think I knew I was going to stay here the second I got back. Well, maybe not the exact second, but when I realized I was happier here, even before Weston and I got back together. That was a good sign. I haven't felt this free in years.

I've already mailed my ring back to Josh with a letter saying he can donate my things. Officially closing out that chapter of my life and getting back on track.

There's a lot of reasons I'm staying. For one, both of the people I love most in the world are here. Time is fleeting, and I don't want to waste a single second away from my family anymore. I can have a really good life here, I know that.

Weston walks into the office holding two coffee cups. I always drink a cup before I come, but I love that he brings me another anyway. Which is good because I have a lot to do today, and it's easier to do things while heavily caffeinated.

"Thank you so much," I say as he hands me my cup of coffee, leaning in to plant a kiss, his lips warm and soft. It kicks my heart beat up a notch. I hope that never stops, the thrill I get from him.

The warmth from the travel cup heats up my hands. I immediately bring the cup to my lips and take a good sip.

"So, what do you need to get done today?" Weston asks as he sits in the chair across from me.

"Actually, I have to have a really important conversation with one of my clients. I'm kind of nervous." Which is true, but I think it's safe to say he's a hell of a lot more than a client now.

"Well, what's making you nervous about it?" Weston leans forward, fully engaged. I love this about him. If there's an issue, he wants to solve it together, and if he can't help, he'll at least listen.

"He's really stubborn, and I don't think he's gonna listen to what I have to say. Even though I know it's what's best."

"I'm gonna apologize on behalf of all men, we have a really hard time admitting when we're wrong," he says with a coy smile. Hearing those words come out of his mouth actually eases some of my anxiety. Because some men may be like that, but not mine. He messed up and owned up to it. He put in the work to fix what was broken. When I think about how good he is to his core, it warms my heart. Loving somebody like this can be overwhelming.

"I don't think you're giving good men like you enough credit. That's why I want to stay here with you." I nervously fidget with my hands as I wait to hear his reaction.

"Do you mean you want to stay in Windy Peaks?" There's a whole range of emotions flying across his face. I can see them also clearly, the concern in the pool of his brows, the excitement, and the slight smile on his face.

Standing, I walk around my desk and plant myself on his lap, looping my arms around his neck. "More specifically, I want to stay here with you. I don't want to spend another minute apart. I wanted to talk to you about this for a while."

His hand rubs up my back. I'm not sure if he's trying to reassure me or himself. "I don't want you giving up your career for me."

"I won't be. I'm fine with leaving New York. I can be incredibly happy here, running the business side of things if you'll let me. And if not, I'm sure there's something else I can find that would fulfill me just as much. What I do for a living does not matter nearly as much as how happy you make me. As getting to be around my grandpa more. I have people I can count on here, West. You have no idea how important that is, until it's gone."

"You are one hundred percent sure?" he asks, hope shining in his eyes.

"I'm more than one hundred percent sure. I miss Windy Peaks. I'm happier here than I have been in New York. I think I felt so restless these last few years because I knew something was wrong, and I know now what it was. I wasn't home. You are my home. I love this ranch."

His hand cradles against my jaw, his thumb gently brushing against my cheekbone. His eyes shine with unshed tears, filled with devotion and love, it makes me realize it was all worth it. As long as we ended up right back here. "I love you, Willow. Always have, always will."

"Ditto," I say with a wink. Because there's no words that can adequately describe the way I'm feeling right now. It's too much. "Thought you were gonna fight me a lot harder on this."

"Wait, was the client you were talking about me?"

"You catch on so quickly. It's astonishing, really." Sarcasm rings through and so does my smile.

"Hey! That actually could've taken a bit longer. I feel like you should give me some credit."

"You're right, I didn't even have to hold your hand and walk you to the point."

"Thank you." He gives me a small kiss on my nose before pulling me into his chest. I have a feeling he's saying thank you for more than one thing right now. "Can we tell everyone you're staying at dinner tonight? Aspen's been bugging the shit out of me about it."

I laugh, tapping his chest twice before saying, "Yes, of course."

One of the best things about Weston is the family I get along with him. I've learned so much from them. Mostly, I've learned to believe that a real family never leaves. And that family isn't always blood, and that's okay. It's a blessing to have either way.

"Shut up!" Aspen's hands slam on the table with a thud as her voice comes out in a girlish shriek. Before I know if she's running over to me and hugging me so tight, she's almost cutting off my airflow.

"Hey, can you let her go before you shut her up forever by accident?" Weston jokes pulling her arms away from my neck.

"I'm sorry, I'm just so excited. It's gonna be so nice having another girl around." She gives me one final squeeze before letting me go and heading back to her seat.

"With her staying, I want to make sure it's okay with you guys if we hire her on?"

"And keep in mind if any of you say no, I will never cook for you again," Mabel interjects as she glares around the table. I know she's joking, but it's still terrifying nonetheless. You would think people would be more afraid of Jack. Wrong. When we were kids, it was the ass chewing from Mabel.

"Hell would have to freeze over for any of us not to welcome Willow home and hire her on. We want her on our team." Maverick says with a big smile.

"Now that you're staying for sure, we need to schedule a once-a-month girls' night," Aspen says, looking from me to Ava.

"Yes, as long as you're okay with me bringing one more girl along?" Ava says, her grin sheepish.

"Did you make a new friend at work? I thought I was your only friend?" Aspen looks downright insulted.

Ava looks for Maverick to the group. "We're having a baby girl!"

The whole table erupts and cheers. And to think, I would have missed all this if Aspen hadn't meddled. I really need to think of something special to say thank you. She's my guardian angel, and no words will ever adequately express my gratitude for bringing me back where I've always belonged.

"Looks like we're going to need to get a bigger table," Jack says, and I swear I see tears in his eyes. I forget that he pretty much doubled as Mav's dad. So this is going to be his first grandbaby.

"And what a blessing that is." Mabel's happy tears streak her face as she leans down and kisses Ava's head, before bringing Mav in for an embrace.

Weston reaches under the table and squeezes my hand. I don't think life will ever get better than this.

Chapter 35
WILLOW

I wake up to an empty bed the next morning, which is unfortunate, considering the steamy, X-rated dream I was having about the very man who sleeps next to me. That's the one new thing our relationship has now that it didn't then. Weston did sneak into my window more times than I can count, but being able to exist like this together, it's everything.

As I start to get ready for work, I can't shake the desire humming through me. I want that man like my heart needs its next beat. The itch for him hasn't stopped now that we're back together; it's grown. I'm at the point where I can't escape him, even in my dreams, not that I would want to. I look at myself in the mirror and laugh. How utterly obsessed I am with that man has changed me. My skin is brighter, no longer dull. My cheeks are constantly flushed and plumped up. It's like being with him has breathed life back into me.

I head to my room, which still has my clothes. We haven't really gotten around to moving everything over quite yet. Maybe after we finish our last tasks with the cabins, we will have more time for it. I pull out an outfit with one thing in mind. One sneaky little fantasy that I can't get rid of. I dream of it nightly, and I think I might be able to bring it to life. I've caught on to Weston's obsession with my pencil skirts, and I know just the one to wear. It fits like a second skin, hugging every curve of my body. Accentuating every single asset I've got working for me. I add a red lip, and it takes my outfit to new levels of office vixen.

I take one final look in the mirror before leaving the room and heading downstairs, where, like clockwork, there is a freshly brewed pot of coffee and a note tucked under my mug. Always with scratch paper he ripped off from junk mail, but the notes he writes are where the love lies. He writes something he loves about me each day on the scrap paper. Reminding me of just how lovable I am.

I get in the truck and drive to work, my thoughts a tangle of filthy thoughts and to-do lists. Usually, my anxiety wins out, but not today.

The first thing I do when I step into the office is send a message to West that there is a private matter I need him urgently for. Hopefully, he gets the hint that I want him to come alone.

I sit on the desk, facing the door, and undo a few buttons on the top of my blouse until the lace trim of my bra peeks out. I swear to God, if that man walks in with his father, I will die.

The door to the office swings open with vigor; someone took the urgency I laced in the text to heart. "What's wrong?"

He stops dead in his tracks when he sees me. His eyes peruse every inch of my body, from my voluminous curls, down the slope of my neck to my cleavage, my stocking-covered legs, and down to where my heeled feet dangle off the edge of the desk.

I cock my head to the side, a saccharine smile stretching across my lips. "Oh, nothing, I just woke up to a very empty bed, which was unfortunate considering the dreams I was having."

Weston kicks the door closed behind him, turning to lock it before slowly stalking forward like I'm his prey. If I'm lucky, he'll eat me alive. "Is that so?"

Bracing my feet on the desk, I inch my skirt up just enough to let my legs fall open and give Weston a peek at what's waiting for him.

He goes slack-jawed before stepping closer between my legs, his thumb cradling my jaw while the back of his hand grips my head.

"The things I have wanted to do to you in this office, Sunshine." He reaches his hand up and brushes his thumb against my plump bottom lip. Desire fuels my next move as I nip at his finger.

"You want to tell me those things?" I say as I cock my head to the side, adrenaline and desire are pumping through my system. I can feel my whole body flush.

"I think I would rather show you." His hands move to my halfway buttoned-up white dress shirt. He grips each side and pulls, sending buttons flying everywhere. My breathing kicks up a notch, and so does the fire burning in my core.

He gawks at my breasts, which are sitting pushed up thanks to my white, push-up bra, and they look good, even I know that. His hands roam of their own accord, he palms one of my breasts, and I throw my head back.

With my head thrown back, it leaves my throat exposed. Weston takes advantage and leans forward, his lips finding my skin. Goosebumps erupt over my body as his stubble scratches against me. "Weston." It comes out as a whimper, but it's the most I can muster.

My hand laces through his hair, pulling him closer to my neck as he kisses and laps his tongue against me. A wild moan leaves my lips, bouncing off the office walls.

I need him to fill this insatiable longing.

His hands glide down to my skirt, bunching it all the way up and taking notice of his second little surprise.

"Are you wearing a garter?" he says, his eyes growing more hooded by the second.

I throw my arms over his neck, forcing him to look my way. "Yes. Do you like it?"

"You could wear a fucking paper sack, and I'd like it," he breaks eye contact, looking down at me, "but right now, I've never seen you look so God damn fuckable. I want to bed your sexy little ass over the desk and fuck you, hard."

My eyes flutter closed, imagining it. It's my exact dream: wanting him to fuck me like that. He grabs my thighs and pulls me off the desk, steadying me, before spinning me around until my front is at the desk.

"I think I'm going to do just that." He shimmies my skirt the rest of the way up, and I go to step out of my heels. "Did I say to take those off?" His stubble scratches me as he brings his lips close to my ear, a shiver violently racking through my body. "You're gonna eave the heels on while I fuck you." He pushes my front down until I'm flush with the desk.

I expect to hear him fumbling with his belt, but instead, I feel his hands grip my ass, spreading it, and then his mouth is on my pussy. His hand reaches around and toys with my clit. My back arches, giving him an even better angle. "Weston, don't stop. Please."

His fingers replace his mouth, the sensation amazing and not enough all at the same time. "Does my girl need to be fucked senseless, now?"

He presses more pressure on my clit, and I try to answer, but it comes out as a garbled mess of moans and pleas.

He stands, and I hear the telltale sounds of a belt coming off and jeans dropping.

"You better grip that desk, baby, 'cause I'm going to fuck you hard and fast."

My hands shoot out to grip the curve of the other side of the desk, just as Weston slides in. My back bows, and my fingers tighten their hold. "Yes."

This is what I wanted this morning. It's in a different setting, but this is even better. In here it's even hotter, with the added thrill of getting caught. It sends my pleasure to higher levels than I thought possible.

Weston groans as he sinks into me, over and over. The repetition feels like matches getting struck each time. "You look so good bent over in those heels, baby. You've been a little cock tease for weeks in those skirts and those damned heels."

All this time I thought he hated my business attire and wanted me back in boots, now I know he might've, but only because it was turning him on.

He keeps one hand on my waist as he reaches forward and palms one of my breasts, working my nipple between his fingers. It adds too much pleasure at once, and the moan that erupts from me would be embarrassing if it didn't immediately make Weston groan.

"God, you sound so fucking hot when you moan for my cock. I need you to reach around and play with that clit. I want you to soak my cock."

His words are so fucking filthy that my body sets aflame. I reach between my legs and rub circles on my clit.

"Good girl, keep playing with yourself. I want you to come for me." The hand on my waist grips harder as he thrusts deeper and deeper.

The fire in my core keeps burning brighter and hotter until I feel like I am going to explode. "Weston, I'm close."

He keeps his rhythm steady. "Good, come for me, Sunshine. Let me hear how much you love being stuffed full of my cock."

As if his encouragement is all I needed, the fire turns explosive and I feel my pussy clamp down on his cock, his groans echoing around the room. "You come for me, so good baby."

This man knows my body like he's the architect who designed it, perfectly sending me over the edge with ripples of pleasure still coursing through me as he joins me on the other side, his own moan adding to my pleasure. It's otherworldly to know you make a man weak in the knees; the confidence that I get from him is staggering.

We spend a second catching our breaths, Weston's body covering mine. I'm not sure how long we stay there, but eventually, there's a knock at the door, and my eyes shoot open. Weston slowly pulls out of me, and I can feel the trickle of come dripping down.

He comes back over me to kiss the side of my neck. My breathing is still erratic and coming in heaves. Whispering in my ear, he says, "Your pussy looks so damn good when it's dripping in my come."

He then stands, and with far too much annoyance, he says to the knocker behind the door, "Come back later, we're on a call." He pulls down my shirt as if that is the biggest problem we are facing. My shirt is ruined thanks to the button-ripping moment.

I turn, and Weston starts laughing as he takes me in, with a ripped shirt and disheveled hair. "Well, uh. I think that might be hard to explain." He looks around the office, his thick brows knitted together, before he strips his T-shirt off and hands it to me.

"I don't think this really goes with the outfit," I say sarcastically.

"Okay, brat. I know that. But for now, we can say you spilled coffee on your white shirt, and I, being the gentleman I am, gave you mine."

I look him up and down now that he's shirtless. My eyes catch on his tattoo. A tattoo for me. Like my own little brand. I shouldn't love it this much, but I love that it leaves no doubt of who holds his heart. "Okay, but I'm still going to go home and change."

I see the twinkle in his eye, "Can I come? I could be of assistance in getting you cleaned up and redressed."

For once, I don't think about all the work; I think about how much I love him and how badly I want him. "Yes, only if you promise to shower with me?" I wink, and he smiles, so devilish I can practically hear his filthy thoughts.

Turns out, today might just be my most productive day on the ranch, yet.

Chapter 36
WILLOW

Weston's truck comes to a stop outside the bonfire. There's already people huddled in a circle around the fire. It glows a soft orange with little flickers of embers, popping every so often. For the first time, I'm no longer feeling nervous. I don't care what people say because I'm freaking happy for the first time in years.

For the most part, it'll just be our close circle of friends here, but I know a few people from town will be stopping by, too. It'll be nice getting to catch up with more people. I saw a few at the fair but was a little bit distracted by Weston.

"Willow, it's so good to see you!" Ava walks up, and somehow her bump is even bigger than the last time I saw her a few days ago at dinner. "Come sit and hang out with his girls for a little bit." She loops her arm through mine and starts pulling me away.

I look over my shoulder back at Weston. He's grinning as he waves at me as I go and sit with Ava and Aspen.

"Okay, so I'm going to need neither of you bitches to judge me when I am downing ten of these s'mores," Ava says as she sticks a marshmallow onto a skewer and puts it over the fire.

"Girl, I can't judge you if I'm right there with you," Aspen says as she follows her motion, shoving a marshmallow over the fire until it's basically a sugar flame.

"Was your goal to have charbroiled marshmallows for dessert?" I ask Aspen as she pulls her marshmallow, which is now completely engulfed in flames, out of the fire and blows quick, rapid breaths at it, trying to stop it from burning too much.

"As a matter of fact, it was. And here I was gonna offer to make you a s'more," Aspen says as she flops her marshmallow on the graham cracker, shoving a piece of chocolate on top and then encompassing it in another graham cracker. She shoves half of it in her mouth and moans.

Ava and I both laugh as marshmallow streaks and drips down the corner of her mouth.

"What are you laughing at?" Aspen says through a mouthful of graham cracker and sugary delightness.

Ava turns toward me. "I don't know why I was worried about you guys judging me when we're eating with someone who's clearly never had a s'more before." She hikes her thumb over to Aspen, who wipes the corners of her mouth through giggles.

I make my own s'more, sans flaming marshmallow, unlike Aspen.

Ava and I take turns poking fun at Aspen, and I don't think I remember the last time I laughed this hard. I don't even remember the last time I had friends like this. Where I didn't have to worry about putting on a show. Where they love me just how I am. Marshmallow-covered face and all.

"I was thinking before the baby comes that we need to have one last girls' night," Ava says.

"What kind of girls tonight are we talking about?" I ask skeptically, not that I wouldn't go, but when Aspen is involved, things can go off the rails.

"I was thinking we should have a sleepover. We can do it at my place. Mav can go and snuggle Weston like old times." She elbows me, and I laugh with her.

"That's a good idea. We can't have their bromance sizzling out now that they're coupled up," Aspen says.

"I'm thinking girly movies that our boys complain about watching, enough sugar to send us a diabetic shock, and stretchy pants only."

Honestly, this sounds heavenly. Especially the stretchy pants part. "I'm in. What do you need me to bring?" I can't tell you the last time I had a sleepover. It was probably in this very town. I didn't have a lot of great friends in college. Mostly study buddies, but genuine female friend friendships, forget about it. Not because there was an option, but because I don't think I was in the headspace to let anyone in.

"I don't know, I'll get back to you on that. We could all run into town together and go to the grocery store and pick up everything we need, and then go to the house when we do it?"

"I think we should take the town in our pajamas. It might mortify the guys, but it's totally worth it," Aspen says.

"I'm pretty sure those boys have been doing dumber shit around town than going to buy groceries in their pajamas," I chime in. "In fact, I have a vivid memory of Maverick daring Weston to run butt naked down Main Street when we were sixteen."

Aspen throws her head back with laughter, her hand going to her chest as tears start to leak out of her eyes. "Oh my God, I forgot about that. Mom grounded them both for two weeks."

"Oh, I remember, Weston had to sneak out of his window to come see me. Each time, he had a new bruise and a scrape from the old frames on the windows." I'm laughing now, too, remembering it all.

"I would have paid good money to watch the ass chewing Mabel gave them. Anytime Maverick gets even the slightest attitude, I threaten to call Mabel, and poof. Attitude gone, and he's giving me everything I want."

"Doesn't he give you everything you want regardless?" Aspen asks with a raised brow.

"Yes. It's very hard being a spoiled wife. You'd know if you and Rhett would stop being weird."

I almost choke on my graham cracker. "She knows?" I ask, shocked. I thought those two were doing a better job of hiding it.

"We're just having fun, and yes. She figured it out about as quick as you did."

"You're in denial, babe. And it's not hard to figure out when it's so freaking obvious. I'm pretty sure half of town knows, and if Weston wasn't so oblivious, he would have pieced it together by now, too."

"Ugh, we really need to stop before we get caught." She nervously bites on her lip while she stares off at Rhett.

"Or you could stop being in denial and admit you have feelings for him, which is why you've been doing this for two years now, three?"

"You guys have been messing around for three years!" I borderline shout.

"Can you keep it down when discussing my biggest secrets? More or less. Sometimes we stop for months." She avoids eye contact, which tells me she's probably on the more side.

"Well, if you need advice on how to stop running from your feelings, I'm your girl," I admit.

"How are things going with you and Weston?" Ava asks before taking another bite of her s'more.

I can't help this smile that forms on my face. "Really, really good. It's just like how it used to be, but better because we're older and know more about life now, you know?"

"I'm really glad I butted in," Aspen says through a smile.

"Me too, girl, me too. Maybe I should butt in on your business next?"

Her face goes ghostly white, and I can't help but laugh. "I'm just kidding... Kind of."

Chapter 37
WESTON

Willow and I sit in the office, which is now officially hers. It's clear by the pictures she has hung up of her own, pictures of us, pictures of her grandpa. My favorite part, though, is the picture she stole from my lock box, now framed and sitting on the desk.

We're ready to press launch on our new website and officially be open for bookings. I expected to feel a level of anxiety, but it's the exact opposite. I've never felt more confident in anything in my life. Maybe it's because this project brought Willow and me together, but without a shadow of a doubt, I know that these cabins were the right move. Having her by my side makes me more confident in just about everything. I'm running the ranch better, I've never been happier at home, and I'm about to expand my business with the love of my life.

"You ready?" Willow looks up at me, her bright green eyes shining with way too much excitement.

I nod. "I'm ready if you are." I affectionately squeeze her shoulder.

"How about we do it together?" She shrugs, a touch of nervousness in her voice.

My heart warms at her thoughtfulness. "You want me to press launch at the same time as you?"

"This is your baby after all." She smiles.

I shake my head "No, this is our baby now. Let's do it." My body leans over hers, and I take a deep breath in, enjoying the thrill her scent shoots through me.

I put my hand over hers, and we click the launch button. Our website is officially live. Now Willow just has to upload our profile to other booking sites; she already has them drafted and was waiting on the website for more information. This was the final piece of the puzzle.

"Are you ready to show your family what you've been up to the last few months?"

"Heck yeah, I am." Rhett and Mav picked up a lot of slack this summer; they're the best brothers a guy like me could be blessed with. We may not be related by blood, but the love is all the same.

We step out of the office and then walk to the barn door. When we swing it open, the whole gang sits outside the office.

"Did you do it, or did you chicken out?" Aspen jokes as she pushes off Rhett's truck. Mav, Ava, Rhett, and my parents stand in front of us looking so proud that my chest hurts.

"Weston was shaking like a leaf, but I gave him the strength he needed to carry through," Willow jokes, her hand in mine, giving me a squeeze.

"Oh brother." Mom laughs, clearly exasperated with our shit. Can't blame the woman.

"You guys ready to drive up?" I ask. The cabins are all on the same road as my parents' place, but a good distance away from their cabins and the rest of ours. They'll get to keep their privacy, and people will get to fall in love with the Wyoming mountains.

"Yes!" Ava says, clapping with excitement. She turns, and Mav opens the back door, helping her in. Before he goes around the truck and hops in himself, Aspen jumps in front, and I take that as my cue to get in my truck and lead the way. In a train-like fashion, we drive to each one of the cabins, so Willow and I can show off our hard work. Some of Aspen's hard work, too; her interior design ideas were phenomenal, and they really added a nice touch.

We stop at the first cabin, gathering in front of it.

"I can't wait to see what you've done with the place, honey," my mom says, wrapping her arm around my waist.

My throws his arm around my shoulders. "I'm really proud of you, son. You had an idea you ran with it. Look what you've done," my dad says, looking up at the cabin, which was in crumbles only months ago. I love my mom with all my heart, but praise for my dad hits different.

I look it over, now with fresh eyes, and the exterior has been restored to its original glory. Flowers, native to these mountains, grow in beds along the front of the cabin, and wild grass covers the front lawn. This land has been in my dad's family for generations, and for him to be proud of the way I'm taking it into the next generation makes my heart warm.

I can't help but look over at Willow and notice she's looking at everyone's excited faces. Pride blooms. I can't wait to see what more she does with this place. This is only the beginning.

Pushing the front door open, we step foot into the new cabin. It's full of bright light streaming in from the windows. The sage green and white curtains are drawn, letting the light spill in. The rugs in the kitchen and living room match; the pattern on them is inspired by the leaves of a willow tree. Just another way Willow is woven in.

The living space only has a couch and a love seat; too much furniture would make the space feel crowded. The kitchenette has a small table. These aren't large cabins by any means, one bedroom plus living spaces, but it's enough to give people a time away. Space to breathe free of the sounds of rushing traffic, sirens, and people.

My family is here all over this place, not just physically, but little touches of other personalities have shown up in these cabins. Pictures of my dad's cattle hang on the wall, and flowers from my mom's garden sit in a vase on the counter. I carry them with me every day.

We finish our tour with the cabin Willow briefly lived in, not brief enough for me.

"Hey, this cabin isn't so bad. I don't know what the big fuss was," Mav jokes.

"Yeah, after about fifty thousand dollars worth of work, it's livable." I slap him on the shoulder with more force than necessary. He trips a little, and I preen.

Willow spins, looking around. I think she's still very partial to this cabin. I don't get it, but I'll let her have her moment with it. It's a little roomier than the other ones. She took a lot of time picking out everything for this one. If my gut is right, it's going to be our most booked cabin.

"You guys knocked it out of the park. These are fantastic." Rhett's smile is genuine. He comes in for a hug, and we slap each other's backs before pulling away. I'm over six feet, but next to him, I feel short.

Aspen clears her throat, grabbing our attention, before she pulls a bottle from her purse, "I think these two deserve a toast." She walks into the kitchen, pulling out a few glasses from the kitchen. "Ava, I brought you apple juice." She shakes the mini bottle in the air.

"You deserve some praise too, you did great work with the design stuff," I say, not knowing the correct verbiage for anything to do with decor, but I do know this place looks great.

She shrugs and bats away my compliment with a smile.

My dad takes the lead on the toast before Aspen turns it into a whole debacle, which is probably for the best. "Here's to Weston and Willow on their new business adventure. You brought life into these cabins again and exceeded any expectation I had. I'm proud of you both," he says before raising his glass. "Cheers," he says before it echoes throughout the room.

We raise our glasses, and I look around, feeling appreciative that everyone I love most in the world showed up in support of our project. Before taking a sip of the champagne, I turn to Willow, and her eyes land on mine. We share a moment, a breath, as we take this in, lost in each other's eyes. Unable to hold back, I mouth, "I love you, Sunshine."

Her eyes sparkle with warmth, and the most radiant smile fills her face.

"I love you too," she mouths back, lost in our little moment together amongst everyone.

We clink our glasses, celebrating our big achievement. We did this *together*, and that's how it will always be from this day forward. The best is yet to come.

Chapter 38
weston

The horse trots down to the last of our rental cabins. The smell of pine fills my nose, along with my woman's sweet perfume, making it the perfect combination of all my favorite things. She sits in front of me, relaxed as can be. A far cry from our first ride together when she came back to town.

"I can't wait for our first booking." She wiggles with glee as we come to a stop.

I chuckle at her excitement as I help her slide off the horse, jumping off myself shortly after. Walking the horse over, I tie her off at the nearest tree branch and walk back over to Willow.

My arms come up around her shoulders before I pull her into my chest, my head resting on the top of her head. "You know what I love most about this?"

"Hm?" she asks, squeezing her hands on my forearms.

"That I get to share this dream with you. That you and I got to build this thing from the ground up. This is only the beginning."

She turns and drapes her arms over my shoulders. God, I can't take my eyes or hands off her. I want her with me all the time for the rest of my life. I've always wanted that, but now, I need that. Life without her is dull, almost as if I'm living in black and white. Now that I'm seeing color again, I never want to stop.

Her eyes twinkle, and a smile is stretched wide on her face, "I'm glad, too. It led me back to you, and for that, I am forever grateful. I love you, West."I feel an urgency rise in me; I need to do this, and I need to do this now. "Marry me, today. Right now."

Her head rears back as her eyes go wide. "What? You're crazy, we can't get married right now."

I shrug, is this a little crazy, sure? You know what would be even crazier? Not doing it. My gut is screaming at me to do this. To make her my wife as soon as possible. "Twelve years without you has made me certifiably insane. I don't care. I want you to be my wife more than I want my next breath." I drop to one knee, "You are my life, and I want to start it, right now, with you. What do you say?"

She gapes at me like a fish. "It's Sunday, who the hell is going to marry us on a Sunday?"

The idea comes to me so clearly, I know it's the right thing. "Is that a yes, Sunshine?" I grab her hands and squeeze them both.

She blinks rapidly before a smile stretches out across her face. Suddenly, she's sixteen, and I'm telling her I love her for the first time in the front seat of my truck while we're parked on a back road. That's what this smile reminds me of. I want to make a whole lifetime of memories with her smiling like this. "Yes. Always yes when it comes to you."I pull her in my arms, and her legs wrap around my waist as her soft hands frame my face. She wastes no time bringing her lips to mine, and I get lost. Lost in the taste of her Chapstick, at her gasping for air when she pulls back. This girl is the air in my lungs, and the blood in my veins. She's all I will ever need for a happy life.

"Let's go get married."

My old truck, the one that holds all our dearest memories, comes to a stop in front of Verns. I give Willow credit because I know she has a lot of questions. I know she's confused. But I have a plan, and it includes our favorite old man.

When I open the door, I look at her, and her eyes are now bugging out of her head. I can't tell if it's the nerves or all the questions she has brewing up there creating internal pressure. Jury is out, but I take pity on her regardless.

"The man behind that door is really important to both of us. I thought we might ask him if he'd be willing to double as minister today."

"My grandpa has done a lot in his life, but I'm pretty sure ministering isn't one of them." She quirks up a brow.

"Come on, babe. Your man has a plan, I promise." I grab her hand and usher her out of the car.

We walk through the back door, and Vern is in his favorite spot, legs stretched out on his recliner and Sunday football on the TV.

"Vern!" I holler out, hoping he can hear me over the TV.

He turns his body around, a big smile stretching across his face when he sees us hand in hand in his kitchen. "Hey, kids!" He snaps the recliner leg down and stands up to meet us in the kitchen. "To what do I owe the pleasure?"Willow looks to me, and I look at her before glancing back to Vern. "Well, now that I've got our girl back, I don't want to let her go. I want to get married. Today. And I'd like for you to marry us."

His smile stretches further, "Well, I'll be damned." He pulls us both into a hug. "I hate to disappoint you, too, but I can't marry you.""Well, actually, you can. You can be an ordained minister in about fifteen minutes on the internet." I hold up my phone and wave it back and forth. "Are you up for it?""Don't you guys want a big wedding. This is a long time coming, you know?"

We look to each other, considering the thought. It comes out so easy. "No. We can celebrate with everyone after, but I think this part needs to be just us." Willow says.

"Well, alright then. Weston, can I talk to you for a second, just us two?" He looks over to Willow, silently dismissing her.

She rolls her eyes as she laughs. "Well, I'll go watch some football, I guess."

Once she's out of the room, his eyes meet mine. "Did you get her a ring yet?"

Blood leaves my face at an alarming rate because, no, I don't have a ring.

"Don't panic, son. I want to offer you my late wife's ring. I know it's nothing fancy like you all have these days, but..."I cut him off as tears fill my eyes, the gesture so impactful I can feel my heart swell. "Fancy isn't what we're going for. We're going for forever, long-lasting and genuine, like something you all had. It would mean everything to give her that ring."

"Alright, son," he nods once, "I want you to know there is no one on earth better suited for her. You are exactly the kind of man I had hoped she would end up with. I'm proud to add you to our family, son."

I feel tears stream down my face as he pulls me in for an embrace. I have a wonderful family, but this man is all Willow has had. The way he loves and protects her is a force to be reckoned with. To be welcomed into their small circle as family is a gift I will forever cherish.

He pulls back, patting my shoulder twice. "Well, let's get you two hitched."

After a quick twenty-minute form on the internet, he's now ordained. We will have to do the whole marriage license bit tomorrow, but the part I care about is happening right now. Marrying the woman who is my everything.

We stand in her grandpa's backyard, surrounded by his bright blooms of flowers, and of course, perfectly mowed grass.

Hand in hand we look over to Vern.

"I've done a lot of great things in my life, the greatest was raising you, Lolo. I am so proud to be marrying you today. Do you two have vows prepared, or should I do the textbook version?

I chime in and say, "I have some," just as Willow says, "No."

She looks at me, surprised. "How do you have vows prepared? We decided to get married one hour ago."

"If you think I need more than three seconds to adequately put together how I feel about you, you don't grasp exactly how much I love you." I mean it wholeheartedly.

"Well then, looks like I will leave you two to your vows, Weston son, you first."

"Willow, I knew from the minute I met you that you were something special. I had no idea until we were old enough to bridge that gap from friends to more, exactly how damn lucky I was. You work harder than anyone I have ever met. I cannot believe how blessed I am to be on the receiving end of your love. You are everything I've ever needed," tears stream steadily down her face, and I let go of one of her hands to brush them away, "and I promise to be the man that you need, every day until death do us part. There is no river I wouldn't cross, sea I wouldn't swim to get you what you desire. There is nothing on this earth that matters more to me than you; you are my life, my family, and my future. I cannot wait to see what life has in store for us. As for me? I'll die a happy man as long as you are mine."

When I finish, I feel a tear trail down my cheek and a shuddering breath leave my lips.

Vern clears his throat. "That was beautiful, Weston. Willow, do you have any words you would like to share?"

She nods and looks back at me, the softest smile dancing across her face. "I think I have loved you from the minute I met you. I looked for reasons to talk to you in school, and once we were friends, I wanted more. I don't think I will ever have enough of you. I think I was born with my soul tied to you. Every time we are not together, I feel like a shell of myself. You complete me in the best way. You steady me, encourage me, and love me like no one else can. You are truly my best friend, and I cannot wait to spend the rest of my life with you. Together, you and I can build the family I dreamed of. I'll love you long after my last breath. Forever."

"I love you, too." I fight the urge to lean toward her and kiss her now, but that time is coming.

"Alrighty, love birds, let's exchange some rings." Grandpa claps his hands together and looks so damn excited to be a part of this.

"Weston, we don't have rings." Her shiny eyes are wide now.

"Well, I've got a ring for you; we can worry about mine later." I shrug. The most important part is that she gets what she needs.

Vern clears his throat. "I'm not sure if you'd want to, but I'd love to give mine to you guys, too. I loved my wife, and I loved the marriage we shared. It would mean a lot to me to see you two follow in our footsteps, if you would like, that is." He runs his hand over his neck nervously.

Willow's tears are back with a vengeance and so are mine. "That would be amazing, Grandpa. Are you sure?"

"Sure about you two making it to the finish line together? Yes. This ring deserves another round of everlasting love."

"Thank you." She grabs the ring gingerly from him after he takes it off, holding his hand between hers for a second. A silent conversation happening between them.

"I don't really know the exact next words, but I think I can pull something together.""Weston, do you promise to love, protect, and always admit when you're being a stubborn jackass?"

My chest shakes with laughter. "I do."

"Willow, do you promise to love, stand by, and accept help from your husband without him having to force it?" He cocks an eyebrow at her.

She sighs heavily before saying, "I do," looking directly into my eyes with a piercing type of love.

"Beautiful, now exchange those rings." Vern clasps his hands in front of him and looks between us.

We look up, and a sense of relief and calm washes over me. I have her, she's mine for the rest of my life.

I grab her hand, steady as ever, and slide her grandma's gold-banded solitaire ring on. It's perfect for her. It's timeless, just like our love.

She slides on my gold band, and I can't take my eyes off it. I have physical proof that I'm as much hers as she's mine. It knits together the last piece of my broken heart, making me whole again, making me hers.

"I now pronounce you husband and wife. You may now kiss the bride." Vern's eyes glisten as he looks between us like he's watching his own dream come true.

My lips lock with hers, and I feel peace like I've never known. I get to spend the rest of my life with the only girl who's ever held my heart.

Epilogue

There used to be days when going to work sounded about as much fun as riding a seatless bike. I'm glad to say those days are well behind me. As I sit and get ready for work, I think about how that's not my life anymore. In fact, the best part of my day is going to work. Actually, that's a lie. The best part of my day is coming home to Weston, but running this business together is a close second.

The last piece of my hair is curled to perfection, so much longer than it was when I first showed up here. I've had it short for so many years. I forgot how much I loved it like this. Spritzing on some perfume Weston gifted me, I take one last look in the mirror. Fully content with the woman looking back at me.

When I get downstairs, I see a pot of coffee for me waiting on the kitchen counter. Weston is reliable to a fault. It doesn't matter how much he has to get done on the ranch; I know there will always be coffee with a love note on the counter.

"Look at mighty fine this morning, Mrs. Taylor," Weston says as he walks through the door, a gallon of paint in each hand.

"When I said I wanted to paint an accent wall, I didn't mean you had to do it the next day." I walk over to Weston as he sets down the paint jugs, and I wrap my arms around the back of his neck, getting on my tiptoes and bringing his lips to mine.

"What my woman wants, my woman gets."

"You're supposed to be helping Rhett and Maverick today?" I question.

He shrugs, "I think they can handle the ranch for a couple of days while I spruce the place up." They work so well together that I don't doubt that.

"While you're on the note of freshening up, do you think we could maybe go pick out some new furniture?" I look around the room at the mismatched couch, love seat, and chair. It served its purpose, but we're making this house our forever home.

"Whatever you want, Sunshine. We can swing into Cheyenne this weekend and go look?"

"That sounds perfect. Are you dead set on painting with me, or could you maybe do a walk and a short drive with your wife? I want to check out the books and maybe swing by Grandpa's place." I cock my head to the side, knowing I'm not playing fair. There is nothing this man loves more than being reminded that I am his wife.

His gaze heats, and I know that I'll be getting whatever I want for the rest of the day and probably a life-changing orgasm later. A win all around. "Of course, baby, let me just go drop these off in the garage."

He picks the cans back up and carries them away while I get the mighty fine view of his ass in a pair of Wranglers that are bordering on too tight, but I like them that way. Showing off his assets. He turns around as he says, "How about we take the old pickup today?"

I'd drive that truck all day long if I had it my way. I love that thing and all the memories we've made in it. "Yes." I practically skip my way to him.

He opens the attached garage door and swats my ass as I walk in front of him.

"I'd say I'm sorry, but I can't keep my hands off your ass when it looks that good. Between the skirt and those heels..." He doesn't finish, lost in thought. I'd laugh, but I love having him this obsessed with me. It makes me feel like I'm glowing from the inside out.

We get in the truck and swing by Grandpa's cabin. We broke ground on it in the spring, the second the snow started to thaw. Weston is convinced it'll be done by the end of summer. It'll be on the smaller side, two bedrooms, but more than enough for him. I'm just glad to have him close. He's getting older, and I don't want to waste a single second I have with him.

The cabin's frame is completely up. You can see the vision coming to life before us. Hopefully, this time next year, there will be a full yard of grass. Maybe even a grandbaby playing in it.

"It's looking good. I'll be mowing the grass here in no time," Weston jokes as he looks over to me.

"You're ridiculous. Let's head down to the office. It should only take me a little bit. We were only one booking away from being booked out April through August, can you believe it?" I turn back and settle into the middle seat, nestled right up beside the love of my life. "I can, you work hard. You've taken my dream and made it even bigger and more successful than I could have on my own."

"I wouldn't say that, but I do think that we work best when we are together." It's probably the truest statement I've ever said. Sure, work can be stressful, but I love every second of it.

"I couldn't agree more." He grabs my hand and admires the ring sitting on it. He brings it to his lips and gently kisses it. "Have I told you lately how much I love being your husband?"

"You have, but feel free to say more nice things to me." He laughs and throws his arm over my shoulders, and I can't help but realize I got my dream. All I ever wanted was a family, something dependable, and I got it.

I can see it so clearly, growing old with him. The babies we will raise together will never have to wonder about being loved; they will know it. Weston loves so loudly, it will be impossible to ignore. We'll get to spend our nights on our porch, watching the sunlight disappear behind the mountain.

What a way to spend the rest of your life, loved by a man like Weston.

Acknowledgements

Writing this book was no easy feat. It was torn apart, rewritten (not once, not twice but three times). I am incredibly proud of the final result. Getting the story right would not have been possible without my sweet angel baby Bryanna. She is one of the hardest working people I have ever met and I am so incredibly blessed to have her in my corner.

My wonderful beta team, Sam x2, Page, Wren and Jess. Thank you so much for your time and your feedback. Every little piece helps make the book the best it can be.

My dear friends, Jessica, Renee, Madison and Caitlin. For allowing me to blab about my stories non stop.

My dear husband who pretends to know what I'm talking about when I'm yapping to him about my books.

This year was a rough one and I never would have made it through without God & Christ.

Thank you to all my dear readers. Spurred On changed my life. It was my favorite book to write and you all showed up for me in ways I never could have imagined. Thank you so much for reading my books.

Also by

Check out book one in the Windy Peaks series, Spurred On:
https://www.amazon.com/Spurred-Windy-Peaks-Elle-Jordan-ebook
/dp/B0DGX42Y9P?crid=3BWQTXIBS1H4P&sprefix=spurred+on
+%2Caps%2C218&sr=8-1
Pre-Order Rhett and Aspen's book
here: https://www.amazon.com/gp/product/B0DPR8G8NW?ref_
=dbs_m_mng_rwt_calw_tkin_2&storeType=ebooks&sr=8-1
Pre-Order Erin and Tate's Christmas love story:
https://www.amazon.com/dp/B0G5H8FTD7?_encoding=UTF8&
content-id=amzn1.sym.8617ee0f-57de-4d6d-8e06-177f827e1ad2

About the author

I spend most my days at my local hospital were I work as a surgical technologist. My off time is spent hanging out with my two fur babies and my sweet husband. I love spending time at the beach with an ice cold daiquiri in my hand and kindle in the other. Though I write contemporary romance, my favorite genre is romantasy.